WITHIN THESE WALLS

USA TODAY BESTSELLING AUTHOR

J.L. BERG

ALSO BY J.L. BERG

THE READY SERIES

When You're Ready

Never Been Ready

Ready to Wed

Ready for You

Ready or Not

The Ready Series Box Set

When You're Ready - 10th Anniversary Edition

THE WALLS SERIES

Within These Walls

Beyond These Walls

Behind Closed Doors

The Cavenaugh Brothers - A Box Set

THE LOST & FOUND SERIES

Forgetting August

Remembering Everly

BY THE BAY SERIES

The Choices I've Made

The Scars I Bare

The Lies I've Told

The Mistakes I've Made

This one is dedicated to my kids,
For showing me just how much love a heart can hold.
You are my everything.

TWO ROADS DIVERGED IN A WOOD,
AND I—I TOOK THE ONE LESS TRAVELED BY.
AND THIS HAS MADE ALL THE DIFFERENCE.
—ROBERT FROST.

PROLOGUE

Within these walls, he became my solace, my sanctuary, and my strength.

Like a white knight, he saved me from a life of gray and showed me a world full of color.

Within these walls, I gave myself to a man who said he would always fight for me and love me until the end of time.

But sometimes, not even love was enough when life got in the way.

When your heart was already damaged beyond repair, what was left to break?

Within these walls, I gave my less than perfect heart to the man I loved.

And then...he walked away.

CHAPTER ONE
GOING HOME

LAILAH

Beep, Beep, Beep…

Ever so slowly, I began to register my surroundings. My ears kicked in first as my sluggish, tired body came awake. I heard the sound of the pulse oximetry monitor as it beeped away in the background, tugging me out of dreamland. Like most days, before I even managed to crack open my eyelids, I'd take account of my surroundings, listening to the world around me and mentally checking off the things I could hear to determine where I was.

Someone wheeled a rickety cart down the hallway, its wheels spinning and squeaking, as she pushed it to its final destination. Across the hall, someone chatted outside a room. Close to me, the ever-present sounds of the equipment beeped and buzzed while monitoring my oxygen and heart rhythm.

All these sounds together could only mean one thing.

I was in the hospital—still.

Most kids had a favorite grandmother's house, or a special friend they couldn't get enough of—I had Memorial

Regional. It had been my home away from home since I was an infant.

It was definitely not the same.

Home was quiet and warm.

The hospital bustled with noise at every God-given hour of the day, regardless of whether the sun or the moon was currently occupying the sky.

Staying here also felt like spending a night in a meat locker. I'd learned through my many years here that heat bred infection, which is why nurses buried patients in blankets rather than cranked up the furnace. Standing barely five and a half feet on my tiptoes, I weighed a little over a hundred pounds. No amounts of blankets could ever keep me warm. I seriously loved heaters.

I rubbed my chest as I took a labored breath though my lungs. It crackled slightly as I exhaled. Biting down on my lip, I tried to ignore it, focusing on my one and only goal for the day.

Going home today. I'm going home today, I chanted.

My eyelids reluctantly lifted, my vision blurry at first until the room came into view. Nothing had changed since I fell asleep last night. I saw the same boring, lackluster eggshell-colored walls and the same white board listing my nurse on shift with a little happy face drawn next to her name.

Grace was working this morning. She was young, around my age, and she'd just recently graduated with her nursing degree. She loved happy faces, hearts, and anything else she could draw with a dry-erase marker. She reminded me of a Disney princess. Even in scrubs, she was over-the-top girlie. I swore, one of these days, she was going to break out into song, summon an entire forest full of small animals, and perform a musical, complete with dancing squirrels and singing larks.

But all that would have to wait for another day because I was leaving—*today.*

What was supposed to be an in-and-out routine procedure

had turned out to be another prolonged hospital stay. I was more than ready to get home to my own bed. I hated hospital beds. They were uncomfortable, hard, and never felt right.

Seriously, who makes these things? Do they actually test the beds out? I know the beds are supposed to be functional, but really, they could add some padding.

I'd arrived at the hospital two weeks ago, expecting to stay a couple of days, to switch out the battery in my pacemaker, but as always, things hadn't gone as planned, and I'd ended up in the hospital—again.

Story of my life.

But not today. Today, I was free—well, as free as my life would allow.

I was born with a heart defect. Basically, my heart was larger than it was supposed to be. It made breathing and mostly everything else difficult because my heart had to work ten times harder than normal. In a nutshell, this little defect controlled my entire life.

It was also slowly killing me, which was why I couldn't wait to break free of this prison. When you were living your life on borrowed time, every second you had to spend watching the days pass by through a hospital room window was one moment less you had to be doing something meaningful.

In my sheltered life, my idea of *meaningful* might be defined as something completely lackluster and conventional, but at least it wouldn't be spent here.

I slowly exhaled another wheezy breath out through my mouth at the exact moment Grace decided to walk through the door.

"Good morning!" she nearly sang.

She gave me her dazzling white smile that was entirely too perky for the ungodly early hour. Her dark curls bobbed behind her as she bounced over to the computer terminal and began her morning ritual.

"Morning, Grace. How are you?" I asked.

"I'm fantastic! The sun is shining, and the birds are singing! My favorite patient is being discharged today! It's a fantastic day!"

Wow, two fantastics in one breath.

The corner of my mouth curved into a smile, mimicking hers. "You're extra chipper today. Any particular reason?" I inquired, knowing she had mentioned going on a special date with her boyfriend last night.

They'd been dating for two years, and she'd been hinting at an engagement for a while. My guess was her boyfriend finally caught on.

Grace played dumb. "I don't know what you're talking about." She held her left hand up to her cheek as she shook her head back and forth.

There, on her ring finger, was a perfect, dazzling white diamond ring that matched her sparkling eyes.

"You got engaged! What a surprise!" I exclaimed.

It wasn't a surprise though. She'd been talking about it since I had arrived.

I really want to be happy for her—no, scratch that. I am happy for her. She deserves all the happiness in the world.

My life is not horrible. It's just different, I reminded myself.

"Thank you! It was so sweet. He got down on one knee in his suit—on the beach, no less—and told me I was the only woman he'd ever want to share his life with, and then he pulled out this ring. It was so romantic."

"It sounds beautiful," I said.

She began to jot down numbers while checking me over. Her brows suddenly furrowed together, causing me to become alarmed.

"What is it?" I asked.

"What? Oh, nothing. I don't think it's anything serious. Your pulse ox reading is just a little low." She bent forward with a stethoscope and listened to my lungs for a moment. "Let me just update Dr. Marcus, and he'll be in to chat with you in a bit."

I nodded absently as she scooted out quickly, leaving me alone with my thoughts.

Looking down at my pointer finger which was attached to the machine that monitored my oxygen levels, I sighed. The reading wasn't terribly low—at least, not enough to trigger an alarm thankfully. I let out a small groan and slumped my head forward in defeat. I knew what this meant—something wasn't right, and Grace hadn't wanted to say anything because it was now above her pay grade.

So, now, I had to just sit here and wait—*alone.*

Sitting around in a hospital, day in and day out, was tedious. There was only so much TV I could watch, so many books I could read, before my head felt like it might explode. Sometimes, the craving for human interaction could become so intense that I'd feel physically ill.

My mother had been here every day, and her company meant the world to me, but the desire and need to interact

with someone my own age was overwhelming. I just wanted someone who hadn't helped me go to the bathroom or didn't watch my every move with anxiety, afraid my next breath might land me back in the hospital.

The book my mother had been reading—something academic, a text book no doubt—was lying on the cushion of the worn blue chair in the corner, forgotten along with her jacket and a notebook. She must have stayed late and left after I'd fallen asleep. She usually didn't stay past seven, but she had been desperately trying to finish her syllabus for the next semester so that she'd have it done before I returned home. She would always be so paranoid whenever I was discharged from a hospital stay. She feared I would have some sort of rebound and end up back where I started—laying back in that room waiting for my next escape. Therefore, in her mind, my need for supervision doubled, tripled even. She'd end up almost killing herself, trying to get everything done in preparation for my return.

My mother, Molly Buchanan, was a religious studies

professor at the local community college. She was probably one of the most eclectic women on the planet. When I was young, I'd once asked her about why she taught religion, but we didn't go to church. She'd smiled sweetly and told me that she loved learning about religions so much that she couldn't pick just one, so she never had. It had made sense to me when I was a naïve child, but now, it just made me laugh. I'd decided years ago after being one of her students that my mom was just overly curious about the behavior of humans and there was no better way to learn the hows and whys of people than through their religions.

I spent what was hopefully going to be my last morning in the hospital eating less than stellar eggs and toast from a tray while I haphazardly flipped through the fourteen channels on TV. After catching up on the news and watching a rerun of *Boy Meets World*, I decided it was time to pack.

Careful of the hep-lock buried in the crook of my arm, I slowly got up and made my way to the en-suite bathroom.

I brushed my teeth and attempted to throw my long blonde hair into a ponytail. I then gathered all my toiletries and placed them in the bag my mom had brought. After returning to the room, I threw the small bag into the suitcase by the bed. Several other items also went in, and after a few minutes, I was ready to go.

I could hear my bed calling out for me, whispering my name. Uninterrupted sleep was something that was seriously taken for granted by those who were lucky enough to enjoy it. Right now, I was exhausted—probably more exhausted than I should be, but I ignored that because I was going home.

After everything in my room had been tidied up, I settled back down to wait out the day. Whenever a nurse told you that the doctor would be with you in a bit, she really meant that the doctor would be in sometime today, so you shouldn't hold your breath. Seeing as it had been less than an hour since Grace disappeared from my sight, I was quite surprised when Dr. Marcus suddenly appeared at my door. Clad in blue scrubs, he ran his large hands through his salt-and-pepper locks.

Having adjusted back to teaching day classes, my mom had finished teaching her one summer course for the day, and she was now sitting in her usual spot in the corner. She was deeply immersed in her book from earlier, scribbling down notes, but she instantly perked up when my longtime handsome doctor came in.

He took a few steps, hesitated slightly, and then walked the remaining distance to the bed. He seemed uneasy, and his eyes were roaming around the room as if they were desperately trying to lock on to anything but me. Finally, he met my gaze, and immediately, I knew he had bad news.

"Hey, Lailah," he said.

"Hi, Dr. Marcus."

"Listen, kid—" he started.

I interrupted him, "I'm not a kid anymore."

"Right. I keep forgetting. Twenty-two. Crazy."

Dr. Marcus had been caring for me since I was a child. I'd gone to other hospitals for more complicated procedures, and other doctors and specialists had seen me over the years, but I'd always been under the care of Dr. Marcus. Besides my mother, he was the closest thing I had to family.

"I've looked at your levels, and it's not happening today, Lailah."

"Why?" I whispered.

He arched his brow, giving me a pointed stare.

"My breathing," I answered my own question.

He nodded. "Yes, your breathing isn't good—I can tell you that standing across the room and your heart is beating irregularly. I'm sorry. I know you wanted to hit the road today, but until we get you in better shape, I can't let that happen."

I turned to my mother, who was staring at me with a sad, concerned expression. Our eyes met, and she gave me a hesitant smile. She wouldn't fight him. I knew that from experience. She followed all doctor instructions to the letter. When it came to my health, she wasn't willing to take even an iota of a chance.

"Okay," I said, turning back to Dr. Marcus, as I tried to fight back the tears. "I guess it's time for bad food and daytime TV for me once again."

"I'll make sure they send up extra dessert," he said with a wink.

His focus then went to my mother and I watched her rise from her chair to join him across the room. Huddled together, I could hear very little of what they were saying, but from what I managed to catch, I was going to be stuck within these walls for quite a bit longer.

Freedom had suddenly vanished before my eyes.

Back to jail I go.

CHAPTER TWO
CHANGES

JUDE

Today was my birthday.

I was twenty-four—wait, maybe twenty-five?

Shit, I should probably know that.

It had been three years since the accident. A celebratory vacation had brought me to California, but it had turned into nothing but shattered dreams and sorrow. Since then, I hadn't cared much about birthdays or any celebrations in general.

It had been three years since I lost her.

I guessed that meant I was turning twenty-five today.

Happy birthday, Jude.

Four years ago, on the day I'd turned twenty-one, I'd spent my birthday bar-hopping and clubbing with my fraternity brothers, throwing around cash like I had a never-ending supply—and at the time, I had.

"Go have fun," my dad had said.

And we had done just that. I couldn't remember half of what had gone down that night. All I could recall was spending the next morning with my head hunched over a toilet while Megan had nursed me back to health.

Tonight, however, I had a hot birthday date with a few

bedpans, a bevy of charts, and if I was lucky, a fifteen-minute break with the vending machine. *Maybe I could really go all out and get a Milky Way tonight.*

For two years now, I'd worked at Memorial Hospital in Santa Monica as a CNA—basically, a glorified orderly who was required to pass tests and earn certificates. While I'd started from the bottom as a janitor, a sympathetic HR woman, Margaret, had taken pity on me after seeing me roaming the hospital halls for weeks. Realizing I'd never leave otherwise, she'd offered me a janitor position, and I'd said yes on the spot. When I'd listed my newly earned Princeton business degree under education, she'd raised her eyebrows a bit, but she never asked any questions. When I'd firmly requested not to have my last name listed on my ID badge for personal reasons, she'd just arched her brow a bit further, handed me my newly made ID, and sent me on my way.

I'd barely left the hospital since.

I had a small apartment across town where I would sleep between shifts and make mediocre meals, but this place was where I lived the majority of my waking hours. I usually worked overtime and took extra shifts when people needed days off just so I could stay within the walls of this hospital.

This was the only type of home I had anymore.

I hadn't really lived a day of my life since arriving here three years ago with blood dripping down my face as I'd screamed out Megan's name over and over, trying to will her back into consciousness. It hadn't worked in the ER, and it hadn't worked in the horrible days that followed either. I'd been walking these empty halls without her ever since, following her ghost around corners and down halls while I tried in vain to just exist.

I couldn't live when everything I'd lived for was dead.

Stopping by the vending machine, I pulled out the loose change in my pocket until I found the exact amount for my birthday-dinner treat. Dropping the coins in the slot, I pressed the correct combination of buttons and waited for the candy bar to push forward before plummeting to the bottom. It dropped with a hard thunk, and I quickly bent down to retrieve it.

Less than three minutes later, I'd demolished the candy bar, and the wrapper was long gone in a trash can. I made my way back to the nurses' station from the vending machine to check back in. I'd just rounded the corner when I came face-to-face with Margaret.

"Hey, Jude. You're just the person I was looking for. Would you mind following me? I wanted to talk with you for a minute," she said.

I gave a curt nod and followed behind her, watching her dark brown bob in all directions, as she briskly walked down the long hall. In a sea of scrubs, she was the oddball dressed in a cheap blue wool suit. It looked itchy, and judging from the red scratch marks along her collar, I was guessing she would agree.

Cheap wool could make people break out into a rash faster than taking a hike through a forest of poison ivy. When I was around nine, our nanny, Lottie, had been instructed to take me shopping for a new wool blazer for Christmas Eve. It was something my mom had always loved doing, but I remembered that year as being particularly stressful, so she'd sent Lottie instead. Halfway through Mass, my father had pulled me out of the service because I couldn't stop scratching. It turned out that Lottie had bought the blazer from a cheap knockoff store, and she'd pocketed the rest of my parents' cash. Needless to say, that was the last Christmas she'd spent with us. It had been quite the adventure for the ten year old boy I had once been. When I retold the story to my friends, there were cops and robbers involved.

As Margaret and I made our way farther down the hall, she continued to fuss with her collar, but I refrained from making any comments. I'd left behind the life of expensive tailored suits and board meetings.

Jude, the nurses' assistant, wouldn't know shit about any of that. He was quiet, he didn't have friends, and he never answered any questions about his past. It had taken awhile, but my coworkers had learned to respect these boundaries. After the first year of turning down every after-hours hangout opportunity, flirty date request, and party invite, they'd quickly figured out that I was a loner with a fortress of thick, impenetrable walls built around me.

I wasn't about to go screw it up by making some snide comment to my HR representative about digging her fingers into her neck. If I were to do that, I might as well give her advice on her 401(k) and offer to look at her stock portfolio.

Margaret unlocked the door to her office and flicked on the fluorescent lights above us.

"Have a seat, won't you?" she asked, gesturing to the seats in front of her desk.

I settled into one of the cushioned wingback chairs and leaned forward, bracing myself for whatever might lie ahead.

She shuffled some papers around her desk and clicked on her keyboard before finally turning her gaze to me. "You're probably wondering what you are doing here."

I nodded.

"Well, you see, there's been some adjustments and—"

My pulse quickened, and I cut her off, "What do you mean, adjustments? Am I being laid off?"

I couldn't lose this job. This was the last place I had seen her, where I'd held her hand. If I weren't here, I wouldn't be able to feel her with me, and I didn't know how to function without her.

"Calm down, Jude. No one is getting laid off. You're just switching departments."

"What? To where?"

I'd been working in the emergency room since my first day as a CNA. It was exactly the type of place I needed to be. The ER was fast-paced and kept my mind occupied. It was also where they'd wheeled us in, battered and bruised from colliding head-on into a Jersey barrier after Megan had fallen asleep at the wheel. I'd been treated and discharged quickly, only sustaining a broken arm and a few bumps and bruises. Megan, though, had taken the majority of the impact, so her injuries had been far worse.

"You're being transferred to cardiology."

I inwardly groaned. All I could picture was old people with aging hearts and their bypass surgeries. My bedpan duties just went through the roof.

"Why? Is there a particular reason?" I wanted to know what I'd done to deserve this hell.

"We just think it would be good for you to do something different," she answered with an encouraging smile.

She'd done this on purpose.

"I don't want to be fixed, Margaret. I'm not your charity case," I said through clenched teeth.

There had been a handful of others like her, but Margaret was persistent. She'd been the one to get me this job, knowing I was a broken, grieving man wandering these halls. She'd probably assumed the job would open me up and give me opportunities to heal and move on. She was wrong. Healing required the desire to do so. I didn't want to heal, and I certainly didn't want to move on. I hadn't left my old life behind and taken a job where my fiancée died to soothe my soul. No, I came here each and every day to mourn the life I'd selfishly taken, and I would remain here to do exactly that— no matter what department Margaret stuck me in.

"I'm sorry, Jude," she whispered. "You weren't the only one transferred. Please don't feel singled out."

"When do I start?" I questioned, trying to calm the anger I felt rolling off me.

"Tonight. You can head over there now if you'd like," she answered with a polite smile.

As she returned to her piles of paperwork, I rose from the chair and made my way out, but I was stopped when Margaret's small voice cut through the silence.

"Oh, Jude?" she said. "Happy birthday."

Every step I took toward the third floor felt more like a mile, creating an expanding distance from the cocoon I'd managed to build over the last three years. Like was probably too strong of a word, but I'd grown complacent in my simplicity. I'd adjusted to my new life and the way it was, and this sudden wrench that had been thrown into the mix was making my mind go haywire.

Megan had never visited cardiology. Glimpses of Megan's parents pleading with me as they'd mentioned her heart flashed before my eyes, but I pushed back the painful memory. After the ER, she'd spent a few short days in the ICU following several unsuccessful surgeries to repair the damage to her brain, but like a speeding bullet to the heart, the wounds had been irreversible and fatal. Just like everything else.

As I approached the nurses' station, my slight hesitation dissipated at the sight of Dr. Marcus Hale. Dr. Marcus, as he liked to be called, was a cardiologist I'd known since my janitorial days. He wasn't like most of the other doctors. He was laid-back without the slightest hint of snobbery. He always arrived for his shifts in sandy board shorts, and his hair would still be wet from surfing. He'd been trying for years now to get me on a board.

The first time I'd met him was late at night when I was called up to clean a restroom. A patient he had been treating had gotten ill. When I'd arrived, I had immediately gotten to work, cleaning up something that should not be described, while they had been busy talking in the room. I'd finished up around the same time as Dr. Marcus, and we'd exited the room together.

He'd let out an exasperated sigh and turned to me. "You want to get a cup of coffee? I'm beat."

I'd thought he was joking. I had been a damn janitor, and he was a cardiologist, who probably made more sneezing than I had in an entire year.

He hadn't been kidding though. Together, we'd walked to the cafeteria and talked over coffee and crappy pastries. It had become a tradition of ours ever since then.

"Hey, Dr. Marcus," I greeted, pulling his attention away from the computer screen.

"Hey, Jude. What brings you over to these parts?"

"My new digs. I was relocated," I answered.

His eyebrow rose in curiosity. "Really? Well, that's the best news I've had all night. Good to have you on board."

I looked around and immediately noticed an old man shuffling down the hall. I inwardly groaned. Then, I felt a hard pat on my back.

"Maybe you'll like it here better."

His encouragement wasn't helping the situation.

I gave him a dubious look.

His rich laughter filled the air. "Okay, maybe not, but you never know. This could be exactly where you are meant to be."

<hr>

AFTER MEETING THE NIGHT-SHIFT HEAD NURSE, WHO REMINDED me a bit of Nurse Ratched, I made my first round on my new floor. I assisted nurses, changed sheets, answered call buttons from patients, and completed all the other duties I'd performed a million times. The job wasn't different just because I had been placed somewhere else. Things were just a bit slower. The nurses moved at a leisurely pace here. The rushed lifestyle of the ER was gone and had been replaced with something much more low-key.

This kind of blows.

The slow pace did offer me a chance to meet some interesting characters throughout the evening. That was one thing that differed from the ER. There hadn't been much of an opportunity for social interaction with ER patients when they were all temporary. They would either be shipped out or moved to somewhere else in the hospital. In the cardiology department, however, the patients usually stayed for a while.

The guy in room 305 was recovering from a triple bypass, and as soon as I entered his room, I knew he had a story or two to tell. Books filled the small space. Leather-bound novels, art books, and books about nearly anything else I could imagine were piled high on almost every hard surface.

"They're beautiful, aren't they? Like a naked woman covered in silk, you just want to reach out and touch it, devour it and own it," the man said with a rich deep voice that hinted at his Latin heritage.

Um…okay…

I wasn't exactly sure how to react to that, so I did my usual noncommittal head nod and carried on. I checked his vitals while trying not to make direct eye contact that could encourage him to talk more.

He smirked slightly at my obvious avoidance, and his chest rose in silent laughter. "I'm Nash," he said.

"Jude," I replied quickly.

His eyes assessed me, taking note of my sandy-blond hair that was in desperate need of a haircut and the tattoos that scrolled across my arms and biceps under the sleeves of my shirt. I was used to this routine. I'd been stared at and brazenly gawked over ever since I started inking my skin. I'd ditched the perfect upper-class appearance I'd been sporting since birth for something a bit rougher.

I was no longer the man I had been before. When Megan had died, I'd left my family and the life I was supposed to have. When I looked in the mirror, I didn't want to see the old Jude, so I'd changed everything about myself. I'd bought a home gym, and when I wasn't at the hospital, I would lift weights, run in the early morning, and work on making sure I never saw what I once had been when I arrived here so long ago.

"You're not much of a talker, are you?" Nash said, cutting through all the garbage clogging my brain.

"Not really," I answered honestly.

"That's all right. I talk enough for two people."

And he did. Within twenty minutes, I knew more about Nash than I did my own mother. A retired hippie, Nash had spent his early years living in communes up and down the West Coast.

As he said, "I was loving life and breathing it all in."

I translated that to mean, he'd slept with a lot of women, and he'd done about every drug imaginable, but I thought he was a man of poetic words.

Later in life, he'd settled down and married—several times. He had a few children, who had eventually had children of their own. He was a writer, and apparently, he was a very successful one. I'd made a mental note to look him up when I got home. His love for filet mignon and chocolate cake had caught up to him, and now, he was paying the price with an extended stint in the hospital.

"But every part of our life is a journey, isn't it?" he said.

I made my way to the door without a response before entering the hallway.

My life was anything but a journey. It was a dead-end.

As I passed by room 307, I noticed the door was slightly ajar. It was a room I hadn't visited yet. I quietly peeked my head just inside and saw a young woman sitting up in bed. Flowing down her back, her long hair was loose and straight, like silky sun-kissed straw. Pale and thin, she looked fragile and angelic. Her gaze was focused up toward the TV positioned across the room in the corner, and she laughed silently, covering her mouth.

That was when I noticed she had chocolate pudding on her finger.

In her other hand, she held a pudding cup. She was

scooping out the chocolate with her finger and sucking on it like a child might suckle a favorite pacifier. I couldn't help the smile that spread across my face at the sight of her using her finger instead of a spoon. It was kind of gross but a little endearing. She slowly continued this process, taking small scoops of the dessert, until the cup was completely empty. She then proceeded to lick the edges clean.

I didn't know why I was so fascinated by this event. Maybe it was the simplicity of it or the sheer goofiness of witnessing something so innocent.

When was the last time I enjoyed something so simple? Have I ever?

Growing up, my life had been all about privilege and clout. I'd enjoyed it, but I didn't know if I had ever taken the time to appreciate something so easy and insignificant.

Have I allowed myself the opportunity?

Before she had a chance to notice the creeper standing in her doorway, I disappeared back into the hallway. The slight smile was still spread across my lips as I set my sights for the hospital cafeteria. I suddenly had a special late-night delivery to make.

CHAPTER THREE

THE GREAT PUDDING MYSTERY

LAILAH

No checklist was required this morning. It took all of a second for my tiny eardrums to recognize the whisper-soft sound of oxygen being pumped into me. As my eyes fluttered opened and focused, I reached up and felt the plastic tubing around my nose. I instantly frowned. My nose was already dry and flaky from the stupid tubes.

Gross.

I hated sleeping like this. It was uncomfortable, unpleasant, and put me in a bad mood, but since my breathing had been a little less than ideal yesterday, I'd been put on oxygen overnight.

The bright side was I at least had machines and monitors on days like these.

Things could be much worse, and when I found myself trending toward the bitter side of the spectrum, I always tried to remind myself of that little fact. I could have been born half a century ago and never made it out of the hospital. In my twenty-two years, I'd done my fair share of complaining. I'd cried myself to sleep more times than I could count. I'd argued with my poor mother. I'd begged and pleaded with her when she brought me back to the hospital for yet another procedure.

But through it all, the rational, realistic part of me knew one very important thing—I was so incredibly lucky to be alive.

I had been fortunate enough to be born in a century with modern technology and in a country with experienced doctors who could treat my condition and help me move from one birthday to the next. Without them, I knew I wouldn't have made it this far. My life would always be an uphill battle, and even though no one knew what the future held for me, I knew I was blessed for the short life I'd had so far. Longevity wasn't a guarantee for me. It was a reality I had come to terms with long ago, far younger than any person should, but it was my reality and mine alone.

Being the repeat offender that I was in this medical establishment, I didn't bother with calling in a nurse to help me. I simply shut off the oxygen myself. Pulling the tubes away, I took a deep breath and wiped my nose, hating the way my skin felt after a long night of the cannulas blowing air on it.

I did a small stretch and quickly glanced across the small room. My mother's latest book was once again lying on the chair, forgotten along with her sweater. An empty cup was sitting on a nearby table. I searched around for my journal. I'd been writing late into the night.

That was when I noticed it. A single cup of chocolate pudding—with a spoon—was sitting on the tray next to my bed.

I looked around as if the hospital walls would somehow divulge an answer. They didn't, and I scratched my head in confusion.

How did that get here?

It matched the same snack-sized pudding cup I'd eaten the night before.

I did eat that last night, didn't I?

My mind wandered back to the evening before.

Lying in bed with my fuzzy slippers on, I'd watched a rerun of *New Girl* to keep me entertained. Dr. Marcus had made good on his promise of getting me an extra dessert. Not only had two helpings of carrot cake been delivered, but there had also been a little pudding cup as well. I'd saved that little morsel for last.

After my tray had been taken away, I'd realized that I'd handed my spoon over with the rest of my dinnerware, so I'd no longer had anything to use for the pudding. I'd sat there, staring at my pudding for a while, as I'd tried to decide if I really wanted to bother the poor nursing staff with bringing me a spoon, or if I should wait until later. Then, I'd remembered the events of the day and the fact that I was supposed to be snug in my own bed. So, I'd peeled the top off and just decided to go for it.

No one had been around anyway, and I hadn't been trying to impress anyone.

So, yep, I'd eaten it with my fingers—after washing my hands first, of course.

My little trip down memory lane proved one thing—well, two actually. I wasn't losing my mind, and this was indeed new chocolate deliciousness perched in front of me.

But from whom?

Dr. Marcus had brought the first one, so I guessed it would be logical to assume he'd brought the second one. A small smile danced across my face. He always did like to spoil me. I made a mental note to thank him when he came in to check on me later.

I got up and readied myself for the day—showering, brushing my teeth, and pulling a brush through my wet hair. Then, I might have possibly eaten that pudding before breakfast.

"Hey, did you, by chance, sneak into my room last night—you know, after I fell asleep—to drop off another pudding cup on my tray for me to wake up to?" I asked Dr. Marcus.

He looked up from the computer screen, his mouth slightly ajar, as he stared at me with a bewildered expression on his face. I really wished I had a camera to capture it.

"Did I what?"

"Sneak into my room? To bring me chocolate pudding?" I repeated, not even trying to hide the grin quickly spreading across my face.

"No, I definitely did not do that. I might be a little unconventional, but sneaking into my patients' rooms late at night is one thing I haven't attempted yet," he answered with a wink.

He finished my checkup and gave me a bit of good news.

"No oxygen tonight Lailah. Let's see how things go. I'll be back to check on you tomorrow," he announced, with a warm, encouraging smile.

My heartbeat was still irregular, and I wasn't feeling all that great. Those were two signs that I wouldn't be busting out of this place anytime soon. All the cozy grins in the world couldn't distract me from that cold hard truth.

The next two days passed by without much change. The only shift in my mundane hospital existence was the arrival of the new nursing assistant. I'd only seen him a handful of times, but each time he passed by my door, I would find myself leaning forward just to catch the last tiny glimpse of him walking by. He was like a Greek god covered in tattoos—and scrubs.

Or at least that's what the nurses were describing him as.

Having spent the majority of my life in a hospital bed, I knew that I was a little innocent when it came to the male species, but I understood *hot* when it smacked me in the face —or walked by my door and the little I'd seen was definitely drool worthy.

He wasn't just hot. He was different.

Different and hot were a deadly combination for all females, even me, and that made him interesting.

He'd come into my room a few times, checked my vitals even, but he had barely spoken a word. He would only mumble a hello or something as he typed on the keyboard. With his head lowered, he would just do his job, methodically taking my blood pressure—which I was sure had gone wonky in his presence—and then he'd move on to the next task. His touch alone had been distinct, haunting almost. It was something I couldn't yet comprehend. When everything had been completed, I would get one brief peek into his haunting sea-glass green eyes as he'd give a quick nod in my direction. Then, he'd vanish.

Each time he had come into my room, I'd wanted to talk to him—ask him something, anything—just to hear him speak again, but I'd never really spoken to people my age.

What would I say?

Hey, did you see Jimmy Fallon last night?

Are college parties as crazy as they are in movies?

Do people really say words like totes *and* fo'rizzle?

Outside of TV and books, I had no idea what went on in the real world. My life existed in and out of a hospital. When I wasn't here, I would be at home. So scared of what the outside world might do to my health, my mother had sheltered me from almost everything beyond the safety of what she could control. I'd been homeschooled since I was in kindergarten, I'd never been allowed to do anything outdoors, and I couldn't remember a single memory of my life that hadn't involved a doctor of some sort.

Besides the tattooed addition to the staff, the other excitement to my life had been the continuation of my special pudding deliveries. Just like the first day, I would wake up to find a single chocolate pudding cup awaiting me as I rose from bed each and every day.

By the fourth day, I'd created a list of potential suspects. Since Dr. Marcus was out, my list was now reduced to three people—Grace, my overly enthusiastic and recently engaged day nurse; the little girl from down the hall, who would sometimes visit me; and my mother who knew I was in need of some cheering up.

Scooting my broccoli around my lunch plate, I looked at my list. Yes, I'd actually written out a list on paper. I had a lot of time on my hands.

Receiving mysterious gifts in the form of pudding was the highlight of my day.

Okay, it was the highlight of my year so far.

My short pink nail tapped against the wood laminate of my tray table as I studied the list and finally came to a decision. It had to be Grace.

Having just had what could only be described as one of the best moments of her life, she'd naturally want to spread that joy to others. Plus, she would sing show tunes down the hallway, and she loved Hello Kitty, so it wasn't a hard conclusion to come to.

Why wouldn't she just deliver the puddings during the day when she was on shift, rather than in the middle of the night?

The answer completely evaded me.

Who needs logic?

I decided to call Grace out on being the pudding stalker the next time she visited my room. Kindness like that couldn't go unnoticed, and I wanted her to know that I appreciated the gesture. I also wanted to see if she could maybe bring me more—just in case the first one got lost.

That could totally happen.

I didn't have to wait long. About thirty minutes later, I heard her familiar humming. Within seconds, she was gracing my door, her beautiful smile brightening the fluorescent-lit room like a ray of sunshine from the heavens.

"Still on a I'm-getting-married high?" I asked.

I shook my head at the comical display she was putting on as she waltzed around the room.

"Mmm…yes. In about six months, I think it will change into an I'm-married high, and eventually, an I'm-pregnant high, and—oh!" She froze mid-waltz, covering her mouth, as she realized her words.

"Grace," I said softly, "you don't have to hide the joy in your life around me. We all have happy moments. Mine are just different than yours."

"I know. I just…I'm sorry. Here I am, babbling about babies."

"It's not a big deal. I've known my whole life that I couldn't have children. It's not a secret or a big surprise. Besides, it's not like I have suitors lined up down the hallway, fighting for my hand," I scoffed.

Her mouth quirked as she joined me and sat down on the edge of the bed. Her silky black hair was pulled into a neat ponytail, and her sapphire blue eyes met mine. She wasn't just my nurse. She was a friend, my only friend.

"That's just because they haven't seen you. You're like Rapunzel, stuck away in that high stone tower just waiting for your handsome prince to come and steal your heart away."

I smiled as she went about checking vitals, and I listened as she carried on about some celebrity scandal I'd heard about on the news. My thoughts wandered back to what she'd said about me being locked away, waiting for someone to steal my heart. Usually so hopeful about my condition, I didn't know why, but my first thought had been that whoever the prince might be, he'd better hurry. I wasn't sure how long this heart of mine would last.

GRACE HAD SURPRISINGLY TURNED OUT TO BE A DEAD-END AS well, and as the week had gone by, my list of suspects had dwindled. My mother definitely wasn't the culprit since I would see her leave every night at eight o'clock. That only left Abigail, the little girl from down the hall.

She actually wasn't a patient of the hospital, but I didn't know how else to describe her, so I always referred to her as the girl from down the hall. I thought she was a grand-daughter of one of the patients, and she would sometimes wander into my room when she got bored of listening to her grandfather.

Abigail bounced into my room right around the time I was snuggling into the third chapter of my new favorite book. The book I was currently reading would always be my favorite, and the one I was about to read would always be my next favorite. I loved reading. I'd spent the majority of my life with my nose stuck in a book. I'd inherited my love for the written word from my scholarly mother, and I had managed to teach myself a world's worth of knowledge within the dusty pages. I'd read everything from Chaucer to Shakespeare to even Anne Rice.

"Whatcha reading?" Abigail asked, her springy chocolate brown curls bouncing behind her as she flopped on my bed.

"It's actually a book about a girl right around your age, maybe a few years older."

"You're reading a kids book?" She ducked down to try to inspect the cover of the worn paperback in my hand.

I'd read this particular book several times throughout my youth, and my copy of it had been well used.

"*Anne Frank. The Diary of a Young Girl.* Who's she?" she asked.

"She was a girl who lived during World War II, and this is the diary she kept."

Inspecting the cover a bit longer, she stared into the black-and-white face of the young Jewish girl looking back at her. "I keep a diary," she replied.

"You do? So do I."

"Really? Aren't you a little too old?" Her noise scrunched up as she looked up at me.

I could see the tiny freckles dotting her rosy cheeks.

"Absolutely not!" I pretended to be offended, but then I added, "But I do call mine a journal just to be safe."

I tickled her ribs, and she let out a little giggle.

"What do you write about?"

"I don't know," she replied. "Papa gave it to me for my birthday. He told me to write what's in my soul, but I don't know what a soul is exactly, so I usually just write what I did at school and stuff I like."

That's right.

I now remembered Grace telling me about Abigail's grandfather. He was a writer and quite the talker. Grace had said she couldn't make it out of his room without getting hit on or hearing one of the colorful stories of his past.

"Your soul is kind of like your heart. So, I guess your papa was telling you to write what you feel here," I said, pointing to the place where her perfect tiny heart beat inside her chest. "Here, why don't you borrow this?" I suggested, handing her the book from my hands.

She hesitantly took it, and her eyes floated up to mine. "Are you sure? You weren't done with it."

"I've read it enough times to have it practically memorized. It's your turn."

Her face lit up with a smile, and she dived into my arms, giving me a hug so big that I had to brace myself from the impact. I laughed and wrapped my arms around her small body.

She reluctantly let go and jumped off the bed before straightening her summery pink dress.

"Well, I'd better get going. Thanks again for the book. I'll bring it back when I'm done."

"No rush. Take your time."

She made her way to the door.

I called out to stop her, "Oh, Abigail? Did you by chance leave pudding in my room?"

"Pudding? Like the kind my mom sticks in my lunch-box?" she asked with a curious look.

I huffed out in frustration, "Never mind." *Back to the drawing board I go.*

CHAPTER FOUR

QUIET LIKE A MOUSE

JUDE

Any day now, the cafeteria lady was going to stage an intervention for my all-consuming pudding habit. Either that, or she'd come up with some ridiculous nickname to call me.

Oh, wait—she already did that.

"Hey, Puddin'. Just the usual again tonight?" she asked with a sweet grin.

I nodded as I paid for my pudding and bottle of water, and then I headed back to the elevator.

Over the past week, I'd gotten used to the girl's schedule in room 307. By eleven, she'd usually be asleep, and I could slip in, unnoticed, and drop off the tiny chocolate snack for her to see in the morning.

It had started out as only a one-time thing. That evening, when I'd seen her licking that chocolate off her finger, I had felt like I was seeing humanity for the first time in years. It was crazy, considering where I worked. Hospitals seemed to be a place where humanity soared. Lives of loved ones or patients themselves would be put into the hands of someone else, and out would come every base emotion imaginable—

overwhelming fear, unending love, unsurpassable joy, and heart-rending pain. Everything would be thrown into one messy basket.

Being inside these hospital walls, I'd seen it all, yet I felt nothing anymore. I'd become immune to it all.

Megan's death had been like an atom bomb to my psyche, obliterating every emotion I'd possessed until I saw nothing. An emotional overload, I guessed one could call it.

Every patient I would treat was just another blank face carrying me to the next.

The only reason I was here was Megan. It had nothing to do with taking care of my next patient or connecting with that person's family. I couldn't remember how to feel anything anymore.

Then, I'd seen her. As if she didn't have a care in the world, she had been eating pudding without a spoon while staying in a hospital, like it was the most normal thing in the world. At that moment, I'd experienced the slightest sense of something other than pain again.

And I'd been supplying her habit ever since.

I didn't know how long I was going to keep up the charade or if I could continue without being caught, but it was the only highlight of my day that didn't feel over-wrought with emotionless shades of gray.

WITH ONE PUDDING CUP SNUG IN MY POCKET, I WAS THE EPITOME of stealth.

I slipped through the door quietly, ignoring the fact that I looked like a creepy stalker, and I stepped into the darkened room like I had a purpose.

I did work here, so there could be a dozen reasons for me entering a patient's room.

Delivering a fudge snack pack was probably not one of them.

Like the many times before, I tried not to linger as I entered the room, but with each passing visit, it became more and more difficult.

The first night I'd decided to do this, I'd quickly done this drop-and-dash routine. I had gone in and out without a second glance.

But then, I'd met her. I'd come to her room and found myself face-to-face with the girl behind my late-night pudding runs. She was shy and timid, her gestures clumsy and unpracticed. She was so different from the polished and sophisticated girls I'd grown up with. Even her name was awkward. It sounded like the classic Eric Clapton song "Layla," but hers was spelled all wrong.

She had made me curious. I'd suddenly wanted to know what else in this world would make her smile.

What made her laugh? Why does she quickly tug the collar of her shirt whenever I enter the room?

Curiosity wasn't something I'd experienced in a while, and it had me lingering a little longer each time I entered her room at night. Eventually, it would become my ultimate undoing.

"Ouch! Shit!" I hissed under my breath as my knee collided with her bathroom door that had been left open.

I froze, listening for the slightest movement. My mind jumped ahead, trying to think of any plausible reason for being in her room at this hour.

Changing her sheets?

No, dumbass, she's in them.

Heard a noise and just coming to check things out?

Yeah, okay. That could work.

Never mind the fact that I was the one making the noise.

Five seconds passed by as I stood in the shadows like a statue, my ears on high alert as I waited for any movement that might signal my need for a cover story.

But nothing happened—no movement, no screaming or shouting.

So, I continued with my weird late-night mission. That was what guys with nothing else to do did at night, right? Delivered pudding to hospital rooms in the dark?

Totally normal.

Pulling the small little snack pack out of my pocket, I carefully dropped it along with the plastic spoon on the wooden tray table next to her bed. I wasn't sure if eating the pudding with her finger was a chosen thing or not. Everyone had their quirks, so I figured I'd give her the option. Hygiene was an awesome thing, especially in a hospital.

The moonlight from the window lit up the wisps of her hair, making it appear as if a golden halo surrounded her face. She looked innocent, yet a wisdom beyond anything I'd seen seemed to shine through her very pores. I wanted to reach out and touch a single strand just to see what angel hair would feel like between my fingers.

Instead, I turned away. I'd done enough loitering for tonight.

Much quieter this time, I stepped lightly to the door. I reached for the doorknob and turned it slightly before making my exit.

Then, a light voice behind me uttered, "You were definitely not on my list."

Busted.

Knowing there was little I could do to escape, I stuck my hands in my pockets and pivoted around on my heels. I found her very much awake. Sitting up in bed in a loose T-shirt and shorts, she assessed me quietly with her knees pulled into her chest.

"Your list?" I asked., turning to flip the switch on the wall that turned on the overhead light. Standing in the dark while she was awake now felt awkward and weird.

"Yeah, I made a suspect list of those with the greatest probability of being the person behind the pudding drop-offs. You were definitely not on it. Huh, I'm not wrong very often," she said with a bit of surprise.

"How does that feel?"

"What?"

"Being wrong."

"Oh...well, I kind of like it. It's thrilling." She gave a sheepish grin.

"So, who was on your list?" My hands still in my pockets, I took a few leisurely steps back into the room.

"Oh, um...well, there was my mom. She was almost immediately taken off. She leaves too early. She teaches morning classes now. She didn't used to because she would teach me in the morning, but obviously, that's not a problem since I'm not in high school anymore, and—oh, wow, I'm babbling."

"So, you didn't go to school?" I took a seat in the tired, worn-looking chair in the corner, hoping that it would calm her nerves.

She looked down and fiddled with her fingers a bit. "No, never. I was homeschooled." she answered slowly. "My mom teaches at a local community college. She used to be a professor at UCLA, but when I started kindergarten, she decided to give up her position as chair of the religious studies department. Instead, she taught nights, so she could be home during the day. I always hated that she gave up the career she'd worked so hard to obtain just to teach algebra and American history to me throughout the years, but she never seemed to mind—or at least, she never showed it. My grandmother filled in at night when I was younger, and then after she died, a nurse helped," she said the last part quietly.

"Who else was on the list?" I asked, moving her away from a topic I had a feeling was rough for her.

"Grace," she answered.

"Who?"

"Grace. She's a day nurse. She has long black hair and wears Disney and Hello Kitty scrubs even though she works nowhere near pediatrics."

"Oh, you mean Snow White?" I asked.

She snorted, and it made me smile. No one I'd known back home would ever snort in public. It was a good, honest sound.

"That's a good nickname for her. It's perfect."

"I didn't come up with it. One of the other guys around here did. He said he heard her singing, and he swore that birds were flocking to the window to listen. So, from then on, she became Snow White."

"She loves to sing. But I figured out it wasn't her either. So, that left Abigail."

"Oh, Nash's granddaughter? I've seen her around. She's sweet, but she'd never share pudding with you. Kids don't share pudding snacks," I said with a small grin.

"That's a good rule to live by," she answered quietly before asking, "How's the knee?"

My eyes flew up to hers in surprise. "You were awake?"

She nodded. "How else did you think I was going to figure out the secret identity of my pudding delivery person?"

"Hmm…smart woman."

"Glad you noticed."

"Do all smart women eat pudding with their fingers?" Leaning back in the chair a bit further, I arched my eyebrow in question.

Her mouth fell open in embarrassment. "Oh my God, you saw that?"

A brief nod and a slight grin that I couldn't contain were my only answers.

She started babbling again,

"I normally use a spoon. Like a normal person. I mean, who licks pudding off their fingers? Gross. And my hands were clean. Like, really clean!" she squeaked.

"It's not like anyone was watching."

I lifted an eyebrow and I watched her head fall to her lap.

"Well, apparently, you were watching. How embarrassing!" she laughed.

"Hey, it's not a big deal, Lailah. We all have our weird habits. I'm sure I have mine. Some people eat peanut butter and pickle sandwiches or dip their chips in ice cream. We're all a little crazy in our own little way."

"I'm pretty sure those examples you just said only pertain to pregnant women," she pointed out.

"What?"

"I really don't think anyone who isn't carrying another person in their uterus would be able to stomach peanut butter and pickles together. That's just gross. And for the record again, I always use a spoon—except for that one time."

"Okay, sure," I answered, letting the disbelief in my voice bleed out.

She huffed in frustration. I couldn't help but chuckle slightly when I rose from the chair.

The sound of my own laugh registered in my ears, and I suddenly felt conflicted. I didn't remember the last time I'd heard anything remotely close to a laugh burst from my lungs. I wasn't sure how I felt about it.

"I'd better get back to work. You need anything else before I go?" I asked quickly, looking around and briefly checking her hep-lock and pulse-ox monitor.

"Oh, um…nope, I'm good."

In reaction to my clinical-sounding tone, she immediately retreated back to the shy and timid girl I'd met days before.

"Okay, well, I'll see you around."

"Okay."

This time, I'd pulled the door halfway open before her lyrical voice once again halted me to a stop.

"Jude?" she called out.

Hearing my name on her lips for the first time made something tighten in my chest. It was something foreign and so long-ago forgotten that I didn't even recognize it.

I turned to face her. "Yeah?"

"Is it all right for me to call you that?" she asked hesitantly, her bright blue eyes looking across the room at the badge that hung around my neck.

I nodded, pulling the plastic ID into my hand. "It's my name."

"Next time, do you think you could maybe come a bit earlier and stay a while?"

A grin I couldn't contain spread across my face, and I found myself nodding. "Sure. See you then."

CHAPTER FIVE
NO OTHER OPTION

LAILAH

Jude is my secret admirer.

My secret admirer is Jude.

Can I call him that? What do I call the person who has brought me chocolate dessert snacks late at night? Is there a name for that?

I like secret admirer, so I'll go with that.

Jude.

Chocolate.

I sighed.

"Lailah? Have you heard a word I've said?"

"Huh?" I blurted out, pulling myself out of the ridiculous wheel of girlish thoughts spinning uncontrollably through my head.

"Are you feeling all right? You've been a little absent-minded today."

"I feel fine. Just a little tired."

After my late-night visit, I'd been wide-awake, my head full of questions, thoughts, and possibilities. My first and foremost question had been, *Why is he doing it? What is his motivation? Is he just being nice, or is it something more?*

I'd quickly dismissed anything having to do with something more and concluded that he was just being nice. That man could easily have any woman he wanted. He could probably snap his fingers and groupies with bedazzled *We Love Jude* scrubs would show up, ready to play naughty nurse. He definitely didn't need to deliver desserts to patients in the hospital to help his game.

Even if in some alternate universe, he could possibly see me as someone more than a patient, I couldn't go down that road—ever. My life was too stressful and emotionally turbulent to share with someone else. Asking someone to step into my world would be like asking him to sign away his own life to take care of mine. I could never do that.

Love wasn't an option for me.

I did, however, like the idea of having another friend. Outside of Grace, I didn't know anyone around my age. Carrying on conversations with Dr. Marcus and Abigail were entertaining, but sometimes, I really wanted to connect with someone on equal footing.

"Well, I need you to pay attention," my mother said, bringing me back to the conversation I was supposed to be engaged in. "I talked to Marcus earlier this morning."

"Why didn't he talk to me?" I hated that she still treated me like a child.

"He was going to, but I asked if I could speak with you privately first. He'll be here in a few minutes."

That doesn't sound good.

"He's been reviewing your test results over the last week and comparing them to the couple of weeks prior," she said, hesitating.

Her eyes turned away from mine, but I saw a single tear trickling down her cheek. Her blonde hair masked her expression, but I knew it was bad.

"Yeah? And what did he find out? What is it, Mom?"

"He thinks your heart is getting worse."

"It's always getting worse, Mom," I said, trying not to let the words settle under my skin.

"It's time, Lailah."

Her words were gentle, but I could see how much it hurt for her to say them.

Congestive heart failure.

I'd heard the words before, and I'd known every treatment and surgery would still eventually lead to this.

"But, this has happened before—when they said a transplant was my only option. They managed to do other things, like replace my pacemaker. I've done just fine."

"There's nothing that can fix this, Lailah. There are no more treatments, surgeries, or procedures they can do. We got lucky after the last time, and Marcus was able to give you a few extra years, but not this time. The only thing that can fix this is a new heart."

Her single tear had multiplied, and her face was now wet with mascara-stained tracks running down her cheeks.

"So, what do we do now?" I asked quietly. *Don't cry, Lailah. Don't cry.*

"Marcus is working on getting you set up at UCLA hospital again. Beyond that, we pray the insurance company does what they need to do."

I nodded, feeling numb, when she came to sit next to me on the bed before pulling me into her arms. Everything had become iffy and unknown since my mother's employer had switched insurance companies last year. Her premiums had gone through the roof, and then add in all the new health care laws, and no one knew what was going on.

The familiar sounds of the room—the beeps, the shuffling from outside the door—all faded away. All I could hear were the roaring in my ears and the words repeating and echoing in my head.

Heart transplant.

No other option.

My mother had spent every dime she had on my medical

bills. We lived paycheck to paycheck in a small apartment on the outskirts of Santa Monica. She wouldn't talk about it, but I knew she'd emptied her savings account and retirement plan to pay past-due bills to the hospital. If my transplant was denied or something happened to me, she wouldn't be able to cover it. It would destroy her.

I hated that it had come to this.

I was the never-ending burden.

"We'll figure it out, Mom," I said against her shoulder.

"Yeah, we will. It's just you and me."

My mom brought in dinner that night, and we sat together on my bed, hunched over a meal of simple sandwiches and fruit.

Whenever we got bad news, my mom would bring in dinner. I thought it was her way of coping. Bad news was something she couldn't control. My mother loved control. She'd practically raised me in a glass dome, trying to protect me from everything that could harm my fragile heart. When things went wrong, she would grow quiet, internalizing and regrouping.

After dinner, she would announce her master plan. When bad news struck, Mom always fired back with some sort of plan. Even if it were as simple as following the doctor's orders or sending me to bed an hour earlier, it would put her back in control of the situation.

Mom loved control.

I feared this would be the one situation she couldn't control with any of her master plans.

It wasn't long after my mom had left that night when I began fidgeting with my hair.

I braided it to the side and then promptly brushed it through with my fingers. I gathered it up into a ponytail but then yanked it out. Finally, I just let the platinum blonde strands fall to my shoulders.

Am I seriously sitting here, playing with my hair?

One conversation with Jude—who was just being nice, I reminded myself—and I'd become one of *those girls* overnight. Feeling utterly ridiculous, I shook my hair out, letting it do whatever it wanted. The fact that I'd changed into one of my nicer tops and a black pair of leggings was just a coincidence.

I am so lame.

Sinking back against my pillow, I picked up my latest paperback and opened it up to where I'd left off. I'd barely made it a page in when I heard a quiet knock at my door.

"Come in," I answered.

The doorknob turned, and Jude appeared, dressed in teal scrubs. He was carrying a chocolate pudding and—

A board game?

"Are we playing Scrabble?" I questioned, tucking my hair behind my ear as I tried not to blush. Placing my book aside, I crossed my legs in front of me and watched him enter the room.

"No, we're playing Operation," he answered, placing the game on the foot of my bed. "I found it in a staff lounge. I think one of the surgeons got it as a gag gift. Anyway, I hope the game choice doesn't bother you, but I thought you might want to do something different."

I glanced down at the goofy-looking man displayed on the front of the box and grinned.

"It's perfect." I let go of a breath I didn't realize I'd been holding. "Just what I needed."

He set down not just one, but two pudding snacks on the bedside tray, and then he dropped two spoons next to them. "One of those is mine," he said with a slight grin.

He turned to pull the chair out of the corner, and he brought it closer to the bed. I considered suggesting that he just sit on the bed with me, but I quickly lost my nerve. The thought of having him so close gave me chills. He handed me a pudding cup, and we both dived in. There were no snide comments about eating it with a spoon rather than my finger tonight.

"So, bad day?" he asked as we began setting up the game.

The cardboard lid came off, and he pulled out the large playing board. The same silly-looking man that was on the cover stared back up at us. His uneasy, wide-eyed expression was amusing, and it was already helping to lift my mood.

"How did you know?" I asked. *Do I look that bad?*

"Just a guess. You look like you need a mental break."

"I do," I admitted. "I really do. It's been a rough one."

"Wanna talk about it?" he offered.

I took the first turn. My tiny tweezers pulled out the little ice cream cone causing brain freeze in the man's head.

No buzzing.

Success.

"Got a while?" I joked, the laughter not reaching my eyes.

"I got time. What else are lunch breaks for?" His warm gaze met mine as he took his turn.

"You mean, you don't have any hot lunch dates?"

"Well, I did have plans."

"Oh, I'm sorry. You didn't have to cancel. I mean, you could still try to..." The words tumbled out of my mouth like an overturned apple cart.

"I'm kidding, Lailah," he said, his hand reaching out to touch mine.

My eyes wandered down to where his hand touched my skin, and I couldn't look away. I felt branded. Like the brief times his fingers had grazed my skin before while he'd removed a blood pressure cuff or leaned over to check my IV block, my heart fluttered, and I felt my cheeks redden. My entire life had been spent being touched and examined. By this time in my twenty-two years, I'd become accustomed to random people invading my personal space, but my body reacted to Jude in a very different and completely new way. It nearly combusted at the slightest touch from him.

"The only hot date I've ever had on my lunch break has been the vending machine. Believe me, there is nowhere else I have to be," he said, pulling his hand back to grab the tweezers.

"Oh…well, okay, if you're sure. I mean, we could always do this another time."

"You're deflecting—on purpose. Come on, tell me about your day," he challenged, calling me out on my purposeful rambling.

"I have to have a heart transplant," I said simply.

Jude's attention to the game immediately ended, and his green gaze met my eyes instantly. "Are they sure?"

"Yeah, pretty sure. I was born with an enlarged heart. I had open heart surgery when I was days old. Since then, I've had several more surgeries and dozens of other procedures. It's kept me alive, but a damaged heart can only last so long."

"Are you scared?" he asked softly.

"Yes, but mostly for my mom."

"Why?"

"I just fear the what-ifs. What if the insurance doesn't go through? What if something goes wrong? What if I don't make it…then who will she turn to?"

"You don't have any other family?" He chucked his empty pudding cup in the trash.

"No, I never knew my father. He bailed before I was born. Since my grandmother died, it's always just been my mother and me. I just hate having to see her go through all of this again."

"What do you mean, again?" he asked, the game now long forgotten.

"This isn't the first time I've been told I need a transplant. My heart started failing a few years ago. They told me a transplant was the best option then, so I was put on the donor list. Then, miraculously, one became available."

His brows furrowed together in confusion. "What happened?"

"I wasn't supposed to know. They don't usually tell you until it's a sure thing, and you're being called in for surgery, but Dr. Marcus was so hopeful. It wasn't his fault," I clarified.

He'd only been trying to do the right thing.

"Finding a match and in the same hospital was like angels bringing me a miracle. He was just trying to make sure everything was falling into place. He came into my room and told me that a woman had been in a car accident, and she was an organ donor. He said we were a perfect match, and it was hopeful."

"What happened?" he asked softly.

"The family changed their minds at the last minute."

Silence filled the room as I stared at our dark shadows against the wall. I finally looked down at Jude sitting back in the old blue chair. He'd grown incredibly quiet and still.

"And you said this happened here—at this hospital?" he asked.

"Yes, here," I answered, wondering why he was asking.

"How long ago?"

"Um…it was right around my nineteenth birthday so it was three years ago. Towards the end of May I guess."

More silence filled the air as Jude remained motionless. I didn't understand this abrupt change in pace.

Did I upset him somehow?

Suddenly, almost startling me, he rose from the chair and turned to me. "I'd better go. I think my lunch break is just about over," he said in an almost monotone fashion.

"Oh, okay," I answered.

"I'm off the next two days, and when I get back, I might be pretty swamped, so I'm not sure if I'll be able to get away," he said rather quickly, taking a step backward toward the door with each word uttered until he vanished.

Looking around the room, I took a deep breath. Then, my eyes returned to the closed door.

I was alone—again.

I stared down at the abandoned board game, which we'd barely begun, and my empty pudding cup lying next to it. At that moment, the reality of my day finally caught up to me.

No amount of chocolate, silly games, or odd visits from nurses' assistants could hide the fact that my heart was giving up on living.

What if I'm not ready for that?

After I'd found out the family had changed their minds, I'd been so upset that I asked Dr. Marcus to do anything he could to hold off on the need for a transplant. He wasn't thrilled with my decision but he'd managed to make it work, finding alternate treatment methods over the last few years. That night had scared me and reminded me of how precious life was.

One life had to be given in order for another to live on. I hadn't been ready for that responsibility yet.

After taking one last look around the room, I closed my eyes. Finally breaking down the walls I'd constructed around myself to keep my emotions at bay, I curled into my bed, succumbing to the emotions of the day and cried myself to sleep.

CHAPTER SIX

SELFISH

JUDE

couldn't remember the rest of my shift after I'd left Lailah's room that night. I just remembered moving through the motions, going from one task to the other, while her words had echoed through my head over and over until they had practically seared themselves into my very soul.

Finding a match and in the same hospital was like angels bringing me a miracle.

The family changed their minds at the last minute.

It couldn't be. It wasn't possible. I wouldn't allow myself to believe it was true.

By the time I'd clocked out and driven home, I'd convinced myself I was out of my mind for even thinking about it in the first place.

But then, as I sat in the dark recess of my lonely apartment that night, I allowed myself to do the one thing I'd sworn I wouldn't ever do again. I let my mind drift back to those horrible moments in the hospital three years ago when I'd found myself sinking into the most selfish parts of me

"You can't do this. She's still in there. You're killing her!" I

screamed in desperation, the hoarse sound of my voice echoing through the stark white hallway.

"Jude," Megan's father, Paul said in a passive tone meant to be soothing.

It wasn't soothing though. It only fueled my aggression even further.

"Listen to me," he said. "This is hard on us, all of us." His voice cracked, and he brought his shaking fist to his chin in an effort to steady his emotions.

Megan's mother, Susan, took a step forward and wove her tiny hand through his and gave it a loving squeeze. I turned away.

"The doctors said there is nothing else they can do. She's gone, son. We have to let her go now."

His words hit my chest like a battering ram. She wasn't gone. I could see her. She was just behind that door.

"Her heart is still beating. I can see her chest rise when she breathes. I can still touch her skin. She's not gone," I stated my case, my voice growing small with every word.

"The doctors said that because she's an organ donor, we could let someone else live. Her heart is still healthy. She'll live on through someone else. This is something she would have wanted Jude. We've already told them yes."

I couldn't fathom it. I couldn't stand the thought of them making this decision, snuffing out her life. They didn't know what the future held.

"How do you know she's gone? What if you're killing her?" I shouted, the words making them wince, as tears clouded my vision. I slumped against the wall and collapsed to the floor.

My future was behind the door. She was my everything. They couldn't have her. I wouldn't allow it. No one would take her heart or her life—ever.

I'd won the battle that day. After a few more rounds of arguing, Megan's parents hadn't had the strength left to fight anymore. I'd planted the seed of doubt in their minds, they'd eventually crumbled. They'd told the doctors no to any organ donations and I'd spent the rest of the day by Megan's side, holding her hand and trying to bring her back into consciousness. I'd wanted to prove everyone wrong and thought I could will her back with my love alone.

But not even love could bring someone back when the mind was lost.

She'd died three days later.

At that time, Megan's parents could have still donated her heart and many of her other organs that hadn't been damaged in the car crash, but by then they'd lost the will to do so. By giving them hope that she'd somehow come back, I'd made those last few days hell for them. Two different doctors had pronounced her brain dead, but somehow, I'd thought I knew better. I hadn't allowed her parents to mourn the way they needed to. I never attended her funeral, and I hadn't left California since.

I'd lived with the guilt of that horrible, selfish day ever since. Megan's parents had been able to look past their own grief and see the bigger picture. They had known someone else could live on even if their daughter couldn't.

Why couldn't I?

I had been selfish, so damn selfish.

Was my selfishness also the reason Lailah was still sitting in a hospital room, watching life instead of living it?

I needed to find out.

My first day off, I spent the entire day caged inside my apartment. I hated my days off. I lifted weights, ate ramen, watched a football game, and by the end of the day, I was stir-crazy. Days like this were why I would end up working so many shifts at the hospital. Unlike most people, I couldn't stand to be alone. When I was by myself, I had nothing but the haunting memories of my past to keep me company. Nothing could stop the feelings of loss and the overwhelming sense of shame from taking over when I didn't have the chaos of the hospital to keep my mind from wandering down that dark, deserted path.

I might not talk much, and my coworkers might consider me a bit odd, but at least the hustle and bustle of my job could keep me occupied. It would also allow me to return to the one place where I still felt Megan. My family had begged me to come home. After canceling my cell service, I'd disowned them and basically disappeared. I wouldn't go home. I had no home anymore.

The trip to California with Megan had been a surprise present from my parents. The night of our graduation from college, our families had gathered together to celebrate our joint success. I had gotten down on one knee and asked the girl I'd been in love with since Business 101 four years earlier to be my bride. Everyone had been thrilled, and to celebrate in the typical style of my outlandish family, my father had booked Megan and me a two-week vacation to California and Maui.

He'd made a speech about how proud he was and how he couldn't wait to finally bring me into the family business. I'd already been in the family business since I was in middle school. Blessed with the gift for numbers and analytics, I had been a gold mine in the eyes of my father. At the age of fifteen, I could predict and evaluate the market better than he could at sixty. I'd fought my way out of the house and gone away to college.

Four years, Jude. That's all you get.

From across the table, he'd held his glass high and toasted us, the happy couple. He'd wished us well on our trip as he'd given me a look that said, *It's time to cash in.*

Fun and games had been coming to a close.

I'd left for California, knowing my father owned my life once again. So, I had done the best I could to make sure Megan and I had the time of our lives in California because I'd been too scared to think about what our lives would be like when we returned.

A week into our vacation, the day before we were supposed to leave for Hawaii, we'd been hanging out with a few new friends we'd met in the area. After staggering out of the party late at night, we'd played Rock, Paper, Scissors in the middle of a deserted street. The loser of the game had to drive back to the hotel.

I'd lost three times in a row.

"I don't want to," I whined, dragging my sluggish feet behind me just for effect.

"Jude! I'm tired, and you clearly lost! You have to drive!" Megan yelled back, walking in front of me.

Her tight black skirt accentuated her ass as she sauntered back and forth in her heels. I took a moment to enjoy the view.

My future wife is hot.

Her tanned long legs went on for miles, and she had beautiful dark brown hair that I loved to run my hands in, and that—

"Are you checking out my ass?" she said, suddenly pivoting around. Her hand shot to her hip, and she raised an eyebrow.

Busted.

"Mmm…maybe. If I tell you how nice it is, will you drive us back to the hotel?" I asked with a wolfish grin.

"Ugh! Maybe we should just stay here for the night," she said.

"No!" I immediately shot down the suggestion. My legs revived in an instant at the thought of spending the night anywhere but in a king-sized bed with Megan, and I jogged to catch up with her.

We finally made it to our rental car a few blocks away, and I slowed the last few steps.

Closing the gap between us, I pushed her against the car. "If we stay here, we'll be sleeping on some nasty-smelling sofa with a bunch of drunk college kids."

"We were drunk college kids just a few weeks ago, if you've forgotten."

"Yes, but we're not anymore, and we have this amazing"—I kissed her shoulder—"wonderful"—I moved across to her collarbone—"huge"—I left a trail of kisses up to her lips where I stopped

and hovered—"hotel room. *I really want to make good use of it, don't you?"*

I could feel her breath growing heavy with each kiss to her skin. By the time my lips were almost touching hers, she was practically panting.

"Yes," she breathed.

"Yes, what, Megan?"

"Yes, I want to go back to the hotel room," she answered.

I couldn't help the grin that spread across my face. I quickly planted a kiss on her lips and slapped her ass. "Good, so you'll drive then?"

Being the loving, agreeable person she was—she'd taken the keys and gotten in the driver's side of the car, ready to drive even though it should have been me.

Those were some of the last moments I'd had with her while she was still conscious. Minutes after that glass had been raining down on us as the screech of metal permanently seared itself into my brain.

I'd looked over at her as the world spun and thought of all the things I wanted to say before we died and couldn't. So many things I could have said in those last few minutes in that parking lot if I'd known.

We'd never lived together. After graduation, we'd boxed everything up, and focused on finally moving in together, but first, we had a bit of fun planned.

After she'd died, I had nothing left of her and nowhere to go where she would still be present. Her parents had taken her ashes and buried them in a family plot near their home in Chicago. I was done with school and I didn't want to go home because she wasn't there. So, I never left California. I never left the hospital. I'd just roamed the halls until Margaret offered me a job.

That was why days off were so difficult. I had no life in California outside the hospital. It wasn't just a job for me. It was where I felt most alive—or as alive as I could be anymore.

When the person you were meant to spend your life with died before that life had a chance to even begin, how would you survive? For me, I'd just kept putting one foot in front of the other, coming back to the place where I could feel her presence the most.

I was like a living ghost.

When I had days that were worse than others, I would find myself returning to that hallway, back to the room where I had held her hand, looked down at her battered and bruised body, and tried to will her back to life. Walking down the hospital halls now, I knew she wasn't there anymore, but she had been once. If I closed my eyes, I could almost see her there.

That was kind of like living, wasn't it?

IN A DESPERATE ATTEMPT TO FLEE MY DARK THOUGHTS AND MY empty apartment, I tried venturing out into the world on my second day off. Early that morning, I threw on a pair of shorts and an old T-shirt, slipped on my running shoes, and took off for the beach. It was at least five miles away from my apartment, which was absolutely perfect. I didn't want to come back home until I was so exhausted that I could barely stand.

By about mile four, I'd established a nice rhythm, and my legs were burning. My feet hit the pavement, one after the other, and my mind went blank as I listened to the white noise around me. It was a weekday, so the streets were mostly absent of laughing and playing children, but there was still plenty of life to listen to. A group of mothers walked by, chatting about whatever it was that moms talked about, lawn-mowers buzzed, and cars zoomed by. I let my mind zone out, and in what felt like a matter of minutes, I found myself staring out at the crystal-blue water of the Pacific.

It was early June. Even though California kids were still in school, the rest of the U.S. was happily enjoying summer vacation. It hadn't quite reached peak season yet for tourism, but it was starting to. The Santa Monica Pier was busy today. I decided to steer clear of my normal run down the pier. Instead, I headed left to cool down and walk through the sand.

I kicked off my shoes and headed down to the water. The sand was warm from the heat of the sun, and I felt the stark contrast when the chilly water from the ocean hit my feet. The turquoise waves were endless, stretching out in every direction as far as my eyes could see. The rays from the sun above flickered and sparkled on the water as it danced its way back and forth to the shoreline.

I'd made it probably a quarter of a mile down the beach when I heard my name being yelled from behind me. I knew maybe four people in the entire LA area—five, if I included my pizza delivery guy—so at first, I didn't respond. But how many people in the world were named Jude? My mother hadn't exactly stuck with the top ten baby names.

I turned around and saw Dr. Marcus approaching me. With sand still in his hair, he was clad in a sleek black wet suit.

"Hey, J-Man!" he greeted me, giving me a hard wet pat on the back. His wet suit was unzipped to his waist, baring his tanned chest and surfer physique.

I had to give the man props. For a middle-aged dude, Dr. Marcus was built.

"What are you doing out in the sun and in my neck of the woods? Did you finally decide to take me up on my offer for surfing lessons?" he joked, grinning, as he looked at me through his shades.

I took a quick glance out towards the waves and shook my head. "Definitely not. I've still got a little too much New Yorker in me to surf any waves," I joked. Immediately, I regretted my words. I'd never told Dr. Marcus where I was from. Trying to avoid any follow-up questions regarding my city of origin, I added, "Just out for a run, and I thought I'd cool down for a bit."

"Nice. Well, I'm headed up, he said as his eyes drifted up to the boardwalk. "Waves are shit today. Want to grab a bite with me? They make great fish tacos." He pointed to a Mexican place just up the way.

I hesitated, worried my little slip-up might bring on an onslaught of personal questions, but Dr. Marcus appeared to be nothing but genuine in his offer. In the many years we'd known each other, he never pressed me for personal information. I didn't know why, but I was suddenly paranoid he would do so now.

"Sure. Sounds good," I answered.

We stopped at his truck, and he did that magical quick-change thing that surfers did. Less than two minutes later, he was out of his wet suit and sporting a pair of shorts and a T-shirt. I looked down at my trashy T-shirt and thought about the fact that I'd run five miles here, so I probably didn't smell too great.

As we walked through the parking lot and entered the restaurant though, I felt the tension ease.

The place was small and had maybe four tables that were all mismatched green and white plastic with a few similar tables outside. The menu was written with a dry-erase marker on a white board, and no one spoke a single world of English. With the laid-back and casual atmosphere, I figured my less than stellar appearance wouldn't be an issue.

We picked a green table outside. I swore the plastic chair legs bowed a little when I sat in it. An old tube television was mounted in the corner with CNN streaming. Dr. Marcus ordered for us—in Spanish, of course. Besides knowing the words *dos* and *gracias*, I had no idea what he had said.

My father had spent a fortune on private language tutors, so I'd have a leg up on several languages when I went to prep school. We'd quickly found out that language was not one of my strengths. I believed my tutor had told my father that based on my aptitude for language arts, I was lucky to have learned English.

"You into trading?" Dr. Marcus asked, pulling my head away from the tiny numbers scrolling across the bottom of the TV screen.

I'd left my old life behind, but I would still find myself checking in every now and then whenever I saw that ticker. Maybe I wanted to see them fail without me—or maybe I wanted to see them succeed.

I was a fucked-up mess.

"No, it's just the dude complex. TV is on, so I've got to stare at it," I said in a hopeless attempt at a joke.

He gave me a doubtful look, but we carried on. After that, we chatted a bit about stupid stuff—the weather, current events, and whether we thought the brand of coffee in the hospital cafeteria had been changed—until our food finally arrived.

He hadn't been kidding. With fresh halibut and handmade tortillas, the fish tacos were amazing. We inhaled all of them in minutes. Letting everything settle, we sipped on beers and ate chips and salsa as we watched skaters and runners pass by. Dr. Marcus seemed to be in no hurry. It was either his day off as well, or he would be working the late shift.

Suddenly, my last shift lunch break with Lailah came rushing back, and here I was, having lunch with her doctor.

No better time to find some answers.

"Hey, Dr. Marcus, you're Lailah Buchanan's doctor, right?"

After taking a swig from his Corona, he slowly pulled the bottle away from his lips and set it down on the table. "Yeah, I am. Actually, I have been since she was an infant. Why?"

That surprised me. "Since she was an infant? But you don't do pediatrics? Did you, at one time?"

He looked out past the sand to the water he so desperately loved. Without turning back toward me, he just continued to stare out at the crystal-blue water as he answered, "No, I've never done pediatrics. There's some history between her mother and me. It's…complicated. When I found out about Lailah, I immediately took her on as a patient. There was no question about it. She saw a pediatric cardiologist as well when she was growing up, but I oversaw everything medically related to her." He paused as his eyes traveled back to the table and eventually to me. "Why the sudden interest in Lailah?" he asked with a bit of suspicion.

It reminded me of the first time I'd met Megan's father. After Megan and I had been dating for about two months, her family had invited me over for Easter Weekend. Her father had followed me around that weekend like a hawk. I didn't think I'd turned a single corner the entire time I was there without finding myself face-to-face with his baby-blue eyes.

"I'm just curious, I guess. I've been in her room and talked to her a few times. I've spoken to a lot of the patients on that floor," I said, trying to take the focus away from Lailah. "It's so different from the ER. Each room I visit, I meet the person and get to know them," I lied.

The only two people I'd actually spoken to were Nash, the crazy writer, and Lailah. In my mind, everyone else I had interacted with on that floor remained exactly how ER patients had been to me—completely faceless.

"Patients do that to you," he offered. "Lailah is special to me. She's got a tough road ahead of her. Both of them do," he said, obviously speaking of her mother.

"Lailah said she almost had a transplant before," I said, glad he had been the one to turn the conversation back around to Lailah.

"Yes, it was devastating."

"Do you know what happened?" I already knew what he'd say.

The date Lailah had given me already confirmed what I feared. As May had been coming to a close three years ago, I had been on my knees in a hospital hallway, begging my future father-in-law not to take Megan away from me.

"The family changed their minds. It happens more than you would think. I stayed out of the entire thing. It was too personal for me. Considering I had gone against protocol and told Lailah about everything before it was final, I couldn't risk my medical license by getting more involved. I can't tell you how much I wanted to beg that family to reconsider."

If only he knew that I was the reason they'd said no…

"But she'll get her chance again, right?" I asked in an upbeat tone.

"I hope so. I really hope so," he said.

We finished our beers, and I insisted on splitting the tab.

"No way. I invited you J-Man," he said, holding up his hands in protest.

"We're splitting it, Dr. Marcus. Otherwise, this is like a date. By paying, you would make me the chick, and I'm definitely not putting a skirt on for you." I grinned.

"All right, all right. I won't pay for your damn tacos, man! Chill." He laughed.

After I turned down his offer for a ride home, we said our good-byes, and I headed down the road toward home. The sun was perched high in the sky, just starting to hover over the water, as it prepared for its dazzling sunset display. I decided to walk most of the way home. I was still pretty full from lunch, and I needed a bit more time to dwell on all the swirling thoughts running through my mind.

It's true.

I'm the reason Lailah Buchanan is still fighting for her life.

Had I been a better person, had I been able to let go of my own selfishness, and had I instead thought of others beyond myself, Lailah would have had…my fiancée's beating heart inside her chest.

Fuck, I can't handle this.

Walking turned into running, which turned into panicked sprinting. As guilty as I felt for that day, as much as it pained me to know that I could have saved Lailah's life, the thought of someone else holding on to Megan's heart killed me—no, it slayed me. I couldn't stand the thought of a piece of Megan living on and me not being allowed to be a part of that. I knew that her heart hadn't made her who she was, but it still would have been hers. It had given her life and had moved blood into her veins.

If there were still something left of Megan, how could I not want to be around it?

Before I knew where I was running to, I found myself at the entrance of the hospital. I took a seat on the empty bench and lowered my head into my hands.

Since the night of Megan's accident, I'd not only destroyed Megan's life, but I'd also apparently ruined Lailah's as well. My Megan was gone, but for me, her memories were still floating around the halls of this hospital like forgotten bits of paper sailing through the wind. But Lailah was still alive, her bright soul shining through everything she did. I thought of her nervous blabbering conversations, chocolate pudding obsessions and the way she never seemed to be let down by the hand she'd been dealt.

Somehow, I had to make it up to Lailah, and I had to make sure she would get another transplant.

I wasn't sure how I'd do it, but for once in my life, I wanted to do something for someone else—no matter the consequences.

CHAPTER SEVEN

THE SOMEDAY LIST

LAILAH

Heart transplant.

Heart transplant.

Maybe if I write it out enough, it will actually sink in.

Heart transplant.

Nope, not working.

I've always known this would be the end game, the grand finale. Why am I having such a hard time wrapping my brain around those two stupid words?

It wasn't this hard the last time around.

Heart transplant.

Nope, still not sticking.

Mom's really hopeful, but me? My usual never-ending ray of sunshine attitude is currently filled with nothing but dread. This time, I feel like I'm going to get caught up in a mighty storm, and there will be nothing left of the young woman I was before.

A knock at my door brought me out of the words I'd been pouring onto the pages of my journal, and I quickly closed it and set it on my lap. Ever since a counselor had told me a while ago that words could help soothe, I'd been flooding black-and-white composition journals faster than my mom could stock them.

"Come in," I answered.

My heart accelerated in anticipation of who it could be. Jude hadn't been by since his odd exit four days ago.

Maybe he's coming by to check on me?

My pulse began to slow the instant I saw Abigail. Her eyes met mine for a brief moment and then went to the floor. She was quieter than usual, and she had a few books tucked under her arm.

Is she okay? Have I done something to upset her?

Rather than her exuberant, mad dash into my room, she slowly walked to my bed and hesitantly sat herself on the edge.

"Hey, Abigail. You're here a bit late tonight. What's up?" I asked cheerfully.

She pulled the books onto her lap. I saw my copy of *Anne Frank: The Diary of a Young Girl* and what looked to be a diary. It was brown leather and embossed with a swirly script that had Abigail's initials written on the front. Perhaps a tad too formal and a little too grown-up for a nine-year-old, but considering it had been a gift from her papa, it didn't surprise me.

"Did you want me to read this because you're dying?" she asked.

Her question took me by surprise, and it required a moment or two for me to respond.

"What? Why would you ask that?"

Tears formed in her eyes, and she looked down at the old photo gracing the cover of the paperback.

"Because she dies at the end. I just thought that maybe since you are here...." She looked around at my hospital room and the many different types of equipment surrounding me. "Maybe it was your way of telling me that you are going to die, too."

God, I'm dumb.

"Oh, sweetie, come here," I said, putting my journal on the tray table next to my bed.

I opened my arms, so she could crawl up into them. Her small body fit perfectly next to mine on the bed. I smoothed down her dark brown hair and wrapped the ends around my fingers.

"I'm sorry. I shouldn't have given you the book without warning you of the sad ending. That was irresponsible of me."

"Did she really die?" she asked.

I just nodded against her cheek.

"Sometimes, the world doesn't go the way we want it to," I offered, continuing to play with her hair.

She nuzzled against me. "What about you?" she asked hesitantly, lifting her head so that her large chestnut brown eyes met mine.

"What about me?" I asked.

"Are you going to die, Lailah?"

I took a deep breath and considered lying. *Lots of people lie to children. Is it really terrible to save them the heartache of knowing the truth if it causes them pain?*

But how many times did adults lie to me when I was young? How many times has my mother watered down the truth to make it more palatable for me?

I knew my mother had done this because she loved me and didn't want to hurt me, but it'd made me feel small and weak.

The last thing a child wants to feel is small.

"I don't know, Abigail. I honestly don't know. The doctors are doing everything they can," I answered honestly.

Her eyes searched mine for a moment longer, and finally, she sank back to my chest. "I hope they figure it out."

"Me, too."

THAT WAS THE EXACT POSITION JUDE FOUND ABIGAIL AND ME IN several minutes later when he walked into my room. My heart did a flip-flop at the mere sight of him, and I was pretty sure the child lying against my chest could feel it also. She looked up as he entered. He immediately froze when he saw the two of us embracing on the bed, realizing he'd walked in on something personal.

"Hey, you're that guy who talks books with my papa," Abigail said, sitting up to face Jude.

Jude's face warmed a bit as he shifted from one foot to the other and smiled at Abigail.

He had a gorgeous smile. His shy, unpracticed grin just barely tugged at the corner of his lips, causing the slightest dimple to appear on his left cheek.

He should really smile more often, like all the time.

"I am. Your papa loves to talk about books," he said with a bit of a chuckle at the end.

That led me to believe that Nash did the majority of the talking in those conversations, and it didn't surprise me. Jude seemed to be more of a listener.

"What are you two ladies up to tonight?" He took another casual step forward before plunging his hands in his pockets.

"We were talking about dying," Abigail answered plainly.

My eyes widened and shot over to hers. There were no tears, just honesty.

Kids could be so strange. I wondered if I had been that blunt when I was her age.

"Oh…well, uh…" Jude struggled for a moment, reaching up to grasp the back of his neck with his hand, as he looked to me for some sort of cue.

I just shrugged, so his panicked eyes continued to wander until they zeroed in on Abigail's journal.

"Hey, what's that?" he asked.

"Oh, it's my diary. Papa got it for me. I'd asked him for a pink one with jewels on it, but he said this one was for real writers."

Like he'd done the night he visited me, Jude walked across the room, pulled the corner chair over to the bed, and took a seat. He leaned in close to Abigail. "Will you read something?"

She scrunched up her nose and shook her head.

"Oh, come on. I'm sure you have some great stuff in there."

"It's all stupid."

"As long as you write about what makes you happy, none of it could ever be considered stupid," I added, rubbing her back in encouragement.

"Okay. You promise not to laugh?"

I looked at Jude over her head, and we both grinned. After both crossing our hearts and swearing an oath, she agreed to read a poem.

"Pandas are cute.

Dolphins are nice.

Sugar is sweet,

Just like you."

We both clapped in unison, and Jude jumped up to his feet to give her a standing ovation.

She hopped out of the room to tell her papa all about it, and her high-pitched giggles filled my room and warmed my heart long after.

"That was really sweet of you," I commented after she'd left.

"You both just looked so sad when I came in. I had to do something to lighten the mood."

"Well, it worked. Seeing her skip out of here was perfect. That's how I usually see her, full of life and energy. I hate to think that I took that away from her."

"You didn't take that away from her," he said, returning to his seat next to my bed. He leaned back and put his shoes up on the rails of the bed.

He looked relaxed and casual, and for some reason, that

made me less so. I suddenly wanted to smooth out my hair and check my shirt for stains.

What shirt am I wearing?

My hand flew to my shirt collar, and I exhaled as I felt the smooth cotton material covering my chest. It was then that I realized he'd witnessed my bizarre behavior, and he was now silently watching me.

"Oh, um…I mean, I just hate that I made her sad," I said, stumbling on my words, as I tried to get us back on topic and less focused on my obsession with my shirt. I needed to change the subject. "So, um…no pudding today?"

"No, the cafeteria has been out," he answered.

His eyes didn't meet mine, which made me wonder if he was telling the truth.

"You've been busy?" I asked, wondering why he hadn't been around in a few days. *Has he purposely been avoiding me?*

"Yeah, I had two days off and I've been running around pretty much from the start of my shift until the very end each day since. Didn't even have time to take a lunch break today, which is why I can only stay a few minutes tonight."

Again, he wasn't making eye contact.

"Her poem was cute." That same shy smile spread across his face as he finally looked up at me.

"Yeah, it was. I'm glad she shared it with us. It's not easy to bare your soul like that even if it is about pandas." I grinned.

"Bit of a poet yourself, Lailah?" His right eyebrow rose to form a sexy arch above his light green eyes.

Sexy arch? Seriously? I need to get a life.

"No, poetry is definitely not my thing. Life is pretty dull around here, so I write."

"About what?"

"Anything, everything. I babble mostly. I'm good at babbling. I write about my days in and out of the hospital. If I'm having good days, I'll write. If I'm having bad days, I'll write. I keep lists," I said with a grin.

"Lists, huh? That's not a surprise," he said, obviously remembering our first conversation when I'd brought up my suspect list. "What kind of lists?"

"All sorts, like types of treatments I've had, books I've read, books I want to read, and then I have *the* list."

"That sounds ominous," he said with a bit of humor.

"It's my bucket list, I guess. I call it my Someday list."

"So, your go-to-Tahiti-and-snorkel-or-skydive list?"

"Yeah, something like that, but mine is a bit different," I said, opening the drawer next to me and pulling out the black and white notebook where I kept my list.

"Can I see it?" he asked, leaning forward.

"No!" I said with a bit too much enthusiasm.

In defeat, he held his hands out in front of him and pulled back. "Okay, don't touch the woman's book. Got it."

"Sorry." I laughed. "It's just…I've never showed this to anyone. But I'll read a few to you, if you'd like."

He leaned back in his chair and nodded. "Yeah, I'd like that. How many things do you have on this Someday list?"

I quickly flipped through the pages until I reached the last number. It was all for show. I didn't need to look to know how many were there. I'd spent many hours with this little notebook. "One hundred and forty-three," I answered.

His eyes scrunched together as he smiled. "What's number one?"

I shook my head, glancing down at the long list I'd made. "Nope, not telling you that one. Pick a different one."

"Okay." He chuckled. "Give me number fourteen."

"Um…put my toes in the ocean."

"What?"

"I want to put my toes in the ocean."

"But you live less than fifteen minutes from the beach," he reminded me.

I sighed. "Ironic, right? That's one of the joys of being me and having my mother as a caretaker. I've been sick my entire life, which means I've had to be cared for since the day I was born. My mother has taken that job very seriously. Walking through sand is hard work. God forbid, I get winded. Therefore, no trips to the beach, and no toes in the water."

His eyes steadied on mine for a moment as if he were thinking through something.

"Give me another one. How about sixty-two?" he asked.

I followed my finger down as I went through the numbers until I found it. "Make a meal from start to finish."

"What does your mom have against cooking?"

"I don't know that she has anything against it per se. She just never lets me do it. If a staff member of the hospital is not waiting on me, then she is serving me. Do you know what it's like to be taken care of like a child when you're a grown adult? It's maddening."

"You're not a child," he said.

The way he looked at me made my cheeks flush with heat.

"Will you share a few with me tomorrow night?" he asked, rising from the seat.

He stretched slightly, and the hem of his shirt rose, revealing a sliver of tanned skin. I should have looked away, but I didn't. I managed to look up in time to meet his gaze as his arms settled back at his sides.

"Yes, I'll share some more, but only if you do something for me," I said, setting down the small notebook on the bed.

"Depends on what it is," he said, arching his brow again. *Still sexy.*

"Bring me more pudding?" I asked, grinning.

He laughed. "You've got yourself a deal."

CHAPTER EIGHT
MOVING MOUNTAINS

JUDE

Sitting on the bench outside of the hospital a few nights ago, I'd been sure of one thing and one thing only. For the foreseeable future, I was going to dedicate my life to making Lailah's future better.

From my own selfishness, it was my fault that she had perhaps lost the one chance at having a healthy, hospital-free existence. *I had to make it up to her.*

I'd caused the accident that killed Megan. I'd gone against the wishes of my fiancée and not allowed her organs to be donated. I had yelled and hurt her family in their time of mourning and grief and I'd turned my back on my own family.

I was a terrible human being.

But with the girl sitting up in that hospital bed, I could redeem myself. Somehow, I could make it all right. I wasn't sure how, but I'd left the hospital that night feeling vindicated and resolved. I'd run home, letting the burn in my lungs reach all the way down to my feet as they hit the pavement, and I knew that somehow I would set things right.

This was what I was meant to do right now.

The next day, when I'd stepped foot in the hospital, dressed in my teal blue scrubs, I'd clocked in, put my name badge on, and realized something.

I am just a nurses' assistant.

I wasn't Jude Cavenaugh anymore. I was Jude, the CNA. I was just a forgotten man who worked in a typical hospital, paid his rent, and after everything was said and done, barely made enough to buy a pizza and rent a movie every week.

Who am I kidding? I can't save the day. I can barely save myself.

The man I'd become couldn't move mountains and make things happen just because I said so. I'd lost that power when I left my old life behind and put on this pair of scrubs.

I'd trudged up to the nurses' station in the cardiology wing, feeling defeated, hopeless, and lost.

At twenty-five years old, I'd managed to screw up so many lives.

How's that for a legacy?

For the next two days, I'd avoided Lailah's room, taking every task I could that would get me out of having to walk into that hospital room. I couldn't stand to see her big blue eyes staring back at me, knowing I was the reason she was still here.

If I had known that someone like Lailah would be on the receiving end of Megan's tragedy, would I have chosen differently? Would I have been able to let go, knowing that a young woman so full of hope and life would get to live on even if my Megan couldn't?

I really didn't know.

And that was why I'd ended up in her room even though I had told myself I wouldn't.

I couldn't help it.

She confused and intrigued me like no other person I'd ever met. She was facing extraordinary circumstances with death staring her in the face. Yet, when I'd walked into the room, her hand had immediately gone to her hair, and she'd blushed.

Why does she do that?

She would babble when she was nervous, and she made lists like an old lady losing her memory. Faced with such challenges, she was the exact opposite of the type of person I would expect her to be.

When Megan had died, I'd become harsh and bitter. I'd closed myself off from everyone I knew. I'd disconnected from the life I was supposed to lead and disappeared. Lailah's life had been one bad event after another and yet she was still facing everything head-on.

When she'd mentioned her bucket list, I'd known I found my mission.

I might not have the power of my old life, but I could still move mountains—well, hills maybe.

I just had to learn how to cook first.

After that, I'd figure out a way to get her that transplant.

"Hey, Nash. Heard you are breaking out of here soon," I said after stepping into his cluttered room.

"Well, I tried to talk that pretty raven-haired girl into running away with me, but she just giggled and said she was already taken."

"Who? Grace?" I asked, moving to his bedside to begin the process of taking his vitals.

"Yeah, she reminds me of an exotic princess. I want to remove those silly cartoon uniforms she wears and cover her in nothing but silk. I'd also like to lick cream off of her until she purrs."

That description stopped me as I was in the middle of wrapping the blood pressure cuff around his weathered bicep. "Uh…well…" I tried to think of something to follow up with, but I had nothing.

He smiled a big Cheshire Cat grin that took up half his face. His white teeth were a stark contrast to his dark complexion. "You weren't kidding. You really don't talk much."

After checking his blood pressure, I pulled the cuff off his arm and walked back to the small cart I'd brought in to enter the information into the computer. "Guess I'm a little out of practice."

"No friends?"

"Not really." I walked back to the other side to check his IV.

"No family?"

"No." I shifted from one side to the other, feeling uncomfortable by the sudden onslaught of questions.

"What about a woman? Surely, a man like you has to have a woman?"

"No, not anymore." The pain from saying the words felt like a sword lancing through my heart—a heart that still beat unlike Megan's who I'd selfishly kept from moving on.

He obviously saw the hurt in my eyes because he didn't say another word. He just allowed me to do my job, moving from one task to another, until I was finally finished.

Just as I was about to leave, I remembered a story Nash had told me earlier in the week. Nash was full of stories. His life was an endless cascading sea of them, and as if he didn't have enough of them to pull from in his real life, he would make them up as well.

With over forty novels under his belt, I'd learned—thanks to Google—that Nash Taylor was one of the most accomplished fictional writers of our time. He'd earned every literary award known to man, and he was also known for being a little flamboyant. Loose with his morals and even looser with his money, the man had a reputation for mischief, which is why he had a slew of ex-wives and several children and grandchildren.

Since I'd met the man, he'd told me so many stories about his life. I felt like I knew his autobiography better than I knew my own. One particular story stuck out more than the others because it could help my current predicament.

In the eighties, during a particularly long period of writer's block, Nash had decided to take a job as a cook. He'd had absolutely no experience, and he'd said the manager was probably either drunk or incredibly stupid to hire him, but he'd thought the job would give him some inspiration. For six months, he'd explored the culinary world.

"I was the worst cook on the face of the earth—at first," he'd said. "But the more I tried, the better I became. Like a virgin, I was sloppy and clumsy to start, but I practiced, practiced, practiced! Then, bam! I became a natural!"

Nash always managed to take every story and relate it back to sex. I would call it some sort of gift, but really, I thought he was just a dirty old man.

"Hey, Nash," I said, turning around.

"Yes, my quiet friend?"

"Could you help me plan a meal? I want to cook dinner with someone, but I seriously can't cook shit."

His lips turned skyward, and his expression warmed.

Thirty minutes later, I'd written out a ton of notes and gotten a bit of a headache from the amount of talking, but I had a meal and a plan.

I KNEW WHAT I HAD PLANNED WOULD PROBABLY TAKE FAR longer than the hour I was allowed for a lunch break, so the following day, I showed up at the hospital, dressed in my civilian clothes, and for once, I didn't clock in. Instead, I headed down to the cafeteria, walking past the line of staff and visitors waiting to pay their tabs, and I gave Betty, the cafeteria lady, a quick wink. She blushed and puckered her lips, giving me a flirty air kiss back, as she waved me back through the kitchen.

Ten minutes later, I had mostly everything set up, and I was in the elevator on my way up to the cardiology unit. I anxiously tapped my foot as I waited for the floor number to light up and the sound to buzz, signaling the door was about to open.

I was edgy...or nervous.

I didn't know. I was definitely something.

Twitchy with a touch of anxious maybe?

What if she hates it? What if something goes wrong, and she gets hurt? How much activity can she handle? Will I be overexerting her?

A million things were running through my mind when the elevator door finally opened, and I stepped into the familiar hallway. I wanted nothing more than to make Lailah's life better. After everything I'd done to fuck it up, it was something I needed to do. I only hoped that by stepping into her world and becoming a part of her life, I wasn't going to do more harm than good.

Maybe I should talk to Dr. Marcus first.

I made a quick stop at the nurses' station, asking if I could borrow a wheelchair. Showing up off shift wasn't normal for me. After a few odd looks from the rest of the staff, I secured my requested item, and I was on my way to Lailah's room when I saw just the man I had been looking for.

Dr. Marcus was standing off in a corner, speaking intently with someone. His voice was low, but it was clear by the way his hands were moving and by the expression on his face that he was passionate about what he was trying to convey.

"Why do you always feel the need to be so independent, Molly?" he hissed.

"I will never depend on a man to take care of me ever again," she threw back. Her arms folded across her chest in anger.

She looked familiar, but I couldn't place where I'd seen her before. The light blonde hair and blazing blue eyes reminded me of someone, but blondes were a dime a dozen in Southern California. She could be anybody.

I tried to look away, aware I was eavesdropping on a personal conversation, but I'd never seen Dr. Marcus lose his cool before. He was what I would call, *California chill*—mild-mannered and always laid-back.

Right now, even though I could only make out part of his

face from the corner I was standing in—okay, spying from—I could see that his eyes were wild, full of fire and heat.

"Do you think that's all this is? Do you think all of this"—he made a gesture meant to encompass the two of them together—"was just so I could protect you? And Lailah, too?"

My eyes widened, and I pulled back further into the shadows, not wanting to give up my position now that I'd figured out he was talking to Lailah's mother.

It was no wonder her platinum locks and petite frame seemed so familiar. Looking at her again, she bore a striking resemblance to her daughter. I'd never met Ms. Buchanan. I'd only heard about her from the few stories Lailah had told me. Most shifts, I usually didn't come in until later in the evening, and she had normally left before I clocked in.

"No, I'm sorry. I know you care, Marcus," she said, hesitantly touching his bicep as the anger began to ebb.

"I more than care, Molly."

Someone rounded the opposite corner, and they pulled apart before saying a quick good-bye and turning in different directions. Lailah's mother headed toward the elevator, and Dr. Marcus marched down the hall where I was standing. I started pushing the wheelchair again, trying to act nonchalant.

"Hey, J-Man. Dressed up for work today?" Dr. Marcus asked as he approached.

He tried to cover up the sadness in his eyes with a smile, but it wasn't working. I could still see it there, lingering behind those deep blue eyes. Pain recognized pain, and I'd been looking at the same set of eyes in the mirror for the last three years.

"I don't clock in until tonight. I'm actually here to visit Lailah."

A bit of surprise danced across his features. "Lailah? Really?"

"Yeah."

I explained my plan to him, and he silently listened,

watching me with the appraising eyes of a father figure. After I finished telling him the details, he grew still. I nervously stuck my hands in my pockets, waiting for some sort of reply. It seemed like an eternity of being looked at like I was one of those lobsters in a fish tank at a seafood restaurant.

Then, he finally said, "That's very kind of you, Jude. I think she'll enjoy it, and she should be okay as long as you don't plan on sticking her on a treadmill while doing any of this," he said with a chuckle.

"I'll do my best to avoid the treadmill," I joked.

"Just make sure you don't get too attached to Lailah. She's innocent—in every way," he stressed. "I have every hope that all will go as planned with her, but I don't want her to get hurt."

My brows furrowed together in confusion. "I don't think you understand, Dr. Marcus. I'm not pursuing Lailah. Listen, I lost someone. She was the one, and it happened a while ago. I can't…I'm not capable of those types of feelings anymore," I said, fumbling over my words.

His hand came to my shoulder, steadying me. "Then, I guess we don't have a problem, do we?"

His eyes met mine, and I could see understanding there. Somewhere along the way, he'd lost his one and only as well.

The only problem was Marcus's ghost was still very much alive.

CHAPTER NINE

PIZZA AND ANGELS

LAILAH

Some days in the hospital would fly by. I'd open my journal, find a groove, and the words would just start flying. Before I knew it, someone would be knocking on my door to deliver dinner. I loved days like that. It made time feel fluid and precious.

Today was not one of those days.

It was barely noon, and I'd spent the last thirty minutes watching the clock slowly tick away, each minute seeming to last longer than the one before, until I was near the point of ripping the stupid thing off the wall.

It was long, endless days like this that made me wonder, *What's the point at all?*

I hated these days. They made me doubt everything—every action, every decision.

I was sitting in a lonely hospital room, staring at a clock.

Is that any way to live? Is it living at all? Why have a beating heart if I don't know why it beats in the first place?

These were my deepest, darkest doubts. I would keep these feelings bottled inside of me, and I'd refuse to acknowledge them until another day like this would creep up on me.

Then, I'd find myself once again staring at a ridiculous clock, wondering why I was even on this earth if I was bound to spend my life in this room.

A soft knock pulled me from the staring match I was having with the clock, and I looked down to find Jude stepping through the door.

Holy crap on a cracker.

I sucked in a breath and tried not to drool.

I'd grown accustomed to seeing Jude in his signature teal scrubs. Many nurses and CNAs would wear a variety of scrubs to work. None were as crazy as Grace with her cartoon characters and weird prints, but Jude was very plain, wearing the same traditional color each and every day I saw him.

He was not wearing teal today.

And he was definitely not wearing scrubs.

Today, he was in black jeans and a fitted black T-shirt that hugged his upper body in a way that scrubs definitely could not. His hair was still in need of a haircut, but it looked like he'd attempted to at least run his hands through it.

I'd love to run my hands through it.

Oh my God, stop it, Lailah.

I didn't know how long I'd been staring at him, but I suddenly realized I hadn't greeted him or even offered a wave.

Nope, I was just sitting there with my mouth hanging open.

"Um…hey!" I finally said with far too much enthusiasm.

He smiled that shy grin I'd seen before, and then he glanced down at the ground before looking up at me.

"Hi. I know I said I'd come and visit this evening, but I thought you might enjoy some company during the day."

"You mean, you can actually come out in sunlight? I was starting to wonder if you sparkled." I laughed.

The joke was obviously lost on him because he just gave me an amused expression and shook his head.

"Anyway, I have a bit of a surprise for you, if you're up for it."

"Does it involve pudding?" I asked.

"Um…no, but it involves chocolate," he answered.

"You should have started with that. Always open with chocolate."

"So, is that a yes?" he questioned.

"To the mysterious surprise? Even though I have no idea what we're doing or where we're going? Hmm…I had an eventful afternoon planned," I started to say in a sarcastic tone. "I was going to paint my nails and watch a soap opera. You know that Stefano was almost murdered, right? Very scandalous."

He rolled his eyes, his grin widening, and he pivoted on his heels. Turning around, he walked the few steps to the door and walked out.

Oh no!

Did I upset him? Is sarcasm not socially acceptable?

Just as I was about to chew off the entirety of my pink thumbnail, the door opened back up, and he reappeared— along with a wheelchair.

My first thought was, *Yay, he's back! I didn't scare him away!*

My second thought was, *Ugh, stupid wheelchair.*

Considering I'd spent the morning cursing the clock and the fates that had brought me to this place, at that moment, I would gladly go anywhere in a wheelchair as long as it was out of this hospital room and with Jude.

"So, where are we going?" I asked, sitting myself down into the wheelchair.

When I bent over to push down the footrests, I saw Jude moving forward to help, but I shooed him away with a wave of my hand. He wasn't working, and I definitely was not as frail as I appeared.

"Nope," he answered, taking a step behind me. His hands brushed the skin of my shoulder as he moved to grip the handlebars.

He took a step forward, and he propelled me down the hall.

"What do you mean, nope?"

"As in, nope, not telling you."

I muttered a curse and heard him let out a small laugh as we passed by the nurses' station. He stopped briefly to let them know that he was taking me for a while. He leaned against the counter as he spoke in low whispers, telling the nurses of our secret destination. His arms bulged against the weight of his upper body, and I eyed several of his dark tribal-looking tattoos that covered his left arm, as I listened to the sound of his low voice.

I noticed several of the single young nurses curiously watching me as he spoke. I suddenly grew uncomfortable under the attention. Having never attended school or social events with my peers, I didn't know how to react to this kind of scrutiny. The desire to run and hide was growing with every passing second.

What is he saying to make them look at me like that?

Grace, who was just returning from down the hall, took one look at me and must have seen my distress. She briskly walked behind the nurses' station before glancing in my direction and giving me a quick wink.

"Have y'all seen my ring yet?" she said loud enough for me to hear.

Girlish squeals followed.

I chuckled, knowing she'd purposely diverted the unwanted attention away from me.

I truly love that woman.

Luckily, Jude had mostly finished at the nurses' station before the squeals erupted, and we made it to the elevator without any other inquisitive sets of eyes following us. He pressed the button, and we waited in slightly awkward silence.

"So, are you going to tell me now?" I finally said.

"Nope."

I folded my arms against my chest and made an exasperated sigh.

He chuckled behind me. The elevator dinged, and the doors parted. He wheeled me around and backed both of us in, so we were facing forward.

"You have the patience of a gnat," he said.

The door closed, and we headed downward.

"I have a great deal of patience."

"Well, not today," he said.

Then, I felt his hot breath against my ear as he bent down behind me.

"Or maybe it's just me who ruffles those feathers of yours."

"Um—"

I had no witty comeback, nothing to say that would equal what he'd just said, because he'd just rendered me speechless. I tried to compose myself, but all that came out was word garbage. His breath against my earlobe alone had reduced me to a mumbling mess of letters and syllables.

Why does his presence affect me so?

I'd grown up in the hospital. I'd spent my teenage years—the most vulnerable time of a young girl's life—being poked, prodded, and exposed to countless people, including several men.

But no one had ever made my skin flush and my heart flutter the way he did.

It was something I'd never felt before—and also something I needed to forget.

Jude wasn't for me.

He couldn't possibly want a mess like me.

Besides, a life outside these hospital walls wasn't something I could think about right now. Hope was an emotion that could give the smallest man the strength to move mountains. But if a man was given too much hope in a dire situation, that four letter word would suddenly crush him, weighing him down by the impossible belief that things would somehow get better when there was no chance in hell they ever possibly could.

Until I knew more about my transplant probability, I was staying far away from the idea of hope.

"I don't have feathers," I finally answered, finding my voice again.

"What?" he asked.

The elevator once again dinged, and the door opened. He pushed the wheelchair forward, and I took a look around, but all I saw was the same boring hallway that covered every floor. That wasn't much of a clue.

"You said my feathers were ruffled. I don't have wings. I'm not a bird," I pointed out.

He pushed the wheelchair to a set of glass doors. I looked in and saw people in scrubs and regular clothes walking around, carrying trays.

We're at the cafeteria? Is he buying me lunch?

I looked up and found green eyes staring down at me.

"Every angel has wings, Lailah," he answered.

He pushed me through the double doors, and rather than finding a spot in the line with the rest of the folks waiting to grab a bite to eat, he took a turn toward the kitchen.

"What are we doing?" I asked.

"Relax! We're almost there," he said from behind me with an amused tone. "Hey, beautiful," Jude said, greeting someone.

My head flew up to see who he was addressing

Is he introducing me to his girlfriend? That would not be my idea of a fun afternoon.

An older woman, probably in her late sixties, with long silver hair twisted up into a complicated bun, looked up from the cash register and batted her eyelashes at Jude. "Hey, Puddin'," she answered. "This your girl?" She glanced down at me with a wrinkled warm smile that reminded me of my late grandmother.

"This is Lailah," he simply answered.

"Well, your stuff is all back there and ready to go. Take as much time as you need, hon."

His large hand went to her tiny shoulder and squeezed it for a moment. "Thank you for this," he said before pushing the wheelchair forward once again.

Another set of doors and a few seconds later, we were in the cafeteria kitchen.

I took a look around, noticing the huge stainless steel commercial refrigerators, ovens, and countertops. Everything gleamed and shined under the fluorescent lights. On the counter located in the center were several shopping bags from a local grocery store my mother and I would pass on the way home from the hospital. Next to the bags were stacks of produce, different types of meats and cheeses, and a chocolate cake.

"What are we doing in here?" I asked as my gaze continued to wander around the large space.

"We are cooking lunch," he said.

My expression must have shifted to extreme surprise or maybe fear because a loud, booming laugh came tumbling out of him. It was the first real laugh I'd heard from him, and it was beautiful. So many other times I'd caught him laughing, it had been timid and apprehensive, as if he wasn't sure he was allowed the pleasure of doing so. Hearing this laugh felt real, like I was finally seeing and hearing his soul.

"You look mortified," he finally said, still chuckling.

"Maybe slightly, but I'm more surprised. We're cooking? Really?"

A smile tugged at his lips. "Yeah, I can't take you to the beach—you know, without busting you out of the hospital and getting fired. So, I figured I'd do this. It's not much—"

"It's perfect," I said, interrupting him.

"Good," he replied. "Let's get to work."

"Before we start, I do have one quick question," I said, looking down at my current seating arrangement. "Do I have to sit in this thing all day? You know, I can walk."

"Oh! Sorry. I was just trying to stick to hospital policy. Yeah, you can stand up. Just no treadmills."

"What?" I asked, completely thrown off by his comment.

He grinned, moving forward to offer me a hand, as I stood. I'd normally decline. I liked being able to do things by myself, but the idea of touching him again was too tempting.

Just because I know he isn't for me doesn't mean I don't want him to be.

A girl can dream.

When his hand slid into mine, I felt that same sizzle I'd felt when his breath caressed my ear. Feeling instant heat, my stomach clenched, and my pulse started to race.

And it had nothing to do with heart failure.

Our eyes met as he helped me up.

"Nothing. Sorry. Lame joke," he mumbled quickly. "Let's make some lunch. I'm starving." He let go of my hand and turned to the counter. He began pulling things out of the bags and started setting them out.

"So, what are we making?"

"I thought we'd do something simple since it's your first time in a kitchen, and I'm a terrible cook."

I made a snorting sound before bringing my hand to my mouth. "You are supposed to be teaching me how to cook a meal, and you don't know how to cook?" I asked, still holding back laughter.

He folded up the reusable grocery bag, set it on the counter, and turned to me. His expression was once again light and amused. The awkwardness he'd been carrying moments earlier when our hands touched had seemed to dissipate.

"I didn't say I couldn't cook. I just said I was a terrible cook. There's a difference."

"Oh, okay. So, what terrible food are we having today?" I asked, peeking around at the various things lined up on the steel counter.

"I thought we'd go easy and make pizza. How badly could we mess up pizza?"

"That sounds like a challenge." I laughed.

"Well, let's at least try for edible. I had some help. Abigail's grandfather, Nash, gave me some pointers, so I'm pumped." He shook his hands out and stretched out his neck like he was preparing for a fight. "Yeah, we can do this."

I giggled. "Okay, let's go for it."

He'd thankfully bought prepared dough, and all we had to do was roll it out.

It was easier said than done.

"Don't you just roll it with a rolling pin?" I asked, looking around for one.

"I thought you threw it up in the air?"

"Only if you have a twisty handlebar mustache and happened to be named Luigi. I think beginners roll it out."

We searched high and low for a rolling pin and managed to finally find one on the back of a corner shelf.

Jude pulled the sticky dough out of the bag and plopped it down on the clean counter. "We need flour." Half of the dough was still stuck to his palm.

I went on another mission to find flour, and luckily, that didn't take nearly as long. Pulling out a large handful from the canister, I coated the dough and the counter, and then I sprinkled some on his hands.

"Help me get the rest of this off," he said, holding up his fingers still covered in dough.

Making sure my hands were properly floured, I started moving my hands over his, taking off bits of dough as I went. Our fingers brushed and wove together while not a word was said. He watched me as I did this, his eyes taking in every movement like he was studying it.

"All done," I said softly.

He seemed to come out of his trance. "Good. Okay, I'll roll it out."

With the addition of flour, we managed to roll out the

dough without too much fuss. It wasn't round like delivery pizza, but it was flat and didn't have any holes.

"What about sauce chef?" I asked, admiring our oddly shaped pizza.

Digging around in one of the shopping bags, Jude held up a bright green and red jar a moments later.

"Nash recommended this expensive pasta sauce. He said it would be better than anything we attempted. I didn't argue." He popped the lid, and we spread a little over our budding masterpiece.

"So, how does a grown man in his twenties not know how to cook?" I dug around the remaining ingredients and found the cheese.

"Same way as most, I guess—laziness and the invention of ramen."

"I seriously doubt that—at least, the laziness part. No, there must be some other reason," I said, ripping open the bag of shredded mozzarella.

I dipped my hand into the cold bag and started sprinkling the cheese on the pizza. It looked like large pieces of snow falling—or at least, I thought it did, but I wasn't sure since I'd never seen snow.

"Well, I can tell you, I'm in good company. I can guarantee you that most men in their twenties who aren't married or involved usually live off of take-out menus and anything that can be made in the microwave."

The only thing I heard in that entire explanation was the fact that he was single. What I should have focused on was the fact that he was dodging any sort of real answer, but the female side of me—the one that never had a chance to crush on a boy in homeroom or dance with a boyfriend at the home-coming dance—didn't notice any of that.

It shouldn't matter that he was single. I should have ignored it, but my stomach did a flip-flop the instant the words left his mouth.

Jude was single, and he was here—*with me.*

No, it doesn't matter.

It doesn't change anything. Of course, it couldn't.

Denial was something I always excelled in.

After the pizza was properly covered in a good coating of cheese, we moved on to toppings.

"So, what do you like on your pizza?" He grabbed the bags and began pulling out more toppings than one pizza could possibly hold. There were mushrooms, artichoke hearts, olives, pepperoni, ham, green peppers, onions, and about a dozen other things.

"Um…whatever you like is fine," I answered, glancing around at everything.

His eyebrows went up in amusement. "Lailah, I might not know you very well yet, but I can tell when you're lying. You're not very good at it. Right now, you're looking at half of these things like they're going to jump up and attack you. Just tell me what you don't like, and I won't add it."

"Okay, but don't laugh."

He schooled his face, trying to keep the grin that was threatening to take over his face. "No promises."

"I hate mushrooms," I started, looking down at the counter rather than up at him. "They're weird-looking. And bell peppers taste funny. They're never quite cooked but not quite raw either. Like, why is that? Also, you're so sweet, but half of these things I can't have because they're too high in salt, and I'm on a low-salt diet because of my heart. Do you hate me yet?"

I risked a glance up and found him smiling a lopsided warm smile that stole my breath.

"How about cheese?" he asked.

"Love it."

"Good. We'll have plain cheese then." He scooped the pizza up, balancing it with one hand on the pizza tray we'd found on one of our many search-and-rescue missions around the kitchen, and he paused in front of me. Grabbing my chin, he looked at me with those celadon green eyes. "And no, I definitely don't hate you."

CHAPTER TEN
FALLING

JUDE

Our first attempt at making a pizza actually turned out quite well despite several false starts and roadblocks. As I pulled the pizza out of the oven, noticing the perfectly baked crust and the browned cheese, I realized something startling. Lailah and I made a great team.

I'd never expected that from this little adventure. I'd planned this afternoon as a way of payment. I owed the woman standing in front of me a debt. She might not understand or realize that, but I did, and I was going to do everything in my power to make sure that her life was better from now on.

What I hadn't planned on was enjoying the time I spent with her so much. Ever since I'd spied her licking chocolate off her fingers, laughing like no one was watching her, I'd been intrigued by this girl with pale blue eyes and hair the color of wheat. The more time I spent with her, the more my fascination turned into something genuine.

She wasn't just a debt or an obligation. I genuinely enjoyed being around her.

It was as if I'd been underground for years, locked away

in a dungeon of my own making and unable to break free. After meeting Lailah, I felt as if my chains had melted away, and I had finally crawled up to the surface to catch my first blinding glimpse of the sun.

Lailah was the sun, and I was dazzled by her soothing, pure presence.

I knew it was selfish of me to crave her companionship just to fill a void in the remnants of my heart, but for the first time in three years, I felt a flicker of hope in my life. After everything that had happened with Megan and her family, I was sure my life was over, and I'd be nothing but an empty shell wandering these halls for eternity. But if hope still lived inside of me, then perhaps a friendship with Lailah was exactly what I needed.

Always seeming to be one step ahead of me, Lailah rummaged through the drawers of the massive kitchen and found a pizza cutter. She held it up with the intent to do harm to our cheesy masterpiece.

"Whoa there, Chucky. Why don't you give me the sharp object, and I'll cut the pizza? I'd rather not return you to Dr. Marcus with a missing appendage."

Her brow rose in defiance, but she handed over the spinning wheel of death easily. Her arms folded across her chest, pushing her breasts together under her dark blue sweater. Locked in a trance, my breath suddenly faltered. My fists tightened at my side, and I quickly looked away.

What the hell was that?

Choosing to ignore my body's obvious confusion, I devoted my attention to cutting our pizza. Moments later, I plated each of us a slice. At the counter, she sat back down in the wheelchair, and I made a chair from a step stool.

"It's perfect," she said after taking the first bite. She looked casual and comfortable, leaned back in the wheelchair with her legs propped up against the edge of my step stool. It was the most relaxed I'd ever seen her—at least around me.

I took my first bite, and I was actually surprised. "Huh… how about that? It's pretty damn good."

"So, does this mean you're going to make pizzas from scratch now?" she asked as she took a napkin to the corner of her mouth.

"Hell no. Gotta get my delivery boy through college. Besides, I wouldn't have my sous chef."

The second the sentence left my lips, I had a vision of Lailah standing in my kitchen, laughing with streaks of flour covering her nose and cheeks, as I stepped in behind her, wrapping my arms around her tiny waist, and kissed her shoulder.

No, not Lailah. Always Megan. Always.

I shook my head, trying to erase the image from my mind. Guilt swept through my gut, and I felt sick.

"Jude, are you okay?" she said, cutting through the fog in my mind.

"Yeah. Fine." The words were barely more than a whisper. I didn't even bother trying to cover up the despair seeping through every pore in my body.

Her hand touched my knee, and I jerked back instantly. I knew she was trying to be comforting, but after the crazy mind tricks my brain was doing, I couldn't allow it.

I couldn't allow any of this.

"Sorry," I said, not even looking up to meet her gaze. "I'm not feeling well all of a sudden. Do you think we could cut this short?"

"Oh, um…sure. Just let me clean everything up," she said, quickly jumping up to start gathering everything back into the bags.

I rose from my spot on the step stool. "Don't worry about it, Lailah. I'll come back in a few and take care of it all."

"But you did so much, and look at all this food. I should at least help pack it, especially if you don't feel well." The words were tumbling out of her.

The obvious shift in my mood had made her nervous, and she was now reverting back to babbling.

I rested my hand on hers, desperately trying to ignore the feel of her soft skin beneath mine. "It's fine. I can handle it." I finally looked up at her.

Her eyes were wide and uncertain, and I watched as they searched mine for the hidden clue or missing piece that she couldn't figure out. She knew I wasn't sharing something, and she was right. But she didn't know that it wasn't just something. It was everything.

There wasn't much conversation during our elevator ride back up to cardiology. I stood behind her as she studied her nails and then watched the different floors light up.

We said a quick good-bye. I made yet another excuse about not feeling well and needing to rest before my shift, and then I bailed. I didn't think I took a breath until the elevators closed behind me, and I was moving downward, away from the cardiology department and Lailah.

I went back to the cafeteria, which was a great deal slower now that the rush had cleared out. I walked into the kitchen and proceeded to bag up all the unused produce, leaving it there with a note that said it was up for grabs. It would find a much better home among the kitchen staff. I wouldn't know what to do with anything that had an expiration date.

I sadly looked down at the unopened cake I'd bought. *We didn't even make it to dessert.*

Another note went on the cake.

I finished up cleaning, wiping down the counters and washing the few dishes we'd used. Once I was done, I thanked Betty and started to make my way out of the cafeteria.

"Hey, Puddin'. You forgetting something?" Betty asked, holding up two small cups of chocolate pudding.

I gave a weak smile and shoved my hands in my pockets. "No, not tonight. Thanks."

I spent the next hour doing what I did whenever I would
start to feel like the waves were pulling me under. I wandered
the halls and found myself back at the place where I'd held
her hand for the last time, where I'd bent down and kissed
her bruised cheekbone before telling her I loved her even
though I knew she couldn't hear me, where I'd listened to her
heart beat for the last time.

During the first year or so, I'd just walk the halls. Sometimes, I'd rest against a wall or even sit on the floor if it were a
really bad day. After I'd started taking classes to become a
nurses' assistant, I'd come back after a particularly bad class
about trauma patients and found a bench where I usually sat.
I didn't know who had decided to put it there, but I had my
theories, and they all revolved around a certain woman
in HR.

For the longest time, the bench had made me angry.

I remembered thinking, *How dare someone meddle in my pain
and invade the sanctity of my personal hell.*

But the longer the bench had stood there, the less and less,
I'd felt anything. As the days had passed, I'd let the numb-
ness of my life take over until nothing was left but my grief
and memories.

In the hallway where I'd screamed and begged for
Megan's heart, I sat down on the cool wooden bench situated
across from the room where I'd lost my soul mate, and my
thoughts began to drift back to Lailah.

I'd laughed today, felt emotions beyond despair and loss
today.

With Lailah, I'd felt human for the first time in years.

*Is friendship bringing these emotions to the surface again? Or is
it more?*

Leaning forward, I rested my head on my hands. I looked
across the way at the closed door to the room that had once
been Megan's.

It was so long ago, but if I closed my eyes, I could still see her. I remembered the way her hair had smelled in the morning after she just showered and the sound of her laugh when I told a joke. She was supposed to be my forever, but I'd lost her.

That was the end. My story was done.

Months after she'd died and I'd taken my position at the hospital, I'd come home late one night. I'd felt so tired that I had basically been sleepwalking to my doorstep where I'd found someone sitting.

"Who the hell are you?" My voice sounded hoarse and strained from the lack of sleep.

I'd pulled two shifts in a row, trying to make more cash to build up my savings account so that I could purchase a car.

"Nice to see you, too, brother," Roman said, rising from his spot at the foot of my dusty door. He brushed the dirt off his tailored suit pants, no doubt cursing under his breath about the damage it had done.

Only my brother would travel in Armani.

"What are you doing here?" I asked, rubbing my eyes and blinking several times. Maybe if I squeezed them tight enough, he'd disappear.

"Attempting to bring you to your senses," he answered, looking down at my dark uniform in disgust.

"Ah…well, let's do that inside, shall we?"

I pushed past him to unlock the door. He followed me in. I set my keys on the kitchen counter and turned in time to watch him assess my pocket-sized apartment.

His eyes wandered over the empty white walls and lack of furniture. The card table and folding chairs basically said it all. I was poor and barely making it.

He probably figured he could swoop in and write an extra-large check, and then we'd both be back in New York by morning.

Too bad that wasn't happening.

"So, are you done with this ridiculousness yet?" He took a seat on one of the plastic folding chairs.

"You think I'm ridiculous? After everything I've been through in the last few months, you think I'm ridiculous, Roman?"

"I think you were handed a bad hand, Jude—the worst fucking one imaginable, but the way you're handling it is shit. She's gone and you've giving up, man. You're twenty-two years old, and you've just rolled over and cashed out."

I lunged forward, grabbing the collar of his crisp white shirt. "She was my fucking fiancée, and she died!" I roared.

I pulled tight on the fabric, and it bunched together in my fists. His hands went up, the universal white flag of surrender, and I pushed him back into the chair.

"I don't expect you to understand that since you seem to have a new flavor every other week, but she was it for me. You don't get more than one of those in a lifetime."

He studied me for a moment and then adjusted his shirt and jacket. Looking at Roman was like looking into a mirror. We had the same pale green eyes and dark blond hair, but that was where our similarities ended. Roman was like our father, cold and calculating. He never let anyone in unless the person was useful for his own personal gain. I was my mother's child, meaning I actually loved someone other than myself.

There could only be one reason for him flying all the way out here. He needed me.

"Why are you really here, Roman?" I took a step back to lean against the counter.

He looked up at me with an emotionless gleam in his eyes. "We need you, Jude. No more playing around, no more games. The family needs you."

I pushed off the counter and paced around the room. "Unbeliev-able. I should have known that this wasn't about me. It's always about you, isn't it, Roman? Not performing well enough for Daddy? Need a little help? Well, fuck off. Handle it yourself."

"Listen, you little twit, your family needs you. Mother needs you," he said, knowing he'd just hit a nerve. "Doesn't she mean anything to you?"

"Of course she does!" I yelled. "But this isn't about her. It's *about you and Dad. You need me to come pull you out of whatever mess you've gotten yourself into. Well, forget it. You wanted complete control of the company? You have it." I took several long strides and pulled the door wide open. "I think you and my front door are well acquainted. Have a nice flight home."*

His hard gaze met mine as he walked a few steps forward and paused. "If you do this—if you walk away, you understand that there's no going back? Father won't forgive you. You'll be cut off, forgotten, and disowned forever."

"Sounds perfect," I answered, not turning away from his harsh stare.

I knew my stubbornness meant I'd never see my mother again. I could never go home and hold her, and I'd forever be a failure in her eyes. But I also knew that I'd never be anything but what I was now. I was already a failure. It was best if she never saw it.

Roman took the remaining steps and walked over the threshold. He turned, his gaze downcast and his brows furrowed, like he was choosing his last words carefully. "How did you know she was the one?" he asked, catching me off guard.

"What do you mean?" I stepped forward in anger.

He took a step back and held out his hands again in silent surrender. "I'm not trying to cause another fight. I just want to offer a bit of parting wisdom, little brother. If she was the one, why are you alone at twenty-two? Surely, life wouldn't be so cruel."

I squeezed my eyes shut, holding back the wave of emotions threatening to take over. Keeping my voice even and my anger checked, I replied, "When you've lost the one person who makes life worth living, give me a call and let me know what you think about the cruelty of it all."

My brother had made good on his threats that day.

I hadn't heard from my family since, not even my mother.

The only information I had were the brief financial updates I would hear on the news, but I tried to avoid anything related to the family business.

I was nothing more than a help line for Roman when

things got rough. He'd always wanted all the glory, but he had never been willing to put forth the effort to achieve it.

When he'd shown up on my doorstep that night so long ago, I'd had a glimmer of hope that he'd come because he cared, but I should have known better. All my brother cared about was the bottom line at Cavenaugh Investments and whom he would be taking home that night.

As I sat on that familiar bench, looking down the hallway where I'd spent countless hours over the last three years, his parting words came back to the forefront of my mind.

If she was the one, why are you alone at twenty-two? Surely, life wouldn't be so cruel.

No, life really was that cruel because as I withered away the afternoon, silently sitting on my bench, I thought about Lailah and the life she'd had and all the opportunities she'd never gotten to experience. Making a meal together today was only the tip of the iceberg for her. Dozens of things she'd missed out on were written in that book because she'd spent her life in a hospital.

What if she never gets the chance to do any of them?

That was the definition of cruelty—keeping a special person like Lailah locked inside where no one could see the fire in her spirit and the beauty in her soul. The ironic part, the real twist of the story that made the fates laugh and cackle high up in the clouds, was the realization that I hadn't even seen the extent of life's cruelty yet because in that moment, I realized two things.

One, I was falling for Lailah Buchanan.

And two, she was dying.

CHAPTER ELEVEN
THE PROMISE

LAILAH

"I'm going to miss you," Abigail said softly, wrapping her small arms around my neck. "And I'll come visit you every week."

I held her in my arms as her tiny body wrapped around me. Squeezing my eyes tightly, I knew one thing.

She isn't going to come back.

I'd heard this promise of visits along with promises of phone calls, letters, and emails from many friends throughout the years. But after the first few attempts, the effort to keep in touch would taper off and eventually stop altogether.

It didn't make me angry. It was the way it was supposed to be.

Life carried on outside these walls.

Abigail's grandfather, Nash, was being discharged today. He would no longer be confined to a hospital bed. His life was moving on, and so too would Abigail's. She would have no more visits to the hospital and no more long conversations with me. She was leaving, going back to the life she'd had before she was introduced to scary things like heart surgeries and IVs. Her world would return to the simple life of a nine-year-old, which was exactly how I wanted it to be. No little girl should have to grow up so quickly.

I hugged her a bit tighter, sending a million wishes for her future with every firm grasp.

"Keep writing," I said into the crook of her neck. "But don't do it to please your grandfather or because I said so. Don't write what you think you're supposed to. Write what makes you happy even if you write about pandas and dolphins every day for the rest of your life."

She pulled back from our embrace, and the tiniest smile kissed her precious face. "Well, I do like pandas," she said with a faint giggle.

At that moment, her mother appeared in the doorway to collect her. I gave Abigail another quick hug, and she hopped off, sprinting out the door and down the hallway back to her grandpa's room.

***

I thought about Abigail for the rest of the day, seeing her little cherub face in the back of my mind, as I reread *Anne Frank: The Diary of a Young Girl* and later wrote in my journal.

Would she be a writer or grow up to do something entirely different? The world was at her feet, and she didn't even know it. None of them did—the normal ones; the ones who didn't have to worry about the day to day, hour to hour, and minute to minute; the masses of people who woke up each and every day not fearing the hours ahead and the day that would follow; or those who didn't have to wonder if they'd be around to celebrate the next holiday.

How easily people took life for granted when it had so easily been given.

How I wished for such simplicity.

When the sun started to settle in the horizon and my dinner had gone cold, I reached into the drawer by my bed and pulled out the list I'd created so many years ago.

One night, while sitting at home in my room, I had curled up in my bed and watched some ridiculous high school drama flick. The plotline was the typical he-said, she-said with a bit of show tunes thrown in. It was horrible, and I would deny ever seeing it to anyone who might ask. But as I had sat there, watching these girls in cheerleading uniforms trying out for school plays, crying over boyfriends, and arguing over prom dresses, I'd realized my life would never be anything like that.

Except for the medical drama in my life, I'd never had any of the highs and lows that came with being human. As the teenyboppers had sung about broken hearts and stolen dreams, I'd pulled out a fresh notebook and started this list. It had become a way to almost purge my soul and let go of the life I'd never had. I'd known I would never do any of the things written on the pages of this journal, but seeing them would at least remind me that I could have, if things had been different.

I cracked the worn spine and ran the pads of my fingers over the pages of my Normal list, my Someday list. My eyes wandered down each item until I stopped on the last one listed on a page near the middle of the book.

62. Make a meal from start to finish.

A wisp of a smile tugged at my lips as I remembered standing in the industrial kitchen of the cafeteria, rolling out pizza dough with Jude. Reaching down to where I'd set my journal next to my legs, I grabbed the pen I'd used and uncapped it.

Feeling like something monumental was about to happen, I took a deep breath and slowly drew a dark black line through number sixty-two.

He'd done that for me. Jude had made one dent in my Someday list.

For one day, I'd felt real and whole, and finally, someone had looked at all of me instead of just the broken parts.

But like all the other times I'd spent with Jude, as soon as he'd begun to open up, he'd fled. Without warning, his mood had gone from light and teasing to edgy and quiet.

What makes a man act that way? Regret? Guilt? Did I do or say something?

I didn't know much about life on the outside, but my instincts told me something much deeper was going on with Jude. He never shared anything personal, and from what I'd learned from the gossip Grace told me, he was about the most antisocial person in the hospital. He was known to take every shift he could. He apparently had no known friends, and he never attended any social functions.

What self-inflicted prison is he holding himself hostage in, and why?

FINALLY STARTING TO GIVE IN TO MY HEAVY EYELIDS, I BEGAN TO nod off when I was stirred back awake by a noise in my room. My eyes fluttered open, and through my blurry sight, I saw Jude standing by my bed.

"Shit, I'm sorry. I didn't mean to wake you," he apologized, pulling chocolate pudding out of his pocket. He placed it on the tray table next to my bed and set a spoon on top.

"Not planning on joining me anymore?" I asked, motioning in the direction of the single snack pack.

"You were asleep. I didn't wanted to disturb you."

"Well, I'm awake now. We can share." I pushed myself up in the bed until I was in a sitting position.

I took the pudding from its perch on the tray and began pulling the foil wrapper from the top. I watched while Jude looked around the room as if he were deciding where to go. His eyes wandered to the chair where my mom always sat, before finally traveling back to me.

He took a step forward and sat on the edge of the bed facing me. His knee brushed mine under the blanket, and I became very aware of how close we suddenly were. Tucking one leg under the other, he crossed his arms across his chest and leaned forward.

Oh, okay, so even closer now.

Hello, heart rate.

"So, are you going to share? Or are you just going to hold it all night long?"

"What?" I said in confusion, waiting for my brain to kick back into gear.

I could smell the scent of his soap or aftershave or whatever the hell it was that made him smell so mouthwatering. It was like rainwater, pine, and something earthy all wrapped up in a Jude burrito.

"Our pudding. Hand it over," he instructed, reaching over to snatch the dessert from my hands.

"Hey!"

"You snooze, you lose," he mumbled, his mouth now full of the stolen pudding he'd just shoveled in it.

"That's just mean—stealing food from a sick person," I teased.

He visibly winced, and I instantly regretted my words.

"I was just kidding, Jude," I said, placing my hand on his.

Touching him was becoming something I couldn't stop myself from doing. My hands and fingers wanted to reach out to him whenever he was near. It was as if I didn't have a choice in the matter.

He placed the pudding on the tray next to us and glanced down at our hands. My frail small fingers were lying gently over his callous large ones. Slowly, as if giving the gesture purpose, he turned his hand over so that our palms were touching. Stretching out his fingers, he caressed the pads of my fingers with his own until he intertwined our fingers and held my hand.

I didn't think I'd taken a breath since his hand had started moving under mine. His eyes finally met mine, and I saw something I'd never expected to see in those faded green irises shining back at me.

Desire.

His free hand reached up to the forgotten pudding and pulled a spoonful from the small cup.

"Open your mouth," he said softly.

Taking a quick gulp of air for courage, I parted my lips as he brought the spoon to my mouth. It slipped past my tongue, and I closed my mouth around it, remember him doing the same thing moments earlier. Never breaking eye contact with him, I sucked the chocolate off the spoon as he pulled back. He dipped it back into the pudding and took a bite himself, sucking and licking the same spoon I'd just touched.

It was the single most erotic event of my life.

"See? Now, we're sharing," he said.

He dipped the spoon in the cup and fed me once again.

"Well then, I guess you're off the hook."

We continued taking turns until nothing was left but trash. He tossed everything in the wastebasket near the bed, keeping our hands joined.

"Will you tell me more about your Someday list?" he asked.

His gaze found the worn notebook lying next to me where I'd left it when I drifted off to sleep.

"Sure," I answered, grabbing the notebook and placing it on my lap. I opened it up and scanned the pages, remembering the hours I'd spent creating it, writing and re-writing it as I came up with new things to add to it.

"Pick a number," I said, recalling our earlier game.

"One," he replied.

"Nope. Try again," I said, not ready to divulge that particular one just yet.

"Okay, how about ten?"

"Go on a roller coaster."

"Hmm...Disneyland or Six Flags?"

"Oh, I don't know. I've never really thought about it," I answered.

"Well, think about it now. Are you a big roller-coaster girl or more of an it's-a-small-world person?"

My mouth twitched as I tried to hide the smile blooming at the corner of my lips. "Mickey Mouse, all the way."

"Good answer. Okay, another one. Thirty-eight."

"Um..." I scrolled through the list. "Oh, go to prom."

His face twisted in amused disgust. "No, I need to scribble that one out. Give me a pen." He looked around for a pen.

I grabbed the one near my thigh seconds before he did, causing us both to laugh.

"Be glad you missed out on that rite of passage. It's way overrated."

Holding the pen against my chest, I asked, "So, I take it yours was awesome?"

"The best," he answered sarcastically. "My date got trashed in the limo on the way there and ended up in the ladies' restroom. I sat outside and listened as she alternated between hurling and tossing every curse word at me that she could think of. Even in her alcohol-induced haze, that girl could fling some obscenities. I'm pretty sure I hadn't heard of half of them."

"Well, I'm still keeping it in there. A normal life isn't about just the good things. It's about the ups and downs. Whether or not prom is a good or bad experience, it's an experience all the same."

"Okay, good point. Did I mention she ended up making out with the prom king? And it wasn't me by the way," he added with a half smile, causing the tiny dimple in his cheek to make an appearance.

"So, I take it, she didn't become the love of your life?"

His expression went blank, and his eyes became vacant.

"No. No, she didn't. Seventy-two," he said absently, his voice hoarse and soft.

"What?" I asked before catching on. "Oh, um…okay." I scanned the list and easily found the number he'd asked for.

"Have my heart broken," I said softly, realizing it probably wasn't the best one to reveal considering the current devastation written across Jude's face. *I should have just picked the one above it—go to a movie theater.*

His eyes searched mine. "Why would you want that?"

"For the same reason I want a crappy prom. You can't live a normal life without the heartache. It's all part of the package. My life has been nothing but surgeries, procedures, and living from one test result to the next. I'd gladly trade all of that for a little normalcy. Give me a terrible prom and a hot, sticky day at Disneyland. Let me fall in love even if it means I'll get hurt in the end. At least then, I'd know that I'm living."

His fingers brushed mine as he took the book from my lap. He shut it with one hand and set it aside. His gaze never left mine as he shifted forward, narrowing the gap between us. My heart beat faster, feeling the warmth of his body as he came closer to me. His palm cupped the side of my face, and I leaned into his touch.

"I want all those things to happen for you, Lailah. I want to see you cross out each and every item on that list, if that's what it takes to make you feel alive or normal. The truth is, you are far from normal. You are light-years away from the word. You are exceptional. The word *normal* would be an insult to your very nature. I get that you want to experience everything under the sun, everything that life has robbed you of by shutting you out and keeping you prisoner to this bed, but there is one thing I will not allow." His fingers slid into my hair, and his eyes fluttered close ever so briefly before he whispered, "No one will ever break your heart. I can promise you that."

CHAPTER TWELVE

IT'S GETTING HOT IN HERE

JUDE

Since clocking in, I'd been moving through the motions of my duties, half-assing my job. I'd barely made it through a minute without thinking about the night before. My revelation regarding Lailah, my realization that whatever was going on between us went far beyond the boundaries of friendship, led me to one absolute conclusion.

I had no idea what I was doing.

I'd spent the last three years feeling nothing but pain and regret. Few other emotions had filtered through my psyche since I lost Megan.

Lailah made me feel…everything.

I was at odds with myself. An internal tug-of-war was pulling me in two different directions, and I had no idea which way to go. Behind me was my life with Megan. She had been my future, and when that had ended, I hadn't wanted to move on. I hadn't known how. I'd refused. I never expected there to be anything else. Now, when I looked ahead, there was this bright, shining path that scared the shit out of me. Lailah was a wild card, and I had no guarantees that I wouldn't end up right back where I'd started—broken and alone.

I wasn't sure if I could risk my heart again, but maybe I already had. What if I'd already given a piece of myself to the girl with the infectious laugh and the shy, innocent smile? Perhaps I was a goner from the start.

Shaking my head, I walked down the hall toward her room, and then I halted mid-step.

Maybe she deserved better than the man who had destroyed her future. She was too fragile to know the truth. *Hell, I was too fragile to admit it.*

Two broken hearts—we would destroy each other before we even had a chance to begin.

But no matter how many reasons I gave myself to stay away, I would still end up back at her door, ready for more chocolate pudding, nervous babbling, and brief glimpses of heaven.

Her zeal for life was addictive, and I needed my fix. I needed the light only my angel could bring.

I'm a selfish bastard.

My knock was answered by her lilting sweet voice. I turned the knob, opened the door, and found her standing by her bed, folding a few shirts. Several piles of clothes were neatly laid out on the mattress.

"Laundry day?" I asked, gesturing to the stacks of clothes.

"Um…no, not quite." She put down the pink shirt she'd been folding and pivoted around to face me. She seemed hesitant and on edge. "I've been discharged," she announced.

"What?"

"Dr. Marcus is letting me go home. He said since I'm healthy, or as healthy as can be expected, considering…" She trailed off since we both knew where that sentence was going.

Considering she's dying…

"He decided it would be best for me to stay at home while we wait for news on the transplant."

I glanced up and saw tears in her eyes. She wasn't happy. She was upset.

Seeing that I'd noticed her stray tears, she quickly brushed them aside and turned back to her clothes and continued folding.

"When?" I asked, watching her in the moonlight streaming in from the window.

"Tomorrow morning. I could have left before dinner, but I wanted some time to pack, and…"

To say good-bye to me.

She hadn't said it, but I could feel the words hanging in the air. I was the reason she wasn't happy about leaving. This should have been a celebratory moment for her, but I'd taken that from her. By being here and interrupting her life, I'd taken the one normal thing away from her—going home.

Step away. Let her go.

"Well, that's great news," I said, trying to muster up a bit of fake enthusiasm.

She turned back around, and I saw surprise and maybe a touch of hurt in her eyes.

"Um…yeah, it's awesome." She gripped the shirt in her hands and then tossed it on the bed.

"I mean, no one wants to—"

"What is your deal, Jude?" she yelled, taking several strides toward me.

"My deal?"

"Yeah, you're sweet and endearing one minute and then brushing me off the next. I don't get it. What do you want from me? Am I a charity case? Do you get off on hanging out with the poor sick girl but then tire of me easily?"

Closing the last few inches between us, I got in her face. "You have no idea what you're talking about," I hissed.

"No," she answered, "I really don't. You don't tell me anything. You are this big, giant mystery that I know nothing about. Why is that, Jude?"

"It's too much," I simply said.

"You mean, I can't handle it," she inferred.

"That's not what I said, Lailah."

"No, but that's what you meant. You're just like everyone else. I'm too fragile. I'm too weak. Let's sugarcoat the truth, so it doesn't upset Lailah. God forbid that we upset her," she said in a mocking tone. "Well, I'm neither weak nor fragile. I've endured more pain than most people see in a lifetime, so don't think for one single second that I can't handle anything you can."

"I know you can."

"Then, why put me through all this? Do you even care a little about me?" Her voice was quiet and timid.

"I care too fucking much, Lailah."

Without a second thought, I grabbed the nape of her neck and pulled her body to mine before fusing our mouths together. She gasped in surprise, pulling back slightly, but then she surrendered, melting into me completely. My hands tightened around her waist as I deepened our kiss. I knew this had to be her first kiss, and I intended to make sure it was well worth the wait.

A new war raged inside of me. My hands wanted to feel every inch of her skin, trace every line of her body, and lay her back on the bed to devour her. My fingers shook as I steadied myself.

She's innocent in every way.

Dr. Marcus's words came back to me like a bucket of cold water on a hot summer day, and I stilled. I needed to be the man she deserved even if I never lived up to it. Being pawed and felt up in a hospital room wasn't the way she needed to remember tonight.

With my breath coming out in heavy puffs, I touched my lips to hers, letting myself taste heaven one last time. I pulled back slightly while reaching up to run my hands through her silky strands. She watched me with wide, curious eyes, and I smiled.

"Did I just knock another one of those numbers off your list?"

Pink stained her cheeks, and she nodded. "What was that, Jude?"

I raised my eyebrow in amusement. "That was a kiss. Did I not do it right? Because I'd be happy to try again."

"No!" she yelped. "I mean, yes! Crap!"

A sly smirk spread across my face. "It's okay, Lailah. Breathe."

Her eyes fluttered closed, and she took a deep breath, letting it slowly fill her chest. I couldn't stop myself. I leaned down and briefly touched my lips to hers.

"Everything needs a beginning," I said, lifting my eyes to hers. "This is ours."

"But I'm leaving."

"Yes, and I will miss seeing your beautiful face here, but I don't live here."

Something must have clicked just then because a goofy grin slowly spread across her face, and she blushed again.

"You don't even know where I live. Oh God! You'll have to meet my mom!"

The angry blonde I'd seen in the hall with Marcus suddenly flashed through my mind, and honestly, the thought of meeting her was a little frightening.

Lailah laughed, the sound of amusement echoing each note. "You're nervous!"

"Maybe a little, but I'll be okay," I assured her.

She gave me a doubtful look, but I wrapped my arms tighter around her waist and squeezed with assurance.

"Besides, we'll have to figure it out if we want to start working on that list of yours. I think a trip to the ocean is in order."

Her eyes lit up at the idea. I couldn't wait to get my hands on that list and start crossing out each and every one of those one-hundred-and-forty-three mysterious adventures.

"So, what do we do now?" She nervously bit her bottom lip.

I leaned in close, millimeters from her lips. She sucked in a breath, and her eyes widened in anticipation. A grin I couldn't stop swept across my face as I placed a chaste kiss on her cheek before taking a step back.

"I'm going to go try to explain my extremely long absence from my duties to my supervisor," I said.

A faint blush appeared on her cheeks.

"And then I will need to play a little catch-up. I'll take my lunch break in a while, though and sneak back in here. It is your last night, and I do have a duty to deliver your dessert."

"Yes, you do," she answered.

I took a step back toward the door, keeping my eyes trained on her, until my outstretched hand felt the cool metal of the door handle. I turned to make my exit, still smiling like a fool.

Then, she called out, "Jude?"

"Yeah?" I answered, whipping back around.

"Just bring one pudding tonight. We'll share again," she shyly suggested, red blotches staining her already pink cheeks.

"You got it."

God bless the creator of pudding.

"Tell me something about you, something I don't know," I said.

We were leaning back against her pillow, sharing the single pudding cup I'd brought, as requested.

I'd raced through the rest of my duties, making sure I had everything ticked off and accounted for before going to lunch. I hadn't wanted to be negligent, but I also hadn't wanted Lailah to wait up until after midnight for me. I'd clocked out and grabbed a quick sandwich and a cup of pudding from the cafeteria before racing back upstairs and wolfing down my sandwich almost whole. If the nurses had noticed me visiting Lailah's room more than needed, no one said anything. I wondered if that was Dr. Marcus's doing.

When I'd slipped back in here, I hadn't bothered with the chair or the end of the bed this time. I needed to be near her. Side by side with our legs entwined, we shared one spoon and started a game of twenty questions.

"Um...what do you want to know?" she asked, dipping the spoon into the creamy, dark dessert.

"Anything."

She thought about it for a moment and finally answered, "Ever since I was young, I've always wanted a sibling. I didn't really care if it was a brother or sister. I just wanted to spend time with someone my age. I guess that comes from being alone all the time," she said. "Do you have any siblings?"

I nodded. "A brother."

"Older or younger?"

"Older."

"Do you like him?" she asked.

I let out a thoughtful breath. "*Like* is a strong word. Tolerate is probably more appropriate. But it's been a long time since I've seen him."

"How come?" She took a small bite of chocolate between her lips.

I watched the spoon dip into her mouth and reappear as I thought about how to answer.

How much should I tell her?

I'm neither weak nor fragile. Don't think for one single second that I can't handle anything you can.

She'd been treated like a porcelain doll her entire life. If I did the same, I'd be no different than anyone else in her life, and I wanted to be different. I wanted to be the one she could trust.

My conscience took that moment in time to remind me in

detailed flashbacks of a younger, broken, and more desperate version of myself begging for Megan's father not to give up her organs.

I told that asshole to take a hike.

The past couldn't be undone. There was nothing I could do to change what had happened in the hallways of this hospital three years ago. The only thing I could do was make the life of the woman next to me better in every way possible.

Would anything change if I were to tell her that I was the reason she didn't get that heart?

No. So, why bother?

It was a terrible, horrible lame excuse. In the back of my head, I knew I was still trying to protect her. I was doing the same thing that her mother and doctors had done her entire life—sugarcoating and suffocating the truth—but I was also doing it to protect me.

So, I'd do what I could and tell her everything else but that awful moment in my history. It would be more than I'd told any other person on the planet since the day I arrived in California.

"We had a falling out. I haven't spoken to anyone in my family in almost three years."

Her eyes met mine and softened. "That's awful. How does that even happen?"

"Well, it's a long and complicated sad story."

"I've got time."

"Okay, but first, I need to explain something," I said.

I reached down and grabbed my ID badge. It had the trademark dreadful picture with bad lighting and my blank expression slapped on the front. Underneath was my name—Jude C.

"I don't even know your last name," she said before covering her mouth with her hand. She looked mortified.

As I peeled her fingers from her face one at a time, I noticed she felt warmer than normal. "You feel hot. Are you feeling okay?"

"What? Yes, I'm fine. You're just trying to change the subject!"

I let it go, but I made a mental note to check her later. "No one knows my last name. It was something I asked for when I was hired. My last name is…well-known."

Her eyes narrowed. "Are you, like, a prince or something? Is this the part of the movie where I get to move to a castle? I don't think I can walk in heels."

"My last name is Cavenaugh."

There was no reaction. She just stared at me, trying to put all the pieces together.

"Like the bank, Cavenaugh Investments in New York? The family who makes the Trumps look like paupers? They've been all over the news lately. You must get confused with them all the time. Don't they have a son named Jude who—" Her hand went to her mouth, and her eyes widened.

"Hasn't been seen publicly for three years," I finished her sentence.

"They just keep saying he's on vacation or too busy in meetings," she said absently.

"My brother and father have always been very good at lying. God forbid that we have a family scandal. They get away with it because I wasn't around much in the years prior to…me leaving. People barely remember what I look like anymore. I was away at college for so long that the public lost interest, and that left my brother, Roman, plenty of time to soak up the limelight."

She looked at me, her eyes searching my face, as if seeing me for the first time. This was what I'd feared—that she would see me differently.

Am I still Jude? Or would I forever be Jude Cavenaugh—heir to a multibillion-dollar company?

She continued assessing me, her eyes traveling over my features, down the length of my inked arms, and back up to my messy tresses. I took a deep breath, closing my eyes, as I waited for the altered tone or the shocked gasp to come.

What I got was pudding on my face. I opened my eyes in amazement and found her giggling. Leftover pudding still clung to her pointer finger, and she was just leaning over to lick it off.

I stopped her, pulling the single digit into my own mouth and sucking it clean. Her eyes heated from the contact, and then they went round with unheard laughter when she once again saw the pudding smeared down my right cheek.

"You don't look like him. You're a little rougher looking," she said, still giggling at her mess.

"Well, that was the idea. New look—"

"New life?" she finished.

I felt myself wince.

Screeching brakes, shattering glass, Megan screaming.

I can't get to her.

Then, silence. Nothing but silence.

"Something like that," I mumbled. "So, whom do I look like?" I managed, blinking rapidly to pull myself back from hell. *Stay in the present.*

"Jude. Just Jude."

"Yeah?"

"Yeah."

"So, are you going to help me out with this?" I pointed to the glob of pudding still clinging to my skin.

Her eyes traveled to where the direction of my outstretched finger, and I could see the hesitation. Finally, she leaned into me, her long strands of hair tickling my arm, as she nuzzled into my chest. I could smell the fruity essence of her shampoo as her warm, wet tongue darted out to touch my skin. I instinctively moved my hand to her waist, pulling her closer, and I reveled in the feel of her. She didn't show an ounce of innocence as her body molded to mine. Her mouth moved lower, leaving a trail of wet kisses, until it found my eager lips.

I groaned, feeling the timid touch of her heated fingers brush against the fabric of the top of my scrubs. My hand slipped under her shirt as I lay back, pulling her with me. The instant my hand touched her bare skin, I knew something was wrong. My eyes flew open, and I stilled, startling her.

"You're burning up." I gently laid her back down on the bed.

"It's just hot in here," she replied, sitting up to adjust her shirt.

Her hands flew to the collar of her shirt, and I watched as she retreated back into her shell. *Was she afraid I had changed my mind?*

I took a look at her cheeks. I'd mistaken the faint blush I saw earlier for nervousness or passion, but it wasn't due to any emotion at all.

Lailah was running a fever.

I let out a puff of air as I prepared to be the bad guy.

She was definitely not going home tomorrow.

CHAPTER THIRTEEN

MEETING MOM

LAILAH

Any speculation as to what was or was not going on between a certain CNA and me was made crystal clear when Jude's dormant alpha tendencies came bubbling to the surface in a major way the second he felt my feverish skin. He'd flown out of my room and demanded the nurses call Dr. Marcus. I could hear him from my bed as he barked orders and expected immediate results.

The powerful surname he'd just revealed to me suddenly seemed fitting.

I should have been embarrassed. I should have been shrinking down in my hospital bed, rolling my eyes, and counting the minutes until the sound of his deep voice had quieted in the hall and I had the chance to chastise him for his overbearing behavior.

But I did none of that.

Instead, in my fever-induced fascination, I'd watched as he marched out of my room, his gait full of hurried purpose. I'd been listening as the deep timbre of his commands reminded me of the fight we'd had when I accused him of not caring. Then, I thought of the kiss that had followed.

He kissed me.

And now he's taking care of me.

It turned out that over the next several hours, I'd need all the help I could get. The fever gave way to chills, which then transitioned into vomiting and cold sweats. I'd caught a virus that was aggressive and, of course, un-responsive to antibiotics. The irony of living in a hospital was that it was actually one of the cleanest, germ-infested places to be. There were so many sick people all stuffed into one place. No matter how hard the staff tried to keep it clean, it was still a giant petri dish for bacteria and viruses.

Dr. Marcus told me this particular virus had to work its way through my system before I'd feel human again. Within a few hours of becoming feverish, I was convinced that it was trying to kill me.

The moment news of a fever spread, everyone entering my room slapped on a hospital mask, except for Jude.

For the remainder of his shift, he didn't leave my side, and he stayed with me well past the time he'd clocked out. After his earlier heroic display, no one seemed willing to step up and argue with him about leaving, not even Dr. Marcus. Although, he didn't look too pleased when he walked into my room to find Jude lying beside me on the bed.

I drifted off sometime around five in the morning after Jude had seen me at my absolute worst. He'd held my hair as I heaved and cried in the bathroom. Drying my tears, he had gotten me a glass of water and helped me back into bed, only to carry me back into the bathroom when the nausea and sickness started all over again. He never complained or seemed repulsed, but I guessed it was due to his job.

I just hadn't wanted to be part of his job—or at least, not this part.

Vomiting mere hours after my first kiss wasn't exactly how I'd pictured it.

Maybe an hour or two after falling asleep, I awoke, hearing the door snap shut. My eyes peeked open, and I peered over to find a sleeping Jude next to me. Sitting in the blue chair, his large frame was bent forward, and he was resting his head on his forearms.

Lifting my hand, I winced, remembering the IV that was now connected. Clear fluids were being pumped into my body to counteract the lack of food and water. I softly raked my hand through his hair, careful not to wake him. I heard a shuffle of feet, reminding me that the door had shut and awoken me moments earlier.

I turned to see my mother standing by the doorway, watching me. Her eyes were frozen on the man sleeping next to me while my fingers stood completely frozen in Jude's unruly hair.

"Dr. Marcus didn't call me until this morning," she said softly, her gaze still fixed on Jude.

"It's just a virus," I said. "Rough night though."

I watched as she took him in—his scrubs, the scrolling dark ink on his arms, and back to the place where my hand was resting in his hair. I started to pull my hand back, but I stopped myself.

You are an adult, Lailah, I chanted, as I willed my fingers to continue their previous path through Jude's thick hair.

"And who is this?" she asked, her tone clipped and formal.

She wasn't wearing a mask as well. Apparently, she wasn't afraid of catching whatever I had either.

Jude stirred under my fingers, his hair falling into his eyes as sleep drained away. I turned away from my mother's rigid stance by the entrance to see soft moss-colored eyes staring back at me.

"Good morning," he whispered.

Even though I felt like I'd been run over by a Mack truck, then dropped off the side of a bridge, and stomped on, I couldn't help the grin spread across my lips.

"Morning."

My mom made a sound in her throat, and I snapped back,

sitting up further in bed. I cleared my throat and took a deep breath.

"Mom, this is Jude..." I looked at him, asking for permission.

He gave me a single nod as a go-ahead.

"Cavenaugh. He's a nurses' assistant here in the hospital, and we've become quite close," I said, trying to muster up as much maturity as possible.

Speaking up to my mother was something I'd never mastered. Having her in front of me always made me feel small and weak.

As I'd expected, Jude's last name was lost on my mother. Her nose was usually buried in a textbook, or she was standing in front of a classroom. Either way, she really only paid attention to current events if they had to do with religious conflict or medical research. Everything else—politics, fashion, celebrity gossip, or business reports—was filtered out and forgotten.

Being the gentleman he was, Jude rose from the tattered old chair and went around to the other side of the bed to formally greet her. Standing over six feet tall, he dwarfed the petite frame of my mother.

"Very nice to meet you, Ms. Buchanan," he said cordially, offering his hand to her.

She glanced down, and I bit my lip, waiting for her to take it.

"Likewise," she finally said, taking his hand.

"Jude stayed with me and took care of me all night," I said with as much enthusiasm as my frail state could manage.

By the way her lip tightened into displeasure, I would have thought I'd said, *Hey, Mom! Jude and I had wild-monkey sex right here in this very bed! Want to see the video?*

"Well, thank you very much, Mr. Cavenaugh. I'll be able to take it from here." Her voice was liquid ice. She'd lost control of things, and she didn't like it. To her, life was always about control.

"With all due respect, Ms. Buchanan—" Jude started, that deep commanding Cavenaugh tone returning to his voice.

It sent shivers down my spine and made me wonder what he had been like in his alternate life.

"Jude…" I said softly, cutting him off, before he had the chance to give my mom the lashing she deserved.

As much as I wanted to see someone finally dish back what she'd been serving for as long as I could remember, I didn't want my mother to hate him. The bad-boy thing wasn't very appealing when I counted on my mother to manage most of my life. I needed her to like my boyfriend.

Boyfriend…mmm…

Warm fuzzies.

"You're tired. You were up all night. Why don't you run home and take a nap, shower, and then meet me back here for lunch?"

I could see the turmoil in his eyes. He didn't want to leave. Last night, as Jude—the nurses' assistant—had barked orders to those who earned double and triple his salary, I'd figured out fairly quickly that he had a driving instinct to protect others. Or maybe it was just me.

Yep, more warm fuzzies.

"Okay," he relented.

He walked back over to my bedside, not caring that my mother's eyes were shooting virtual laser beams of death at him, and he bent down.

"I'll be back in a few hours," he said.

When I nodded, he followed up with a list of instructions, "Try to drink some water. Have your mom use that cool washcloth on your forehead, and try to sleep." He squeezed my hand and gave a quick kiss to my forehead. Then, he was gone.

I looked up at my mother looming in the empty space by my bed, glaring at me as if I were a deviant teenager, and I huffed out a frustrated breath.

Mother—One.

Adulthood—Zero.

"Are we going to talk about this?" my mother asked moments after Jude had left my room.

She paced several steps toward the bathroom and then pivoted back, retracing her steps, only to do the same thing all over again. She looked a bit agitated.

"Talk about what?" I asked, sinking further into my blankets. A chill traveled up my spine, and I buried my hands under the sheets, trying to cover as much skin as possible.

"Why haven't you told me about your secret visitor?"

"Jude isn't a secret. I wasn't trying to hide anything from you. You were just never here when he visited."

"And you never thought to tell me that you were… *befriending* a man who worked in the hospital?"

She'd said the word *befriend* as if it were dripping in gasoline and would likely light on fire at any given moment. It pissed me off, and it was a problem that needed to be taken care of quickly.

"Listen, Mom, I wasn't trying to deceive you. Jude has been a friend to me. He's kept me company on lonely nights."

Her eyebrows rose.

I quickly pulled my hand out from under the blankets and lifted it to silence her rebuttal. "I know what you're going to say. He was a friend. That's it. I know you think because I've been in this bed and behind these walls for the majority of my life that I am innocent about the ways of the world, and to some extent, you're probably right but not about this. Friends, I swear."

She made a garbled humph sound in her throat and pulled her arms to her chest. "And now? That parting display of affection I saw on his way out? That wasn't how you say good-bye to a friend, Lailah. I might be a little out of practice, but I do remember that."

That stung a little. I knew she didn't mean it to be harsh. My mother was direct, demanding, and straightforward, but she was never vicious or vindictive. Her personality came from necessity. I didn't know much about her past, but I knew she'd been abandoned by the one person she thought she could trust—my father. I didn't think she'd ever gotten over it. Since then, she'd fought for everything in life, and I knew my illness had only made that ten times harder. She'd spent her life caring for me, so she could never fit in a love life.

"And now, we're more," I simply answered, not knowing exactly what to call Jude and me.

The word *boyfriend* did sound nice, but he hadn't said it, and I certainly wasn't going to go around calling him that without audible proof from him. Friends with benefits just sounded dirty, and we definitely weren't there yet. Flashes of his lips on mine while his hand had moved up the back of my shirt danced around in my head, and I felt my cheeks redden. While I was hoping for more than friends, I was looking forward to the benefits part.

My mother shook her head in frustration before leaving the room. I was sure she was going to find Dr. Marcus to have another one of her secret meetings that I wouldn't be privy to. We wouldn't want to talk about my own health in front of me.

I let the annoyance melt away, and I snuggled back down in my bed, allowing my thoughts to drift back to Jude. Whatever our label was—friends or something else—I wanted it to continue even though I knew that I shouldn't. I was selfish for not pushing him away. My life was at a crossroads. Who knew which path I would end up traveling on? Was it fair to ask him to walk either of those roads with me? Even if I were lucky enough to get a transplant, there would be no guarantees it would be successful.

But were there ever any guarantees in life?

I'd told Jude that I believed a normal life was about the good and the bad. The ups and downs, not knowing where our lives would eventually end up—that's what made us human.

Isn't that what I want—a normal life with no guarantees?

If I've been living from one bad moment to the next with very little good in the middle, couldn't I just take Jude as my wild card? Couldn't he be my savior from all the bad I've had to endure?

But a normal relationship was about give and take.

If Jude were my replacement for all the bad in my life, could I be his?

But what if I were the opposite?

<hr>

THAT ONE SINGLE QUESTION KEPT REPEATING THROUGH MY thoughts as I tried to catch a few quiet moments of rest before my mom returned. I tossed all the blankets off of me and then promptly tugged them back around me several minutes later when I became ice cold. When I gave up on the notion of sleep, I instead pulled out my laptop and entered the one name doing laps in my head.

Thousands of search results popped up on Google. Many weren't specifically related to Jude but rather the family as a whole. I found financial reports and glamorous photos of who I assumed were his parents at charity events and other elite social gatherings. I scrolled down further and found an old article entitled "The Cavenaughs Find Gold Mine in Youngest Son."

Looking around the room, I felt like I was betraying some sort of secret trust between Jude and me. *Why do I feel the need to do this? Shouldn't I just ask him?*

But my finger pushed down on the touchpad, and I pulled up the article.

I scanned the text, pulling out the bits of information I found relevant, and my mind skidded to a halt about a third of the way down after the introduction where the journalist had written about the vast accolades and accomplishments of the Cavenaugh family.

Jude was smart, like really freaking smart.

He'd also been groomed from nearly infancy to take over the family business.

According to this article, after showing a love for math at an early age, his parents had sent him to the best schools money could buy. From the time he was in kindergarten, he was privately tutored. The journalist commented that the money had been wasted because all the tutors in the world couldn't teach Jude the one thing he'd possessed since birth—instinct. From the age of thirteen, rather than partaking in after-school activities, Jude had helped his father make major business decisions.

A knock at my door startled me from my reading, and I quickly slammed my laptop shut in shame.

Grace breezed through my door like a breath of fresh air in autumn. "Good morning, sweets. Heard you had a rough evening. You're not trying to leave me again, are you?" she asked with a wink.

"Ugh, not anymore."

The mask over her face hid her smile from me, but I could see the crinkles around her eyes, so I knew it was there, buried under that ugly disposable covering.

"Well, no matter. We'll get you out of here soon enough."

Unlike times in the past, I wasn't as eager to get home. I still wanted to, especially knowing I'd still see Jude, but when I was here, I could see him practically every day. *Would that be the case outside the confines of the hospital? Or would it be different?*

I had so many unanswered questions.

"Hey, Grace. Do you know anything about the Cavenaugh family?" I blurted out.

"Like, *the* Cavenaugh family?" She moved around the room as she began checking my vitals and replacing my fluids.

"Yeah, I was, um…watching the news the other day and something about them popped up," I lied. It was a white lie, so it didn't count.

"Well, if they weren't in a movie or on a TV show, I don't

pay much attention, but I do know a few things about the son."

My heart sped up, but I tried not to appear the slightest bit affected. "Oh?" I asked.

"Yeah, he's gorgeous—not as gorgeous as my Brian, of course." She took a seat on the edge of my bed next to my feet to finish our chat.

"I thought he hasn't been seen in a long time," I offered.

"Oh, not him. I'm talking about Roman Cavenaugh, the oldest one. He's been in the gossip magazines since he was in high school. He's one of those men who are hard to tame. Everyone always wants to know whom he is dating or where he was last seen. He's like the George Clooney of the business world."

"And the other brother?" I asked, adjusting my blankets so that I didn't have to look her in the eye.

"Oh, right. What's his name? Jude! Oh, hey, like our Jude. They do kind of look alike, except ours has all the tattoos and muscles. I don't know honestly. He really never became much of a public figure. It's always been Roman. The press speculated that Jude became extremely introverted after his fiancée died."

Fiancée?

Died?

"Really?" I croaked out.

"Yeah, the family didn't release many details until months after the fact. No one even knew he was engaged. Of course, the only Cavenaugh anyone ever paid attention to was Roman," she said with dreamy eyes and a shrug.

Jude was engaged? And he lost her?

I felt pain and sadness for him. All of it boiled up like an inferno until I felt dizzy from it.

My heart began an erratic rhythm that had nothing to do with my sudden education of Jude's past.

Grace rose from her spot at the end of my bed and resumed her routine. She turned her back to me as she disconnected the empty fluid bag from the IV stand. "Speaking of Judes, what's going on with you and our Jude? I heard he caused quite a commotion around here last night."

The room started to spin, and beads of sweat trickled down my forehead while I tried to vocalize an answer. All that came out was a bunch of useless syllables. Grace's head sharply whipped around, and I saw her surprised expression through the haze of movements before she reached out to grab my call button.

I heard her shout the words, "Code Blue," right before I passed out.

CHAPTER FOURTEEN
TWO ROADS

JUDE

was in turmoil, utter fucking turmoil.

I felt it churning within me, boiling up through my veins like a poison I couldn't get rid of.

There was no chance of sleeping. The sun streamed through the flimsy curtains of my bedroom, and I sat up in bed. Running my hands through my hair, I looked around my modest bedroom.

Jumping out of bed, I gave up on any chance of catching shut-eye, and I did what I'd wanted to do since walking through the front door of my apartment two hours earlier. I started to get ready to go back to her.

When I was with Lailah, pure air would fill my lungs, healing me throughout, for what seemed like the first time in years. She gave me purpose and made me want to see the sunrise again. The moment I left her side, the guilt would come rushing back like a punishing ocean current.

I don't deserve any of this.

Nothing I'd done in my life up to this point afforded me the luxury of enjoying a single minute of happiness with Lailah.

I'd caused the death of my fiancée. I hadn't driven us into oncoming traffic, but I'd looked into her tired, droopy eyes, smelled the lingering alcohol on her breath, and still handed her the keys, knowing I shouldn't have.

Because I had been selfish.

When she had been beyond repair, needing to be put to rest so that her family could mourn, I'd prolonged everyone's suffering by trying to prove our love could survive anything —even brain damage. I'd listened to her parents sobbing behind me as I'd held her hands in mine. With tears pouring down my cheeks, I'd begged her to come back to me, but she hadn't.

I'd hurt so many lives when I lost Megan, including the one person I'd never expected.

I didn't deserve Lailah.

But I would take her. I'd take everything she gave me because I was selfish and tired of being alone. And I'd offer her everything I had left to give.

Surely, life wouldn't be so cruel.

It was ironic that I was taking advice from the one person I despised.

My brother hadn't suffered a day in his entire privileged life. He knew nothing about loss or pain. As his words echoed in my head, I couldn't help but wonder if they held a bit of truth.

A twinge of guilt shot through my gut at the mere thought of anyone replacing Megan, but my brother was right. She was gone. I thought my world had ended when she died three years ago. Yet, here I was with air filling my lungs and blood pumping through my heart, and I felt everything because I was alive. I was still here.

My self-imposed exile had stripped me of everything I once was. I'd left my family, friends, and home.

Isn't that enough?

I am still here. I am still alive.

Thirty minutes after giving up on sleep, I was showered, dressed, and driving my piece-of-shit car back to the hospital.

When I'd said I left my old life behind, I wasn't kidding.

My parents had figured out fairly quickly that I had an affinity for numbers. I wasn't like the guy in *Rain Man* or anything. I couldn't solve equations in my sleep. I was more like the guy in the casino who gets accused of cheating at the slots, but they can't prove anything because he was just really damn good. I was one of those. I saw patterns and simplicity while others saw chaos. I was always two steps ahead of the market, seeing trends and pitfalls before anyone else did. Ever since this little discovery, all my father could see were dollar signs. There was no soccer or swim team for Jude. Instead, I'd gotten to sit in on board meetings and listen to hour-long conference calls.

It's good training, my father would say.

He hadn't seemed to realize that I was also smart enough to see through his shit. I'd known exactly what he was planning. I'd managed to get away for college, but he'd still had his claws digging into my back, blowing up my phone whenever he'd needed something or flying me home when it had been too important.

I'd managed to keep most of it from Megan, but she'd known that life after we graduated would be different. I would be different. I'd spent every night of our last vacation awake, watching her sleep while worrying about what would happen when my father took over again.

Leave, a voice in my head had said. *Just run away with her*, it had pleaded.

But I hadn't done that because I'd felt obligated to my family. They were my blood, and I'd thought I owed it to the company and the people who worked for us to ensure the survival of the business.

That all had ended the night Roman visited, begging me to come back. He hadn't given a fuck about Megan or what I was going through.

Dollar signs—that's all I was but not anymore.

I'd resisted every inclination to invest any extra change I had leftover month to month. Instead, I'd put some away, managing to save a meager couple hundred to cover a month of rent if needed. I was poor, dirt fucking poor.

If only Daddy could see me now…

My clunker of a car pulled into the parking lot behind the hospital, and I looked up at the building that had served as my refuge since moving to California. This was where I worked, but it was also where I could feel Megan—in the hallways, walking through the ER, in the tears of the mourning families.

It was my living monument to her, and I was the groundskeeper.

I moved across the parking lot and looked up to Lailah's window on the cardiology floor as if it were a bright white beacon steering me to shore.

The hospital couldn't just be a memorial anymore. It had to be more.

I had to be more—for her.

As soon as I approached the nurses' station, I knew there was something amiss. Nurses on this floor moved at a slower pace than the ER. They would normally chat about their lives and gossip in the hallway.

Today, they were in hyper mode.

The nurses on duty were buzzing around, agitated and on alert, like they'd been spooked. Something had happened, and they were still working their way down from the adrenaline high. I'd seen it before a dozen times in the ER. Each and every person on this floor—hell, in this hospital—was trained for an emergency, but it didn't mean that it wouldn't scare the shit out of someone when the time finally came.

And in a place like this, it always did.

I looked around, trying to find someone I recognized. Day-shift people were mostly unknown to me as we would only see each other in passing, and since I wasn't the most social person on the staff, I knew even less people.

But I did know one person.

Snow White.

Where is she?

I scanned the floor and finally saw her appearing from Lailah's room. A mask was covering her face as she briskly walked to the nurses' station. She glanced up at me from across the counter, and that was all it took. Her eyes told me everything I didn't want to know.

I took off running down the short distance of the hall toward Lailah's room, but I was stopped short when I was grabbed from behind. My fist came up, and I turned to swing at whoever was keeping me from entering that room.

"What the fuck, Marcus?" I growled.

"She's sleeping and stable now."

"Now? Now! What the hell does that mean?"

The grip he had on my arm lessened.

"The virus she'd caught got worse. Her fever skyrocketed in a short time, and her body went into distress. We were able to stabilize her and bring down the fever. Now, she's resting."

While he was talking, all I could think of was that I wasn't here. She could have died, and I wasn't here. She could have slipped away from this earth, and I would have never seen her smile again, never felt the joy of her tenderness. I'd known this girl for only a short time.

How did she come to matter so much to me?

"Can I see her?" I swallowed down the lump of emotions I felt welling up in my throat.

"Yeah, but first, I think we need to talk."

I should have known this was coming. After my demanding display last night and the fact that her mother knew, it was only a matter of time before this happened.

But why does it have to happen now?

I glanced at Lailah's closed door. The need to break through it and crawl up next to her was burning inside me.

"Okay," I agreed.

By the look Marcus was giving me, I knew that there was no way I would get out of this.

He started toward the elevator, and I followed, hating that every footfall was one step further away from her.

She could have died.

The thought replayed in my head while we silently slipped into the elevator and rode it down to the cafeteria. I already knew where we were headed. This had been our tradition long before Lailah. We'd have crappy coffee and conversation where he'd do most of the talking, and I'd listen.

Taking a look at his rigid gait and tight expression, I guessed our roles would be reversed tonight.

We stood in line, ordered, and took a seat toward the back of the cafeteria. It was around eleven in the morning, so the traffic from lunch was just starting to filter in, but it was still relatively quiet.

Marcus leaned back in his chair and set his steely gaze on me. "Anything you want to tell me, Jude?"

No J-Man today. Just Jude.

"What do you want to know?" I took a long gulp of coffee that tasted like mud.

"I want to know why you lied to me."

"I didn't lie to you, Marcus—" I started.

He cut in, "No? You didn't say that you'd stay away from Lailah? That you'd be a friend and nothing more?" His eyes were blazing.

During our conversation regarding Lailah, I'd never made any promises to Marcus and I couldn't help but wonder where all this was coming from. "Look, I didn't plan for this. I didn't go into this expecting for any of this to happen."

"You said you weren't capable of loving anyone else, Jude. I trusted you," he spit.

His use of the word *love* felt like a blow to my knees, spiraling me back to the night I'd proposed to Megan when I'd sworn I would love only her for the rest of my life.

"But I do love her," my voice croaked out in disbelief as I stared down at the table, lost in my own head. Knowing something and acknowledging it were two entirely different things.

"You don't sound so sure."

"No, I'm sure. Just surprised. I didn't think I was capable of it either."

I finally looked up at him and found him watching me. Those punishing blue eyes worked and processed me like he was dismantling a clock or contemplating the space-time continuum.

"What changed?"

"Lailah. She changed everything. She makes me feel human again. I don't dread living anymore."

"But what are you doing for her?"

"What?" I asked.

"You just said how she makes you feel. What are you doing for her? What do you make her feel? I care about her far more than I care about you, buddy. If you want my blessing on this, tell me what you're doing for my girl?"

My gaze narrowed as I looked at him, really looked at him. "What's your connection to Lailah and Ms. Buchanan?"

"I'm Lailah's doctor," he answered in a clipped tone.

"Okay," I relented, letting it go for now.

Eager to return to Lailah's bedside, we rose from the table and threw our shitty coffee into the trash before heading for the elevator. As the doors slid closed and we made our way skyward, I felt Lailah's presence growing as the gap between us lessened.

"You never answered my question," Marcus said, cutting the silence like a knife.

"What question?"

"What are you going to do for Lailah?"

The elevator dinged, and the door opened. Both of us stepped off onto the worn laminate floor, and I gazed down the hall toward my sleeping angel.

"Everything. I'll give her everything."

CHAPTER FIFTEEN
IRELAND

LAILAH

Shapes slowly took form as my eyelids hesitantly lifted for what felt like the first time in centuries. I moved to rub the sleep from my eyes, but my hand was restrained, encased in a warm tenderness I instantly recognized. I turned my head and found Jude's soft green eyes staring back at me.

"Morning," he whispered, bringing my hand he was holding up to his lips.

The touch instantly sent shivers running up my spine, and it had nothing to do with my fever or sickness.

"Morning? What time is it? How long have I been asleep?" I asked, my voice still groggy and tired.

I moved around and noticed the absence of the aches and nausea I'd had previously. I actually felt a great deal better. I wasn't at one hundred percent, but I definitely felt an improvement.

"Just over two days. Marcus purposely kept you asleep the first day, hoping you'd fight off the illness quicker that way. It seemed to help because your fever finally broke, so he was able to pull back on the meds. You've been asleep ever since."

I've been asleep for two days?

Looking up at him, I noticed the deep dark circles under his eyes and the redness that rimmed his pupils. His shoulders sagged under the weight of his exhaustion, and his clothes were rumpled and worn.

"And you? How long have you been without sleep, Jude?" I asked.

He ran a tired hand through his messy hair. "I'm okay," he replied.

When I gave him a pointed look, he amended, "I've had a few hours of sleep here and there. I didn't want to leave. I couldn't leave you, Lailah."

I wanted to argue. I wanted to tell him that he was being ridiculous. He needed to always take care of himself first. But as I watched him, tired and exhausted while speaking with such conviction at my bedside, I thought of everything he'd gone through in his past, and I knew that I couldn't.

He was scared of losing someone else.

What sick, twisted sort of fate did I pull him into?

"I'm not going anywhere," I tried to assure him, knowing I had no grounds to make such promises.

Like second nature, my fingers met the unshaven rough skin of his cheek, and he immediately leaned into my touch.

"I know," he answered.

The elephant had officially landed in the room.

There were no more candid talks of dying and no more what-if conversations. The stakes had been raised. We'd gone from casual friends to so much more, more than I even had words to describe, and death had no place with the type of feelings we now shared.

How could we grow something from ashes? How could we expect a rose to blossom in the shadows?

Whatever this was, whatever I was feeling for Jude, I wanted it to grow. I wanted to see where it would take us, and neither of us could allow that with death looming over us.

That little bastard I liked to call *hope* came wiggling back into my mind. I couldn't help but wonder if Jude was my sign that everything would work itself out.

Why else would I have been given a chance at love so late in the game if I weren't going to be saved in the end?

"What are you thinking about?" He leaned forward to rest his elbows on the edge of the bed.

It brought his head inches from mine, and I could smell the lingering scent of his shampoo in his hair.

"How do you know I was thinking at all?"

He lifted his hand and brushed his fingers over my forehead. "You get these cute little lines and creases up here when you're deep in thought."

"I do not!"

"Do so. I'm a master in all things, Lailah. You can't argue with the master."

"You couldn't possibly be a master yet. I'm not that easy to crack," I debated.

"No, you're not, but I've been paying attention. It's been hard not to," he said.

His eyes darkened slightly, which caused my cheeks to flare up.

"Okay, grand master, if you know me so well, why don't you educate me?"

He grinned, rising from his chair. I felt the bed dip an instant before his body brushed up against mine as he positioned himself on his side, facing me. I turned slightly under the covers, so I could face him and admire the view.

I never thought I could enjoy a hospital bed, but Jude just made living here much more bearable. Then, the thought of my mom or Dr. Marcus walking in while Jude was in bed with me made me incredibly nervous. Apparently, adult Lailah had taken a hike while I was passed out.

As if reading my thoughts, Jude said, "It's Dr. Marcus's

day off, and your mom is teaching right now. Besides, I haven't left this room in two days. I think it's safe to say our little secret is out."

There were so many things to process in that statement.

"How is my mom handling it? How did you manage not to leave when you had to work? Oh my God, you didn't lose your job because of me?"

"First, you babble when you're nervous, like right now," he said with a warm smile. "Your mom isn't a giant fan of mine, but we're making it work. No, I did not get fired. I managed to stay in here because I'd refused to wear a mask, so I was not allowed to work until I demonstrated that I was symptom-free. So, when I can prove I still have no symptoms tomorrow, they'll allow me to clock back in."

"But, Jude, all those lost hours…" I said, feeling so guilty.

"I wouldn't have been anywhere else, Lailah."

His hand reached up to my waist, and I could feel the heat of his hand searing through the fabric of the blanket. My eyes wandered down his body, admiring the way his gray T-shirt clung to his expansive chest. His dark jeans were worn and faded but hung off his hipbones at just the right spot.

"Second, you blush when you're embarrassed or turned-on. So, which one is it right now?"

My brain went back on, and my eyes flew to his. "What?"

"You're blushing. Are you embarrassed or turned-on?"

"You're crazy!" I answered, deflecting.

His grin widened into something mischievous, and his little dimple became even more evident. He leaned his head forward, nuzzling it into the curve of my neck where he slowly began scattering a trail of hot kisses up to my earlobe.

"I think it's the latter," he breathed into my ear.

Our lips met in a fevered kiss as we chose physical touch over words.

I could have lost you, his body said through his desperate touch.

But you didn't, my kiss answered back.

I sank further into the warmth of his chest, so he could feel me alive and whole before him.

Our movements slowed, tenderness replacing fiery passion, before he finally pulled back.

"I'm sorry. I shouldn't have done that," he said, leaning his forehead against mine.

"Why?"

"You've been asleep for two days. You've been through hell, and I'm mauling you in your bed. You're still recovering. I should wait until…"

Until I'm not sick?

That might never happen.

His eyes met mine, and we both let the statement hang in the air, unfinished, until it eventually blew away.

The big, giant elephant was firmly back in place, and neither of us chose to address it.

"On today's menu, we have a lovely selection of rice, saltine crackers, chicken broth, and—wait for it—apple sauce. Mmm…" Jude announced, uncovering my lunch that had been delivered moments earlier.

"Wow, that sounds…"

"Horrible?" he finished, placing the plastic tray on the large wooden tray table.

"I was going to say a weird combination, but yeah, horrible is a good descriptor as well. Although, the rice doesn't sound too bad."

"Well, good. Eat the rice then—slowly though. You haven't had solid food for a few days."

He took a seat in the chair that he'd used as a bed for the last several nights. I took the small cup of rice in my hands. It was lightly buttered, but otherwise, it was tasteless. I took a hesitant bite and nearly moaned. It could have tasted like cardboard, and I would have still loved it. Lack of food had greatly reduced my pickiness over hospital food in that moment. Three bites in, I realized the room was dead quiet. I glanced up to find Jude watching me with hooded, intense eyes.

"Do you always make those noises when you eat? I don't recall that from our lunch date. I think I'd remember a moan like that escaping your lips."

"Um…" was all I managed as a comeback.

His mouth turned into a wolfish grin, and he chuckled. "You're blushing again."

"Well, how can I not when you say things like that?" I said, finally finding the ability to speak.

I picked up a packet of crackers and chucked it at his head. He laughed hard and caught them in midair. He then proceeded to tear open the clear plastic package, and he stuffed an entire saltine into his mouth, giving me a goofy grin as he did it.

"So, give me a few more from the Someday list." He crammed the last cracker into his mouth.

It made me wonder how long it had been since he had a decent meal. I made a mental note to ask Grace to pull a few strings and get him some food. For now, I had to make do with what I had. I handed over the applesauce I had no intention of eating, and he gave me a wary look. When I pushed it further into his hand and raised my eyebrows, he relented and closed his fingers around the plastic cup. I tossed him a spoon and then reached over to the drawer next to me to grab the worn notebook I kept in there.

"What number is it going to be today?" I cracked the spine to once more find the handwritten list I'd meticulously created over the years.

He studied me as his gaze narrowed. My attention drifted to the page in front of me, and my heart fluttered at seeing the first thing I'd written on the list so long ago.

"Twenty-five."

I breathed out a sigh of relief, but I felt myself turn instantly pink at the mere mention of that particular number.

It wasn't number one, but it was an important one, and I'd drawn a dark red line through it just days earlier.

"It's been crossed out," I said, unable to look up at him. *God, will I ever grow up?*

"What was it?" he asked, his voice low and husky.

"Be kissed until I'm breathless."

I met his gaze, and the corners of his mouth turned upward into a cocky grin, revealing just the slightest hint of that single dimple on his cheek.

"Fifty-one."

I couldn't help the small smile that formed on my lips as I found that particular one. "Have an entire conversation in only text messages."

"So, you want to be a teenage girl for a day?" he joked.

"Come on, Jude!" I whined, tossing my napkin at him.

He ducked, and I heard a soft chuckle escape his beautiful lips.

"Sorry, I just don't get it. Being able to hold a conversation with you without your nose buried in a phone is one of the most appealing things about you."

My eyebrow arched in amusement.

Do I have horns I'm unaware of?

Not having a cell phone is my most appealing feature?

"Okay, not one of the most. There are several—no, hundreds of other things I find much more appealing, sexy even. Shit, I'm digging myself into a hole here. Just put me out of my misery and take over?"

I covered my mouth with my hand, trying to stifle the laughter bubbling up. "It's just one of those things that normal people do. They have conversations over emails and text messages. They share secrets and inside jokes that no one else knows about because nothing was uttered outside of cyberspace. I think people feel bolder with their words when they are hiding behind a keyboard. I guess I just wonder what it would be like."

"To be bolder with your words?" he asked softly. "What would you say?"

"I don't know. I've never even had a cell phone. I probably wouldn't be able to type more than three words without messing something up."

I tried to dismiss the topic with a wave of my hand.

But he persisted as he asked, "If you could ask me anything in a text message without fear of those cheeks blushing or my reaction, what would you ask?"

I knew what I wanted to ask him, but fear took over, and it was suddenly guiding my every move.

Would he be angry that I knew? Would it hurt him to talk about it?

Do I really want to know?

I looked into those beautiful jade eyes, and I knew I couldn't ask about his fiancée. I wasn't ready to know. I wasn't jealous or angry that he hadn't shared that part of his life with me. It was the fear that once he did, I'd be faced with something I already knew deep down. I should let him go. He deserved better than a second chance that had very little hope. The elephant in the room might have been firmly planted in the corner by this time, and we'd managed to dodge and weave around him well, pretending the possibility of my death didn't exist, but it didn't make it any less true.

I was selfishly allowing all this to happen, knowing he'd already lost someone before and knowing it could happen again.

"Why me?" I asked.

"Why not you, Lailah?" he argued, leaning forward to take my hand. "Why would you ask that?"

"You could have anyone. Why would you—"

"I don't want anyone else," he answered, halting my words. He reached out to graze the tender skin of my cheek with his thumb. "I want you."

I had no words as I watched him push away my lunch tray

before crawling into bed with me. I was speechless as I felt his solid arms wrap around me and pull me close. I should let him go, but I wouldn't. I needed him—his touch, his tender and healing words, and the way being around him made me feel. I felt restored and renewed in his presence, and that was better than any drug or treatment a doctor could prescribe.

"Tell me one more, and then you're going to get some rest," he instructed as he rested his head on the pillow and closed his eyes.

My notebook was still open in my lap, and he'd made no attempts to peek at the pages currently on display.

"Are you going to pick the number, or shall I?"

"You pick it this time," he answered.

I scanned the page with my index finger, trying to find one that was both interesting and not too embarrassing.

"Visit a foreign country."

His eyes peeked open, and he smirked. "Any foreign country? Or do you have a preference?"

I thought about it for a moment. "I don't know. I guess I just never thought it would come true, so I never took the time to pick a specific place."

He traced his fingers down my arm, a trail of gooseflesh rising as he went, until he finally intertwined them with my own and squeezed.

"Pick one now, anywhere in the world. Where would you go?"

There were so many places in the world. How could I pick just one?

My mind sought a single destination, remembering history class with my mother and movies I'd seen, and one place stuck out in my mind above all others. "Ireland," I answered.

"A beautiful country for a beautiful woman," he replied. "Let's go."

I laughed, loving the sweet timbre of his voice. "What? Now?"

"Yep, close your eyes."

"You're insane."

"Probably. Close your eyes, Lailah," he commanded.

I gave a halfhearted huff and did as I had been told. I closed my eyes and settled further into the pillow.

"Okay, imagine us in one of those European cars. They're compact and boring-looking. Everything is on the wrong side. We're driving down a small road near the picturesque Ireland countryside."

"Wait—we're already there?" I asked, cracking my eyelids open just slightly.

"What do you mean, we're already there?"

"I mean, how did we get there? Did we fly?"

"Of course we flew."

"You're a terrible storyteller."

He huffed, which made me laugh. "Okay, fine. It was a very normal, boring flight. You slept most of the way. After renting our awesome, tiny car, we checked into a quaint little bed-and-breakfast, and we had a quickie to get over our jet lag. Now, we are touring the countryside."

"Why just a quickie?" I asked with a snicker.

"How about this? I took you seven different ways, starting with up against the door of our room because I couldn't wait a single second longer after our long-ass flight. Better? Or would you like more detail?"

My eyes flew open to find his blazing green irises staring back at me.

"Um...nope. I think I've got it." I gulped. "So, we are driving down the Irish countryside?"

His wolfish grin was the last thing I saw as my head fell back against the pillow.

"I'd take you for a long drive around the Ring of Kerry. We'd stop along the way to take pictures and hike off the beaten trail. The sky would be gray with small dots of blue where the clouds thinned and broke. The air would taste salty from the ocean. The grass would be so green that it would almost look unreal as if a painter had swirled it directly from a brush. Can you see it?"

With every word that sprang free from his lips, a picture began to form in my head. Clouds formed, and grass grew. I could taste the ocean air against my tongue, and I could hear birds flying above us.

"Small farms with ancient stone fences dot the landscape for miles with crystal-blue water in the distance. If you look out far enough, you can see a set of islands. Maybe we'll take a boat later in the day and climb the ancient stone steps up to the top?"

"You can do that?"

"When the weather is right, and today, it's just perfect," he answered.

"You've been there?"

"With my mom when I was really young."

I listened to the soft murmur of his voice as he described our idyllic day in Ireland. The deep cadence and even tone eventually began to lull me to sleep. Soft, warm lips touched my forehead moments before I felt sleep pulling me into its tight grasp.

"This was just a placeholder, Lailah," he whispered. "Someday, we will have our day on the Irish countryside along with countless other perfect days. You aren't going anywhere. You can't…"

As the last remaining bits of consciousness were swallowed up by darkness, I swore that I heard him say, "Because I love you."

CHAPTER SIXTEEN
PLACE HOLDERS

JUDE

hated leaving her, but I had to make arrangements. I had plans, ones that involved favors and provisions. I listened to her breaths even out as her head shifted lazily to the side. I pulled the notebook out from her grasp and set it on the tray table beside her. I didn't bother sneaking a peek at the mysterious list hidden within.

I'd already done that. I might be an asshole for disrespecting her wishes, but I'd had good intentions. I wanted to make each and every one of her dreams come true—minus the one I'd promised her would never happen. I couldn't help but want to surprise her a little along the way.

Lying in bed with her while creating a vision of us walking along the countryside of Ireland had given me an idea.

Place holders.

What if I could do that with more of her dreams?

She was stuck here within the walls of this hospital, but that didn't mean she had to be walled in.

So, while her eyes were closed, I'd snuck a peek.

I'd respected her enough not to look at the top of the list. I knew number one was off-limits, and honestly, I wanted her to share it with me when she was ready. It was obviously important to her. So, in my five-second glance while her eyes were closed and her mind was across the Atlantic, I'd found my first place card.

And now, I was on a mission.

"YOU'RE INSANE." GRACE LAUGHED AFTER I'D EXPLAINED MY plan for the evening. She was behind the nurses' station, checking charts and punching things into the computer.

I leaned forward, shaking my head at her ridiculous attire. She was wearing Minnie Mouse scrubs today. Each Minnie Mouse scattered all over her was dressed in a pair of tiny pink scrubs. It was nauseating, but on her, it seemed to fit.

"You're not the first person to tell me that today. Will you help me?" I asked.

"I'd do anything for Lailah. What do you need?"

I went over my plan, watching as her eyes lit up and softened. She nodded her head and offered her help where she could. I left a few minutes later, ready to tackle my next task. I was grateful Lailah had an amazing friend like Grace.

I'd barely made it down the hall when I heard my name being called out behind me. I swiveled around and found Margaret and her itchy wool suit hot on my tail.

"Jude, you're just the person I was looking for. Care to take a walk with me to my office?" she asked as she tugged at the hem of her blazer.

"Sure, but you know I'm not actually clocked in, right?"

She took in my appearance and gave a hesitant nod. "Yes, I'm aware, but I'm afraid this can't wait."

Fuck.

I followed her to the elevator where we took one silent, awkward ride down to the floor where HR was located. When the door opened, I motioned for her to exit first, and I followed behind, letting my mind run rampant as I thought about my less than stellar behavior over the past few days.

She is going to fire me.

My plans, my precious plans, will be destroyed.

As Margaret unlocked the door to her office, it dawned on me that with the idea of losing my job, my first thought had been the idea that I wouldn't be able to carry through with my plans for fulfilling Lailah's Someday list. It'd had nothing to do with sitting on the bench, staring into the room where Megan had died.

I shoved that thought back down to the recess of my brain to ponder another day, and I took a seat across from Margaret in the sparse small office. She leaned back in her chair and folded her hands neatly in front of her. Her eyes darted down at the scattered papers on her desk and then back up at me. She didn't want to be here either.

"I heard you've been spending a lot of time with a certain patient, Jude."

"Yes, I have," I answered, not bothering to elaborate or explain.

"I was told you might have feelings for this patient that go beyond professional."

"I do."

She let out a long sigh. "Look, the hospital can't do anything unless the patient or her family file a complaint—"

"And have they?" I asked, interrupting her.

"No."

"So, why am I here, Margaret?" I asked coldly.

"Because there has been some concern about your job performance, Jude. You made quite the commotion the other night, and it didn't go unnoticed. I get that you feel for this girl—"

"I love her," I corrected.

Her eyes widened at my confession, and she immediately diverted her attention back down to her desk. "You just need to be careful."

"Are you reprimanding me or moving me to another department?"

"No. No, I'm not doing anything yet. I just want you to be more cautious," she warned, her gaze finally meeting mine.

I saw compassion and understanding in those watery blue depths. The firm grip I didn't realize I'd had on the chair suddenly lessened, and I sank back slightly. "I'll do that. Thank you for looking out for me."

"Of course, Jude. That's all I've ever tried to do," she said with sincerity and warmth.

It was the same warmth she'd had when she found me swimming in grief, unable to leave the hallways where I'd lost my fiancée. It was the same emotional qualities she'd probably had when she placed that bench along that lonely wall so that I'd have a place to sit, knowing it was useless to assume I'd move on without Megan.

But I had.

Somehow, I'd managed the impossible, and even though my heart still felt like it was slowly mending itself back together again from a horrendous accident, I was moving forward again.

Lailah was my way out of that hallway and back to the land of the living.

"Hey, Margaret, can I ask you for a favor?" I leaned forward.

Anticipation replaced fear as my plans for the evening took shape.

Curious, prying eyes followed me as I tried to carry in one single load what probably should have been three. Bags were slung over my shoulders, grocery sacks were in my hands, and about a million other things were stuffed anywhere else I could fit them.

With the two fingers I had free, I managed to pry open Lailah's door, not bothering to knock. The noise I had made as everything balanced on my shoulders fell forward against the door was an announcement in itself. I pushed forward and nearly fell on my ass. I really should have made two trips, but I'd known when I got up here and saw her, I wouldn't want to leave.

When I heard her giggle, I looked up and melted.

"Are you moving in?" she asked, her champagne-blonde locks brushed the bare skin of her knees as she bent over her journal. Her blue eyes sparkled with amusement at the sight of me tumbling into her room.

In that moment, I knew I'd do anything to bring that smile to her face.

"Do you think they'd let me?" I began the lengthy process of setting things down—first, the grocery bags and then the large equipment strapped to my back.

"Hmm…I don't know. The bed is awfully small for two people," she replied.

I glanced up just in time to see her eyes widen at the realization of her words. The way she'd said it had been light and joking, but all I'd heard was the possibility of the two of us back in bed together.

"I mean, you know…it would just be uncomfortably small. I might kick you and steal the covers and—"

"I think I could manage." I grinned, letting my gaze run down the length of her body.

The gray shorts she was wearing did little to cover her long legs, and I had trouble tearing my eyes away from her milky white skin. She was usually so covered due to the frigid temperatures of the hospital that it was rare to see so much of her.

"Are you feeling okay?" I asked, immediately stalking forward to feel her cheeks and forehead.

"Yes, fine. Why?"

"You're usually more bundled than this," I said, motioning to her bare legs.

"Oh, I, um…" she fumbled over her words, turning red and casting her gaze downward.

"You, um, what?" I asked softly, brushing my fingers over her thigh.

"I don't have anything nice to dress up in, but I thought I could at least try to look...sexy."

Her eyes were transfixed on the caress of my hand against her skin. She took in a gulp of air and released it slowly as I sank down next to her.

"You could be in a designer dress or a hospital gown, and I'd still find you irresistibly sexy either way. It doesn't matter to me what you wear...or don't wear," I added with a smirk. "I'm attracted to you—your laugh, your voice, the sexy way your breath catches when I kiss you. None of that has anything to do with what you choose to put on your body."

As soon as the last word left my lips, she was on me, kissing me with passion I hadn't known she possessed. Just when I'd thought I figured out this shy, innocent girl of mine, she'd knock me flat on my back and remind me just what an amazing mystery she was to discover.

Pulling back, she gave me a pleased, happy smile, letting me know that she was very happy with herself.

"So, does this mean I should change into pants then?" she asked, placing her hand over mine and running it down the length of her thigh.

Innocent, my ass. This girl is a quick learner.

"No, these are fine. I mean, we don't want to make more laundry for your mom," I answered, digging my fingers into her flesh.

A sheepish grin appeared on her face, and she tried to cover it with her hand.

"So, if you're not moving in, what's with all the stuff?"

"Well, first, you have to promise me that you won't get mad at me?" I said, bracing for possible impact.

"Why? What did you do? Does it involve my mother somehow? Or something embarrassing? Oh God, is it something involving my mother, and it's embarrassing?"

I let out a chuckle. "No, nothing to do with family members and nothing embarrassing."

"Okay, shoot."

"I took a peek at your list today," I said quickly.

Her eyes grew. "You said it wasn't embarrassing!"

"It's not," I said quickly, holding my hands up in defense. "I swear, it was a quick peek, and I didn't look anywhere near the top. I wanted to surprise you with something, and I couldn't do that without looking on my own."

She let out a disgruntled breath. "Promise you didn't see anything that would make me cringe?"

"There was this one thing that involved whipped cream…" I started, trying to keep a straight face.

When her startled face flew up to mine, I couldn't contain the laughter that came spilling out.

"I'm kidding!"

She playfully slapped my arm and rolled her eyes.

"I held your hair back while you were sick, and I nursed you back to health. You'll have to do a hell of a lot more than letting me see a notebook full of secret wishes to send me running."

"Does it bother you that I haven't told you all of them yet?" she asked, suddenly sobering.

"No, not at all. Don't take my single glance as anything more than I wanted to give you a special night. I know that notebook is sacred to you, and the fact that you've shared any of it with me is an honor. Every time you share another wish or dream from it is like unraveling another layer of you. It helps me get to know the woman I've fallen—come to care about so much."

Coward.

I could admit my feelings to myself and even Dr. Marcus. Hell, I could probably tell anyone passing by in the hallway, but when faced with telling the woman I loved, I'd choked.

Part of me was still roaming that lonely hallway downstairs, mourning the loss of a woman I'd never have, a life I'd never have. As much as I knew it was over and I was moving on, I was scared to do so.

Telling Lailah I loved her was final. There would be no turning back from that moment on, and I knew the second I did so, I'd have to say good-bye to the ghost I'd held on to for far too long.

Two paths and two very different lives were before me.

I needed to find a way to let go of one.

CHAPTER SEVENTEEN

SHAKESPEARE IN LOVE

LAILAH

"We're going to what?" I asked again, not quite believing what he'd just said.

"We are going to the movie theater," he said and then quickly added, "Kind of."

"How do we *kind of* go to the movie theater?" I sat up straighter in my bed and watched as he started shuffling through the many bags he'd brought.

"Well, obviously, Dr. Marcus would frown on me kidnapping you and taking you to a real movie," he said, pulling out what looked like a mini DVD player and setting it on my wooden tray table.

He positioned it toward the wall, angling it just right.

"Since a night at the theater was out, I pulled some strings and managed to borrow this sweet little digital projector from the marketing department, thanks to a favor by HR. So, tonight, we are going to watch a movie of your choice on the big screen—or as big as we can make it," he added.

He flipped a switch, and a bright white square appeared on the blank wall across from me.

"Oh my gosh, are you kidding me?" I nearly squealed.

After he finished setting up the projector, he turned around and smiled. "I know it's not quite your number seventy-one, but I figured we could count it as a placeholder until we manage to blow you out of this joint. Then, we could get you to an actual theater, and you can cross it off your list."

"It's perfect."

"Good, but I'm not done yet," he said, moving across the room to the paper bags from a local grocery store. "What fake theater would be complete without popcorn? I got the unsalted kind from the organic section and popped it at home. It's probably going to taste like shit, but at least you'll be able to eat it. Also, I got you M&M's and pudding, of course."

He brought over a huge bag and upended it on the bed, causing me to laugh. Pre-popped popcorn in plastic bags as well as large bags of M&M's—both plain and peanut—and lots of pudding came tumbling out.

"You're crazy," I said.

"I've heard that a lot today. So, what do you want to watch, angel?"

He jogged back over to the black bag that had held the projector and removed a sleek black laptop. A little hospital logo was affixed to the top. Apparently, the favor in HR also included a laptop.

"I don't know. What are my selections?"

"Well, I took the liberty of asking Grace what your favorites were, and she volunteered to bring in several during her lunch break," he said, pulling out a case filled with DVDs. "She also threw in a few extras. Pick whatever you want."

I opened the leather case stuffed full of DVDs, and I wasn't surprised to see that Grace had shoved *Frozen* in the first plastic slot. I snorted and moved on, overwhelmed by Grace's generosity. She'd managed to gather up all my well-known favorites like *Ferris Bueller's Day Off* and *Dirty Dancing* as well as others I'd been dying to see but hadn't managed to see just yet.

"This one," I said, pointing to my selection.

"I don't think I've ever seen it. Have you?" he asked, sliding the shiny disk out of its clear plastic home.

I shook my head, and he set everything up before joining me back on the bed. I began scooting over to give him more room on my small twin-sized hospital mattress, but he just pulled me back over before pulling the covers over my bare legs. Then, he grabbed a bag of popcorn for us to share.

"So, my little bookworm picks a movie about the world's most famous playwright," he said.

The opening title of *Shakespeare in Love* scrolled across the screen—or wall.

"It's all fiction, I'm sure, but I like the idea of him basing some of his most famous works on his own life."

Jude was right. The popcorn wasn't fantastic, but I was used to eating bland food. A couple of M&M's and a few kernels of popcorn made a good combination, and soon, I was engrossed in the dramatic life of William Shakespeare.

Gwyneth Paltrow's character, Viola had bound herself, dressing like a man to cover her high-society female form, so she could act in *Romeo and Juliet*. When her deceit is discovered, a fiery love scene quickly follows.

My eyes wandered over to the curve of Jude's strong jaw. He'd shaved since this morning. When he'd kissed me, I'd touched his jaw where my eyes now lingered, loving the raw, masculine feel of his unshaven skin against mine. It was so foreign and unlike anything I'd ever experienced, and I yearned for more.

"You're not watching the movie anymore," Jude whispered.

"Yes, I am," I answered, quickly glancing back up to the movie.

William was unwrapping the binding from Viola's body as she turned and laughed. He was completely enraptured by her, watching her, as she spun playfully until he finally dropped the last of the cloth and took her into his arms.

"No, you were staring at me." His tone was hushed as the love scene played on.

My breath hitched the moment I felt his finger brush against the fabric covering my collarbone, and I shivered as he brushed away loose strands of my hair.

"What were you thinking about?" he asked softly. I turned to find his intense gaze settled on mine.

"When you kissed me this morning," I replied, completely forgetting about the movie playing before us. My eyes shifted to his beautiful full lips, and I felt my tongue dart out to wet my own.

"Would you like me to kiss you again, Lailah?"

"Yes," I answered, the soft sound coming out more like a plea.

"Here?"

The pad of his thumb caressed the sensitive pink flesh of my lower lip as he hovered above me. He didn't wait for an answer, and his mouth descended upon mine. Soft and gentle, he kissed me with aching tenderness that made my heart leap. His arms moved to cradle my body, and he pulled me closer. Then, I felt the warmth of his hand move to my neck.

"How about here?" he murmured against the hollow of my throat.

Rather than answer, I turned my head, exposing more skin. His head moved downward, and his tongue licked a scorching path across my ivory flesh. As his hand neared the hem of my shirt, my breath caught, and his fingers halted.

His eyes met mine. "You just tensed up. Did I make you uncomfortable?"

I shook my head, but my dismissal of the situation didn't go unnoticed.

He quickly sat up. "Lailah," he pleaded, "talk to me."

I rubbed my hands together, avoiding his gaze. "I'm severely scarred," I finally admitted.

Will he look at me differently now that he knows?

I was different though. He'd always known that.

But now that he knew I have physical proof, will it change how he looks at me? Will there be pity in his eyes or sorrow in the way he views my situation?

I'd seen the sad, empathetic looks from everyone else since the day I was born. I'd gotten the shoulder pats and stray tears from those who thought I'd been given the short end at life.

Will he join them once he sees the jagged scar running down my chest?

When he didn't respond, I gathered the courage for a brief glance at him, and I was met with a penetrating warm gaze.

"We all have scars, Lailah. Some are just more visible than others."

"What are your scars, Jude?" I asked, surprised and scared by my own words.

His eyes unfocused for a brief moment as if he'd lost focus with reality. When he finally snapped back, he gave a faint smile. "I'm hiding in plain sight, remember? I'm the estranged heir to a multibillion-dollar fortune. Can't get much more scarred than that."

My eyes wandered over his inked forearms. The swirling black patterns seemed to have no direction, no purpose. They just meandered down his arms without end.

Did he really ink his skin and change his appearance to disappear from society? Or was he trying to disappear from himself?

"Will you show me?" he asked hesitantly, his voice cutting through my thoughts like a knife.

My hands went to the lower hem of my T-shirt, and I took a deep breath of air, squeezing my eyes shut. I never wore a button-down or a V-neck, so in order to show him, I had to show him all of me.

Warm hands covered mine, and I opened my eyes to find his milky-green irises.

"Let me help you." His fingers grazed my sides as he took the fabric in his hands before lifting my shirt over my head.

My heart beat faster, and I took several slow breaths to steady it. As soon as the fabric cleared my head, I instinctually moved to cover the pink line between my breasts that I'd had since birth. The same scar had been enlarged and modified with each surgery, growing along with me as I aged.

"Don't cover yourself," Jude said softly, pulling my hands away from my body. "You're beautiful."

His eyes were everywhere, and that astonished me. When I was shirtless, my scar always took center stage. It screamed for attention. Even medically trained doctors were drawn to it.

The moment Jude's eyes fell on my half-naked body, he saw me, just me. He didn't see my scar or a broken girl with no hope for the future. He saw me, and in his eyes, I saw passion and heat, no sorrow or pity.

"You're beautiful," he repeated, tracing his fingers over the pink skin.

My eyes fluttered close, and I moaned when his tongue traced the edge of my bra, leaving a wet trail across my breast and up to my mouth. Our legs and bodies quickly intertwined as our kiss intensified. His tongue tangled with mine, over and over, as I moved against him. I felt him harden against me, and rather than blush, I kissed him again, finally understanding what it felt like to use this womanly body I'd been given. His wandering touch slowed, and his frenzied kiss began to fade until he pulled back entirely.

"We need to slow down," he said, smoothing back a few wild wisps of my hair, as he gently smiled down at me.

I nodded, dodging his green gaze, as I searched for my shirt.

"Lailah, look at me."

I didn't. I just continued my hunt until gentle fingers turned my head.

"What did I say? Tell me what I did wrong."

"Would you have stopped if I were anyone else, Jude?" I asked, folding my hands over my plain white cotton bra. It was the same boring bra my mom had been buying for me since I was thirteen.

"Why would you ask me that?"

"I don't want to be treated any differently," I spit, finally finding my T-shirt wadded up near my feet.

I bent over to pick it up, but Jude stopped me midway.

"Well, deal with it," he bit back. "I will treat you differently, not because of your heart problem or the fact that you think you're physically fragile or weak. I'll treat you differently because you're different to me. You matter to me. I will not take your virginity in some random hospital when you're still recovering from a virus that nearly killed you. You deserve a hell of a lot better than that. So, yeah, I'll continue to treat you differently because I think you are worthy of more."

"I-I'm sorry," I said, stumbling over my words. "I thought—"

"You assumed I stopped because I thought you were so innocent and fragile? The girl writhing and moaning underneath me was neither of those things. I want you, Lailah. I want all of you in every way, but it won't be here, not like this. I want you slow and tender, fast and hard, and everything in between. When we come together, it will be miles from this place, and I will spend hours helping you cross out that number on your list," he said with a wink.

I opened my mouth to chastise him, but he spoke before I had the chance, "I know it's got to be on there somewhere."

"It is," I answered. "Number one hundred and twenty-one."

He smiled and bent down to brush a kiss across my lips.

"So, not number one then?" He reached back to grab my shirt and handed it to me.

"Nope."

"What could be better than sex?" he joked, the little dimple on his cheek reappearing as he watched the soft cotton fabric float back over my skin.

"Hmm...I don't know. Guess you'll just have to find out."

I WANT ALL OF YOU IN EVERY WAY.

Jude's heated words had continued to play through my mind well after he'd left, and they had been with me again as I rose the next morning.

Slow and tender...fast and hard.

I'd been a mindless, drooling puddle ever since. I couldn't even remember what I'd eaten for breakfast. I'd been staring at the same blank page of my journal for well over an hour when my mother waltzed through the door.

"You're here early," I said, noting her dressed-down appearance. She was in jeans and a flowery blouse. It was different from the business-casual look she would wear when teaching.

"I canceled my classes today," she said with a flick of her hand as she settled into the worn blue chair.

"You canceled your classes?" I repeated, tilting my head in shocked surprise.

Unless I was going into surgery or there was an emergency, my mom never canceled class. Her students must be rejoicing today.

"Yes, I wanted to speak to you—alone," she answered, giving the last word specific emphasis.

"I see."

Here it comes.

"I did a bit of research on your friend Jude," she began.

"You did research, Mom?" I asked, holding up my hand to silence her.

"I Googled him."

A small snort morphed into full-out laughter, and I wrapped my arms around my sides in an attempt to control the roaring inferno. "You...used Google?"

My mom was a teacher, a professor, but she hadn't quite

graduated to the twenty-first century. She carried a cell phone for emergencies. It flipped open and had exactly three numbers programmed into it—the hospital, our home, and Dr. Marcus. The laptop I owned had been given to her by a colleague when he decided to upgrade. My mom had taken one look at the thing and cringed. She used a desktop computer at work and considered it punishment.

According to my mother, all research should be done in a library. Google was for morons and perverts. The fact that she'd used it to look up Jude meant she was flustered and seriously frustrated.

"Yes, I was curious about the boy you've been spending so much time with."

"Mom, he's twenty-five. He's hardly a boy."

She ignored my comment and continued to watch me from her tattered blue throne. "Do you think he'll take care of you? Is that what this is all about? He's wealthy and powerful, so you think he'll protect you?"

I stared at her, my mouth agape, before I let the shock wear off. "Is that what you think of me? What you think of him?"

"I don't know him," she answered.

"No, but you know me. Do you think I'd do that? Hand myself over on a silver platter?" I spit.

"I did," she said softly.

"What?"

"Men promise all sorts of things when they want something, especially when it involves a woman. Your father was no different."

My breath hitched when I heard her mention him. In my twenty-two years on this earth, she'd only ever spoken about him a handful of times. She never brought him up herself, and she always quickly dismissed the subject of him. The majority of what I knew about the man were small things I'd learned from medical records.

"From the moment we met, I was completely infatuated

with him. He made me feel reckless with his constant pursuit. He promised me the moon and the stars, and I believed every word. He said he'd always protect me, but when I became pregnant, he vanished, just like his false promises."

"Mom…" I started, my voice hoarse from the unshed tears I was holding back for the pain my mother had suffered. "Not all men are like my father." I realized then that even after that heartfelt story, she still hadn't revealed his name to me. The only father I knew was faceless and without a name.

"How can you be so sure?" she asked, leaning forward to take my hand in her own.

"I don't think anyone can be. But isn't that what life is all about? Taking a risk on something? Someone? Jude is a wonderful person, Mom—a very poor, penniless person," I added.

Her eyes went wide. "But I thought…he looks so much like…" she stammered.

"He is. That is him. Your Google skills are fine. It's a long story and one you should probably ask him yourself, but just know that I don't expect anything from him, and he doesn't expect anything in return. I know this is stressful for you. I understand that I'm disrupting your sense of control, but please, Mom, let me take this risk, let me love someone."

She nodded, rising from her seat to join me on the bed. I willingly let her pull me into her arms, loving the way I still fit into her small frame. She was controlling and overbearing at times, but she was my mom. She was my home, and every-thing she'd done since the moment I came screaming into this world had been because she loved me.

"Just be careful, my little angel."

I smiled against her chest, remembering how Jude had called me that same sweet thing mere hours earlier. Mom had named me Lailah after the Hebrew angel of pregnancy. When she'd discovered my heart defect during a routine ultrasound, she'd wanted to give me a name that was strong and hopeful. She might not be a religious person, but I thought it was somehow her way of asking for a bit of help to whoever might be listening.

"I will, Mom, I promise."

She gave me a small squeeze, and I closed my eyes, knowing I'd lied to my mother.

There was nothing careful about falling in love.

CHAPTER EIGHTEEN
DANCING IN THE RAIN

JUDE

It had been a little over a week since that horrible day Lailah's fever nearly took her from this world. A fever was so simple for most but extremely deadly for her. It was no wonder her mother had become so controlling regarding every minute detail of Lailah's life. Her mother had gone over the deep end to ensure Lailah's safety, but standing on the opposite side of parenthood, I would wager a mother would do anything and everything to keep her child from dying even if it meant keeping the child from living a normal life.

For the most part, life at the hospital had returned to normal. After my forced few days of vacation, I had been allowed to return to work after I'd shown no symptoms of Lailah's virus, and then Lailah and I had fallen back into our late-night pudding visits. The only difference was the addition of my off-hour daytime drop-ins. A one-hour lunch break wasn't enough anymore, and I didn't have an endless bank account to fall back on. I needed my job. Now, more than ever, the hospital had become my home. I would be here morning, noon, and night, only running home to shower, crash for sleep, and plan.

I was always planning.

Movie night hadn't been the only trick up my sleeve. Since that night, I'd managed to pull off a few other place holders in hopes of making Lailah's prison sentence a bit more palatable.

We'd had an ice cream parlor one afternoon where I'd brought in ten different flavors of ice cream. We'd proceeded to make a sundae worthy of the cheesy name I'd created for my fictional ice cream endeavor.

"A Dude Named Jude's Ice Cream Parlor?" she'd asked with a snarky grin.

"Hey, it took me a really long time to think that up. I lost precious hours of sleep."

"It's cute."

"You mean, it's sexy," I said with a waggle of my eyebrows as I scooped mint chocolate chip onto a cone.

"Mmm…yes, that, too."

I'd managed to keep her laughing all afternoon while I served up ice cream cones to the entire staff who managed to find their way to the ice cream without any directions or invitations. Lailah was ecstatic for the commotion and welcomed everyone, talking to doctors and nurses for hours as I played host.

Who knew Jude, the loner, could be so charismatic?

She'd brought that back—the old, lighter version of myself, the part I'd thought died when I watched Megan take her last breath.

I still visited the hallway. It wasn't often, but I'd been down there briefly—hovering and waiting…for something. For what, I didn't know.

Am I waiting for a divine sign from my fiancée, telling me everything is as it should be? To hear her voice saying it's okay to love again?

Fuck, I don't know.

I still felt the pull between my old life and the new one that seemed to be surfacing, but the guilt was shifting. When I walked the hallway and sat on my bench, looking at the closed door that had belonged to Megan for a brief few days, I would feel guilty for being there, for not sharing this part of myself with a woman who I was supposed to love.

When you love someone, you tell her everything, including the fact that you love her.

But I hadn't had the courage to do so.

It was still there, on the tip of my tongue.

I'd had so many opportunities over the last few days, yet as I lay in bed, holding her in my arms, I knew I'd let the moments slip by like dust in the wind. Each time I had, I would picture myself back in that lonely hallway, and I hated it. I hated that I was still stuck when everything that lay ahead of me appeared so crystal clear, yet felt so damn murky.

THE ICE CREAM PARLOR HAD BEEN SUCH A HUGE SUCCESS THAT I'd waltzed into the hospital today, ready for another one. It was my first day off after six nights straight. After a brief stop at a nearby strip mall, I'd arrived just a few hours before lunch, ready to spend the entire day with her.

"You want another one?" She placed her latest paperback down on the bed as she swung her feet over the side.

Her toes dangled in the air, and I caught a flash of lavender nail polish glinting off her big toe. She watched me drop the white paper bag near her bed, but she didn't say anything.

"Yep, hit me," I answered with a grin.

She looked up at me, her hands resting close to her knees, as her feet continued swaying back and forth.

She's so damn cute.

"Okay, number forty-three—dance in the rain." Her eyes sparkled with unshed laughter.

"You want a place holder for that?" I asked in genuine shocked.

"Yep. I mean, you brought an entire ice cream parlor, complete with sprinkles and cherries, here yesterday. How hard can a little rain be?" She threw in a flirty wink at the end just to spite me.

My nervous babbling girl had quickly transformed into a quick-witted temptress, and I liked it.

"You couldn't have picked something easier? No, you had to go with rain—in the hospital," I added.

"Well," she started, drawing out the word with her melodic voice, "if it's too hard—"

I didn't even let her finish. I just stepped forward, closing the small gap between us, and I grabbed her hand. Her eyes widened, and laughter came bursting out of her.

"What are you doing?" she yelped.

I briskly walked us into the bathroom. "Making it rain," I answered.

I kicked off my shoes and pulled out my cell phone and keys, remembering I still had yet to reveal the contents of what lay hidden in the mystery bag I'd brought.

I mentally shrugged. *That can wait. It's time for some waterworks.*

I turned toward her, and she had this what-did-I-get-myself-into look.

I smirked and lunged, hauling us both into the shower. I reached for the handle and turned. Cold water immediately fell onto our heads from the showerhead above.

"Oh my God, you're nuts! We're completely clothed and drenched!"

"Well, if we were naked, it would just be a shower." My eyes raked over her soaked body, loving the way her clothes clung to every inch. "But now that you mention it, a shower sounds really good right now."

Her breath hitched, and her crystal-blue eyes met mine.

There were so many possibilities in that single moment.

"But you wanted to dance in the rain, so the clothes stay on—for today," I added with a wolfish grin.

Not pushing her against that ugly white tile and showing her everything I wanted to do to her in that moment was physically painful. But I'd made a promise to her and myself. This was not how I would be making her mine. Angels didn't swoop down from heaven to be treated like something ordinary. I'd never been given a gift like the one Lailah was choosing to give me. Until now, I hadn't really considered virginity much more than a drunken interlude one leaves behind in high school. That was how mine had come and gone. Megan had seriously dated someone through much of high school, and although I'd never wanted specifics, I knew they had been intimate.

Lailah's life could pretty much be summed up within the walls of this hospital. Her illness—this defect she'd been born with had soaked up and stolen almost every minute of her existence. I'd be damned if I was going to let it take anything else.

Sliding my hands down her arms, I grabbed her hands and tugged them up around my neck. Warm, wet fingers grasped my shoulders as I found her waist and pulled her closer.

"I hope you don't mind if I dance with you?" I whispered, loving the feel of her body against mine as I began to gently sway us back and forth under the cascade of water.

"Never," she answered, placing her head on my shoulder.

I didn't know how long we stayed like that, slow dancing under the false rain of the shower, while we pretended to be somewhere else.

"Ahem," a stern male voice startled us from our dreamy waltz in the mist.

Lailah's head jerked up from my shoulder as mine turned

to find Dr. Marcus standing in the doorway. His eyes were trained on mine with a look that was anything but friendly.

"You two had better get cleaned up. Lailah, your mother is going to be here in a few minutes. She said she talked to someone with the insurance company, and she wanted to talk to you."

And with that vague statement, he walked out of the bathroom.

I turned back around to find my carefree girl who had been dancing in the rain gone. What remained was fear, just pure fear.

"Lailah," I coaxed, gently cupping her face as I tried to reach her.

I could see her retreating, fleeing into herself, where she felt safe, like a turtle framing itself into its shell.

"Hey, it's going to be okay. Whatever happens, we are all here, no matter what."

She looked up finally, her eyes connecting with mine, as my words soaked in.

"No matter what," I repeated.

She nodded, and I pulled her into my arms, hating Dr. Marcus for his insensitive behavior. He, above anyone, should have known how a remark like that would affect her.

"Let's get you warm," I suggested, shutting off the water, and grabbing a towel off the rack. I wrapped it around her like a burrito. I stepped out of the shower, not caring about my own soaked clothes, and I began gently drying off her face and arms.

She suddenly looked down at me, and her eyes widened. "What are you going to wear?"

I gave a small half smile as I squeezed water out of her long blonde hair. "I have an extra pair of scrubs and a few change of clothes in my staff locker. I've been keeping clothes here ever since you got sick, and I started crashing and showering here."

"You…showered here?" she asked, looking quickly to the shower, like she was suddenly picturing me in there.

"Yep, right there. Bet you wish you hadn't been sleeping, huh? I changed with the door open, too," I said with a grin.

Her mouth gaped, and I laughed, glad to see I'd managed to get her mind off the impending news of her transplant.

"I'm going to go to my locker and change. I'll be right back. Five minutes tops," I added. I grabbed a towel and tried to get rid of some of the excess water dripping off my wet clothes, and then I threw on my shoes.

That will have to do.

I brushed a quick kiss across her forehead, and then I was gone.

Now, I had to find Dr. Marcus.

It didn't take long to find him.

As my shoes squeaked down the hall, I found him at the nurses' counter. He was watching me with the same look of contempt I had for him.

"I think we need to talk, Marcus," I said through gritted teeth.

"I think we do," he answered back.

"Good, let's go for a walk."

I didn't even pause to wait for an answer. As I reached the elevator and pressed the button with water dripping down the sides of my face, I heard him step beside me. My hands fisted at my sides, but I remained silent. There was no need to make a scene in front of coworkers. The elevator beeped, and we entered one at a time, waiting for the door to shut.

"You stepped way over the line," I said.

"You've gone too far, Jude," he said simultaneously.

"I've gone too far?" I sputtered. "You nearly wrecked her in there, Marcus. Where do you get off walking in there, talking to her like she's just another patient? Do you know what that did to her? Just the mere mention of insurance scares the shit out of her. She freaked out that they aren't going to approve the transplant."

His gaze went cloudy and faraway. "I'm sorry. I didn't think. I walked in there and saw...and I thought...and I just—"

"You were thinking like a father, not a doctor," I said.

His eyes jerked up toward mine.

"Look, Marcus, I don't know what history there is between you and Lailah's mom, but I'm not dumb enough to think that it's all medical. There's more going on here, and it's deeper than this hospital. You feel something for those two, and I'm not going to fault you for it."

The elevator dinged, and we made our exit toward the entrance to the staff locker room. I found my locker, undid the lock, and pulled out an extra set of clothes. I couldn't do anything about the shoes, but at least I wouldn't have wet boxers anymore. I pivoted around to find Marcus turned away from me on a bench. His posture was hunched over, like he felt defeated.

"I've loved Molly Buchanan since I was in med school. She's the only woman I've ever wanted."

"Does she know this?" I asked, tugging off my shirt and replacing it with a clean, dry blue one.

"Yes, she knows. It wasn't fair—how we made her choose. I was never going to win. Who would pick the safe, boring brother?"

My eyes widened as I finished dressing and then shut my locker. "You're Lailah's uncle?" I asked, putting all the pieces together.

His head bobbed in a nod. "Two brothers going after the same girl is so cliché. We were from the wrong side of the tracks, raised by foster parents. Brett and I had no one besides each other. I used our personal tragedies as a way to grow, become stronger. I excelled in school and applied for every scholarship I could get my hands on. My brother did the opposite. He had a reputation that was less than upstanding.

"We met Molly the same night at a bar. I was there with some of my college buddies, celebrating the end of a semester.

Brett was probably dealing out by the back door. I met Molly first, and we had a moment and a dance, but he had a way with women, and he ended up winning her heart. Five weeks later, she was pregnant, and he was gone. Molly and I haven't seen him since, and all the while, I've been trying to convince her that I'm not my brother."

"And Lailah knows none of this?" I asked as we made our way back up to the cardiology wing.

"No. I've been by her side since the day she was born, and she has no idea who I am."

"Why?"

"Molly was so angry for so easily falling so easily for my brother's lies. She'd always prided herself on being methodical and making wise choices, and in five short weeks, she was wined, dined, and knocked up. I'd tried to warn her but by the time she started to listen, it was too late. After he left, she never wanted to speak about him again, so she didn't. Because of that, my role was reduced to Dr. Marcus. I was allowed to be around but only in medical capacities. If it wasn't for my occupation, I would have had no involvement in their lives at all."

"A blessing and a curse," I said as we stepped off the elevator.

"Yes, exactly. I've tried to convince Molly that I'm not him, that I would never hurt her, but he broke her, and I don't know if she'll ever trust another man again."

We reached Lailah's door, and I turned to Marcus before we entered. "Keep trying. Don't give up, Marcus."

"It looks good," Ms. Buchanan said with a look of hope in her blue eyes.

"What does that mean?" Lailah asked, gripping my hand as two sets of eyes watched.

"It means," she said, looking up at her daughter, "that I

think things are finally going our way. I spoke with someone at the insurance company today to make sure they had everything they needed. Everything is in order with UCLA—they will do your surgery when it's time and I double-checked they have everything they need. I didn't want anything to go wrong with insurance."

Lailah rolled her eyes, and I tried to keep my smirk from showing. Lailah had said how much of a control freak her mother was, and I had to agree. Seeing the woman in action was scary. She was like a hurricane in heels.

"You seriously called them?" Lailah said, her head shaking back in forth.

"Yes, I did. This isn't something I want screwed up by some incompetent imbecile in a cubicle. I called and confirmed. I was told that everything was in and looked good," she said.

"You're taking the word of the incompetent imbecile?" Lailah asked, repeating her mother's words back to her.

"No, of course not. I spoke with someone who actually reviews the cases."

"Oh my God, Mother, you are too much."

"I get things done," she stated.

"I don't even want to know how you accomplished that," Marcus muttered. "But it's good to hear. Hopefully, it will mean great news for us later on."

Ms. Buchanan had to run off to a class, and Marcus had other patients to see. After a few short good-byes, it was just the two of us again.

Lailah stared out the window, deep in thought. "Do you ever think about what our lives would be like if it was approved? If I did get a transplant and we were actually able to be together outside of this room?"

"Yeah, I do."

She looked over at me, her blue eyes still lost in her pondering. "What do you think about?"

"I think about taking you to the pier and finally dipping

those pretty toes in the Pacific," I said with a tiny smile. "I think about Ireland and that bed-and-breakfast and all the wicked things I promised to do to you."

A quick blush crept up her cheeks. "But what if it never happens?" she asked.

"It will," I said with conviction.

"How do you know? How can you be so sure?"

"Because I refuse to believe that it's not possible. Somehow, someway, we will make it happen. I'm not giving up if you aren't," I said.

She didn't look completely convinced, but she leaned forward. Resting her head against mine, her sign of surrender, she let me take her in my arms.

"What's in the bag?" she asked after a long block of silence.

"Oh, I almost forgot about my little surprise."

She lifted her head from my shoulder, and I quickly got up to retrieve the white paper bag from the floor. I joined her back on the bed and laughed when she eagerly looked inside.

"No peeking!" I exclaimed.

She pulled back, sitting up straighter and throwing her hands behind her back like she'd done nothing wrong.

"Now, I believe you told me about one thing on your list, and I might have given you a bit of a hard time about—"

"The prom?"

"No, not that one." *I suddenly had a fantastic idea.*

"You've given me a hard time about several. So, why don't you just show me?" she suggested with a teasing grin.

"Fine." I reached into the bag and pulled out the small white box.

"You got me a cell phone!" she practically yelled.

It wasn't the newest model, but it was the most I could afford. She could browse the web, install apps, and of course, text.

"I did."

"So, now, I can finally text my other boyfriend!" she said, smiling.

"Cute, Lailah. Really cute," I deadpanned.

I grabbed the box, placed it on the handy tray table next to her, and gave her a meaningful look as I leaned forward. I saw the flicker of awareness in her gaze seconds before I eased her back against the mattress. My hands slid down her arms, causing her breath to hitch. I weaved our fingers together and brought her hands high above her head.

"The only man you will ever call by that title is me," I whispered. I touched my lips to her neck and then moved them up to the sensitive skin of her ear.

Releasing our joined hands, I let my fingers move down the small curves of her body until I found bare skin where her shirt had lifted. My lips joined my eager hands and I nipped and scattered kisses across her bare skin as the pads of my fingers teased at the waistband of her pants.

"The only man who will ever touch you like this will be me," I said with strangled effort.

This game had started out as light and playful, and now, it was turning into something entirely different. Every part of my body was on fire, needing more of her. I'd pushed myself too far, given myself too much, and now, I was dying.

She moaned beneath me, squeezing her thighs together, as if the flames were too much for her to bear as well. Gripping the edge of her pants, I curled my fingers underneath, touching her hipbone, and I gently tugged before kissing the flesh I'd just revealed.

I knew I was playing with fire. This was exactly what I'd said I wouldn't do—not here, not like this.

Fuck, I want to.

I'm going to hell.

"Please, Jude," she whispered. "Just this. Show me what it's like."

Anyone could come in at any moment. We had no privacy,

yet I was still contemplating it. I wanted to give her every-thing, including this.

Continuing my trail, I kissed a path as I slowly inched the fabric down her hips, exposing her beautiful naked skin. I looked up and saw her watching me with hooded eyes. There was no inhibition, just the faint pink flush of passion and anticipation. If I wasn't already rock-hard in my jeans, I would have instantly popped wood from that look alone.

I ran my hands up her legs, over her hips, and in the junc-ture of her slim thighs, parting them until they fell open. My fingers glided over her glistening flesh for the first time, and she gasped. She was stunning, and I was completely capti-vated. I smoothed my finger over her clit, and she instantly moaned.

"Shh, angel. You're going to get us in trouble." I grinned.

She pursed her lips together, a sheepish grin spreading across her face.

"Tell me to stop," I said, running my thumb over her tender skin again.

"No," she breathed

"Tell me you want this."

"I want this Jude. Please."

I bent forward and took my first taste of her. I saw her hand fly to her mouth as she tried to quiet her moans.

I should have known an angel would taste like heaven. Parting her thighs wider, I worked my tongue—going in and out of her core, moving over her clit, licking and sucking her until I felt drunk.

For a split second before I'd made the decision to do this, I'd worried it might be too much, too soon for someone so new to the physical side of love, but seeing her spread out before me, I couldn't resist. I'd had to show her a glimpse, and she'd blossomed under my touch.

She writhed and moved against me, moaning under her breath, as her free hand wove into my hair. We were so caught up in each other in that moment that I thought the building could have come crashing down around us, and we wouldn't have noticed. Luckily, it didn't.

Lailah's mewling became more erratic, and she pulled her hand away from her mouth. "Jude, it's...I can't...too much," she said in staccato sentences.

I looked up to make sure it wasn't her heart, and no, it wasn't. Her eyes were heated, and her face was flush. Never breaking eye contact, I moved to just her clit and flicked over and over relentlessly. Then, I watched her break apart for the first time in her life. Her body trembled and shook, and her awakening was stunning.

Now, how the hell am I supposed to survive the rest of her hospital imprisonment, knowing she can come apart like that?

CHAPTER NINETEEN
TRUTH AND TEXTS

LAILAH

Dear Journal/Diary/Keeper of Secrets,

I know I've never addressed you as a diary or even as an entity at all, but I need you to be my sounding board for me today. I need someone to absorb all my secrets and not let them go. Will you do that for me?

For today, let's talk as friends. You can be...well, you, and I will be me. Tomorrow, you can go back to being a bottomless void where I trap all my errant thoughts and dreams as they flutter and fly by.

Today, I feel...everything—happiness, love, fear, desire, and yes, even that dangerous little emotion, hope.

A new heart.

A new beginning.

A new life.

Could it be possible?

Just like Jude. The line lingered, and I found myself smiling as I rubbed my thumb across my bottom lip. He was thrilling and scary, but he was also gentle, sweet, and really sexy. I laughed at myself and closed the notebook, deciding to come back to it later.

It was starting to get late, just past eleven, and Jude had left for home not too long ago, stating that I needed to rest.

"I'm fine," I'd insisted.

"Then, why are you still in the hospital?" He'd placed a kiss on my lips and disappeared before I could argue.

Dr. Marcus and my mother had been conspiring to keep me here for a bit longer to observe me after my recent illness. I could understand Mom's control and panic issues, but I didn't get why Dr. Marcus had been acting so overly cautious. Yes, I'd gotten sick, and okay, I could admit that it was bad, but I was fine now—well, as fine as someone with congestive heart failure could be.

Whatever.

Until their over-protective antics ended, I was stuck here.

I thought back to my afternoon with Jude, and a smile snuck up my cheeks.

The hospital wasn't so bad. My face suddenly flamed red with heat, and I laughed.

Jude had undressed me and I'd let him do wicked things to me, and not once had I showed one second of embarrassment. I was amazed by my boldness and downright wantonness.

But now, while I'm all alone, I turn pink.

A chirping noise took me abruptly out of my wayward thoughts, and I grabbed my new phone off the tray table beside me.

Jude: Are you blushing?

I looked around as if the phone had somehow made him privy to the going-ons in my room. But no, it was just a text. There was no magic. It was just straight-up technology and a nosy man.

Lailah: And why would you think that?

I sent back my first text, feeling proud of myself.

I was texting my boyfriend. *Awesome.*

I realized that I was about five years behind for that statement to be cool, but the teenager in me who had never gotten to text was rejoicing.

> Jude: Because I know you're thinking about me.

> Lailah: You're cocky.

> Jude: That's an interesting choice of words.

> Lailah: OMG!

> Jude: Hey, look at you. Three texts in, and you're a pro.

> Lailah: Well, I am a product of my generation even if I don't get to participate. :-)

> Jude: Okay, now, you're just showing off.

> Lailah: Someone clearly missed his lessons. ;-)

> Jude: Blame the stuffy education. Typing in incomplete sentences makes me twitchy.

> Lailah: Thank you for the phone.

> Jude: You're welcome. We'll knock them all off that list, Lailah. I promise.

> Lailah: You're crazy.

> Jude: Yeah, but you like me anyway. Night.

> Lailah: Good night. <3

I couldn't help the grin etching my face as I set down the phone. Turning around, I pulled out the notebook housing my long list of dreams. Flipping though the pages, I found number fifty-one. After picking up the pen beside me, I drew a long black line through the words, *Have an entire conversation using only text messages.*

Flipping through the pages, I noticed a few others to cross out, and then my eyes fell to number one.

Quickly, without a second thought, I took the same black pen and placed a permanent line through the one dream I never thought would come true.

~~4. Fall in love.~~

From nearly the first moment when I'd met Jude Cavenaugh, he had been in a mode of constant planning. He'd moved from pudding to cafeteria dinners to cell phones, but he was always planning something for me.

Over the last week, I could tell he was planning something big.

His nose was buried in his phone, and he seemed to disappear into these secret meetings with Grace, Dr. Marcus, and even my mother at the oddest times. After everything he'd done for me, I was a little scared to ask what might be next.

"You've been very secretive lately," I stated one evening during his brief lunch break.

He was eating an egg salad sandwich from the cafeteria and sipping on coffee while I slowly dug at the cup of pudding he'd brought me.

"All in good time," he answered with a wink. He pulled apart another chunk of bread and tossed it into his mouth. He was leaned back in the chair tonight with his feet propped up on the rails of my bed. His floppy blond hair was pushed back from his eyes, making him look younger and more carefree.

My gaze wandered over his long, lean body, admiring the way he'd cared for it. I knew he ran and spent a lot of time lifting weights when he wasn't here. It showed in every move he made. When his body flexed and tightened, the tattoos scattered up his arms seemed to come alive with the slightest movement.

"Do your tattoos mean anything to you?" I asked, looking at the winding black scrollwork that moved across his forearm until it disappeared under his shirt.

"No, not really," he replied. "I was in a dark place when I got them. I wanted to be someone else, anyone else but the person I had been when I came here."

"Did it work?"

"No," he answered. "Ink and a different hairstyle doesn't change who you are. Life does."

I reached forward, placing my fingers on the inked skin and traced the path it made.

"They might have helped me disappear, but I am still a Cavenaugh."

His eyes looked lost as if they had drifted off to someplace in his past.

"Tell me about your family," I said, tugging on his hand.

He got the hint, and set his coffee and the trash from his dinner down next to the bed. He joined me, and I curled into his warmth as I waited for him to respond.

"My family is a variety of things. We were four different people all thrown into one house, but I guess that could probably summarize every family on the planet. Mine just came with the added pressure of a multibillion-dollar corporation."

"Did you say *billion*?"

He nodded.

"My mom is kind and loving, and my father adores her. Over the years, the press has occasionally tried to find evidence of my father cheating, but they'll never find it. They'd have better luck looking for cheating in other areas besides his marital bed," he remarked, shaking his head.

"What is that supposed to mean?"

"Let's just say my father's and brother's business practices haven't always been the most..."

"Legal?" I guessed.

"No, they're mostly legal—or at least they could pay someone off to vouch for it. I have just never been in agreement with the way they do business. For them, it's always been pure greed. How much can we make, and how fast can we make it? It doesn't matter how many companies we have to close, or the amount of people we have to put out of business. It's all about the bottom dollar. If the trend was to expand, we would. If we had to downsize, we'd cut corners until we were making out like thieves. I hated it."

"Is that why you left?"

"It's why I stayed away. It's not why I left though."

Still curled into his chest, I pulled back slightly and found him staring down at me, his eyes full of conflict.

"I was engaged," he confessed, his voice hoarse and soft.

I wrapped my hands around his and squeezed. "I know."

"You do?"

"Yes, I'm sorry. I found an article about you—"

"And it mentioned the car accident," he guessed.

"No, it was actually Grace who told me about that part. She didn't know it was you I was asking about."

He nodded, not making a sound.

"I assumed you would tell me when you were ready," I offered.

"Her name was Megan," he said finally after a long pause. "She was a firecracker and a jokester, and everyone loved her. Every one of my friends thought I was insane for proposing to her the day we graduated from college, but I knew I wanted her by my side when I would have to return home to join forces with my father and brother. Megan and I had two weeks of vacation to enjoy California and Hawaii before my days of fun would end, and I would have to trade it all. God, I remember being so scared about how it would all turn out, having a wife and my demanding father. I didn't know how it could work, but I wanted it to so badly."

"What happened?" I asked.

"Megan and I went to a party. We'd met some random

college students at a bar and they'd invited us back to an end of the year party on campus. I begged her to drive us back to the hotel rather than stay the night. It's all my fault," he answered, his voice cracking.

"Oh, Jude," I said, my heart breaking for him.

He wrapped his arms around me, like I was his anchor, as he held me in silence.

"You stayed here to punish yourself," I whispered against his chest.

He took his time before answering, "I stayed because I had nowhere else to go."

I pulled back, looking into his eyes that were so full of sadness.

"But you had a family, Jude. What about your friends? Didn't they care that you were hurting, grieving?"

"Friends can only try for so long. After I switched my number and disappeared—so did they. And my family made it perfectly clear that they needed me for one purpose, and that was to make money," he answered, his expression growing a bit harder at the mention of his family.

"Besides, my life was over, Lailah. I had no home to return to."

"I cannot even begin to understand what you went through, but to hear you say you thought your life was over pains me in a way I can't describe. You were twenty-two, Jude. You lost someone you loved, but your life was definitely not over. I really hope you don't still think that."

"I don't know what I believe anymore." He sat up and ran his hands through his hair in a frustrated manner. I followed, sitting with my legs crossed beside him.

"Did you ever stop to think that maybe your life had just started?" I asked.

His eyes flew up to mine in surprise. "How?" he asked.

"I don't know, but you said you were scared to death of what might happen when you returned to New York. Did it ever occur to you that by staying here in California, you might have given yourself a chance to create something new, something different?"

He scooted forward, out of my grasp, until he moved off the bed completely. He stalked across the room. "Are you saying that Megan's death happened for a reason?" His words were clipped as he paced from one corner to the next.

My face fell at his angry words. "God, no, Jude. That's not what I'm saying at all."

"Because you have no idea, no clue what she was like or what I went through. She was everything to me!" he shouted, causing me to jump.

Tears fell from my eyes as I struggled to find words to fix this. "I know. I'm sorry. Forget I said anything." The words tumbled out as I tried to grasp on to anything to keep him from leaving this room, from leaving me.

"My break is over. I've got to go." He turned, walked out, and didn't bother looking back.

My palms came to my cheeks, and I let go of the flood I'd been holding back as I mourned a woman I never knew, a woman who still held the heart of the man I loved.

Will he ever be able to let go?

CHAPTER TWENTY
LETTING GO

JUDE

t had been two days since I stormed out of Lailah's room. It had been forty-eight hours since I saw her face or heard her voice. Hell, even our flirty text conversations had ceased.

I'd spent two entire days of work avoiding her. I would make a wide berth around her doorway, and I would take my lunch breaks alone in the corner of the cafeteria while I'd sit and wonder what she was doing. Even as I'd done this—making every attempt to avoid confrontation, to avoid the conversation I knew we'd have to have—I continued with my plan. I'd been taking my meetings that I'd scheduled with various hospital officials to secure proper approvals. I'd gone over lists with Grace, Marcus, and even Lailah's mom, who would eye me with the usual wary indifference.

I was continuing with my biggest plan of all because, deep down, I knew Lailah was right.

The other night, I had stood there, looking my future straight in the face, as I stared into the eyes of the woman I wanted to spend the rest of my life with.

And she wasn't Megan.

Lailah hadn't said those words to hurt or anger me. She'd said them to try to help me heal. Instead of recognizing that when I should have, I'd lashed out in anger, defending a ghost and a memory.

Megan would have been ashamed by my actions.

Megan would never have wanted me to continue mourning her like I had been.

Yet, here I was, three years later, still stuck in the same place I had been the day we arrived in that ambulance. Maybe I was supposed to do that though, so I could end up here.

I didn't know. I couldn't even begin to understand how the world worked.

I needed to let go. I needed to say good-bye to Megan, the woman I'd lost, and to the life I'd once had. And I needed to forgive myself for the mistakes I'd made that led me here.

She might have spent her years cooped up in a hospital room, but the wisdom Lailah possessed was more than most people gained in a lifetime.

I had been punishing myself, living in a purgatory for my sins, and it was finally time to break free.

"You want to what?" Margaret asked once again.

"I'd like to purchase a plaque for the bench on the second floor. Don't play coy with me. I know you know what bench I'm talking about," I said, leaning back into the tall wingback chair that seemed to be my home lately.

I'd dropped by her office early this morning after having had about three hours of sleep since I clocked out. But I couldn't wait any longer. Each hour ticking by marked how long I hadn't seen Lailah, and the passing time was starting to weigh on me.

Does she think I left for good? Is she okay? Does she hate me?
God, I'm an ass.

But I needed to do this before I could step foot in that room again.

I needed to return whole—or at least, on my way. Aside

from flying to Chicago and visiting where Megan was buried, this was the only way I could work it out in my head. I wanted a way to say good-bye—a remembrance, something concrete and real that I could remember.

I'd skipped her funeral service. Too swallowed up by grief and regret, I couldn't bring myself to face our families and friends. So, I never got the chance to say good-bye, to have that sacred moment to wish for more, a better afterlife, for the loved one who had left me.

I needed that now.

"I'm not really the person to talk to about that type of thing, Jude," she started.

"Oh, come on, Margaret. Let's cut the shit, shall we?"

Her mouth fell open.

"I know you pulled strings and got the bench put there. No one else in this hospital, besides you and Dr. Marcus, gives two shits about me. And you're the only one who knows about me and that hallway. It's a little fishy to me that a bench would suddenly appear in that exact spot," I pressed, staring her down.

"They call and check on you," she blurted out.

Stunned silent for a moment, I gathered my thoughts, trying to figure out what she'd meant. "Who? Who calls to check on me?"

"Her parents."

"Megan's parents check on me?"

She nodded. "I don't know all the details, but a few months after she passed, they called here, looking for you. I don't know the relationship between your families, but when the call finally got to me, it sounded like her parents hadn't gotten a lot of information from yours, so they were starting at square one."

Considering my father was still keeping up the scheme that I was antisocial and too busy to do anything but work, I could see my family not running the risk of giving any information regarding my whereabouts out to anyone, even

Megan's parents. Besides a family scandal, the idea of our family business breaking apart could send the shareholders into turmoil. Making them believe I was just quirky and fearful of people after my personal tragedy was better than instigating any inkling of panic.

"I told them you worked here, which surprised them."

"I bet," I said.

"They asked how you were after…"

"Go on," I urged.

"Well, I've been giving them updates ever since," she said quietly, knowing she'd probably broken a dozen laws in giving out an employee's personal information. "They don't call often, just once or twice a year to check in. They love you, Jude."

Even after everything I put them through?

I looked at her for a minute or two, putting it all together —the special care, the job offer, barely a second glance when I'd asked to leave my last name off my badge.

"You've known who I was this entire time," I said, not bothering to phrase it as a question.

"Yes. I recognized you the second I saw your last name on that employment application."

"Yet, you've never said anything?"

"We should all be able to grieve privately, Jude. I wanted that for you. I just didn't realize it would take so long," she confessed.

"I think I'm almost done."

She gave a faint smile, her eyes glistening with unshed tears. "I'm glad," was all she said.

"And the bench?" I asked, wondering how it played into all of this.

"Megan's father requested it. When I told him where you would go after your shifts, he wanted you to have a place to sit. He knew he couldn't change what you were doing, but he wanted to at least make it better for you."

"I'd like a plaque if you could swing it," I finally said, my voice heavy with emotions.

"I'll make some phone calls."

"And, Margaret?" I rose from the chair. "When they call next time, could you tell them that I'm finally happy again? And that I love them, too?"

She smiled warmly. "I'd be happy to."

Leaving Margaret to make her calls, I headed up to cardiology, passing the eyes of every nurse and staff member who had taken a particularly high interest in my social life over the last few weeks. Becoming involved with a patient was front-page gossip—or at least, that was what Grace had told me.

I really couldn't give a fuck.

The hallway seemed endless, and my arms became restless as they waited to finally swing that door open, so I could see Lailah again.

God, I've been a fool.

Hasn't my past shown me anything?

Life is precious. It's there one minute and gone the next. It shouldn't be wasted.

I'd lost two precious days being angry with Lailah for something I'd already known but been too frightened to admit.

Finally making it to her door, I grabbed the knob and knocked. I heard the soft, sweet sound of her voice ushering me in, and I entered before the quiet click of the door sounded behind me.

She was standing, and her back was turned. She was going through a pile of books her mother had probably brought over. Her hand smoothed over the cover of one of the paperbacks, tracing the raised letters of the title.

When she looked over her shoulder and made eye contact with me, she froze. "Jude," she said, her eyes round and wide with surprise.

I took a step forward but stopped.

What do I say first? I'm sorry? I'm an ass? You were right?

I wanted to say them all at the same time, but I didn't know where to begin.

Finally, I stalked forward, removing the air and space separating us. Weaving my fingers through her hair, I kissed her. She gasped, her hands gripping my shoulders before sliding around my neck.

"I'm sorry, Lailah. I'm so sorry," I said between our frenzied kisses.

"No, I'm sorry. I shouldn't have pushed you."

"You didn't say anything I didn't already know."

Grabbing her around her waist, I lifted her, and she instantly responded, wrapping her legs around me. I leaned her against the wall. Sliding my hands down around her ass, I supported her weight to keep the strain off of her.

It also wasn't a bad position for me. I might be choosing the good-guy route to wait until I could have her in a proper bed without wheels, but by no means was I a saint.

With her legs spread and her body pressed firmly against me, I wanted nothing more than to strip her down and forget every reason I had for waiting. Even with my raging hard-on and the heat of her core doing funny things to my brain, my conscience still remembered how much I wanted to love her for the first time in my own bed.

But that didn't mean we couldn't have a little fun until then.

"Lift up your shirt," I whispered against her ear.

A small smirk tugged at the corner of her lips as she pulled the bottom of her shirt up halfway, exposing her smooth stomach.

"Higher."

She did, lifting it up above her chest.

"No bra today," I said as my eyes skimmed over her beautiful body.

"I wasn't expecting company."

"You should not expect company every day," I replied with a wicked grin.

With my hands still firmly holding her up, I bent forward, moving my tongue over that perfectly shaped pink bud until it pebbled and hardened.

"Gorgeous," I remarked before closing my mouth over her tight nipple.

Her head went back, and a long moan followed as her hands raked through my hair. I nipped, sucked, and kissed until she was writhing and moving against me so hard that I was about to blow.

"Jesus, Lailah, I'm going to lose it."

A blush crept up her face as she looked at me. "You are?"

I gave her a dumbfounded look. "You're practically dry-humping me while nearly topless. I'm about to die."

Her head fell to my shoulder, and laughter soon followed. "You're the one who put us in this position," she reminded me.

"Yeah, I know," I said, letting her legs slide to the floor. "I tend to do all sorts of stupid things when you're around."

Her mischievous eyes met mine. "I like when you do stupid things."

"I can tell," I replied with a grin as I stepped back from the wall. *Air. I need air.*

"Why don't you come sit with me, and we can catch up?"

I nodded, and we took our positions on the bed, but this time, I sat up rather than snuggling down next to her. I could still taste her on my lips and feel her touch on my skin. If we had too much contact now, we'd be right where we had been three minutes ago. Right now, I wasn't sure I would be able to stop again.

I'd taken things farther with Lailah in this room than I'd ever planned on, and every step we took over the line was one foot closer to taking away my promise to her.

"How have you been?" she asked, crossing her legs in front of her, Indian style.

"Miserable. Lonely. Spent a lot of time thinking about Megan and my past...and the life I was supposed to have with her. You were right, Lailah. I was punishing myself. I'd always told myself that I stayed because it was the only way to be close to her, but she's not here. She hasn't been here in three years."

Lailah took my hand.

I continued, "I have though. I've been here for three years, lost and alone, holding on to a life I was never going to have. Then, you appeared and showed me what it was like to live. I remember looking into this room that first night and seeing you eating pudding off your finger. It was so simple, so *human*. I wanted that. You make me feel human again."

"I don't ever want you to think I'm trying to replace her," she said. "For the last two days, I've been so afraid that you wouldn't come back, and if you did, you would resent me."

"I should have never stayed away," I said, tugging on our joined hands.

She unfolded her legs and crawled onto my lap, and I let my arms fall around her.

"I know you aren't trying to replace her. You're too good-natured to even try. She was my first love, and my heart broke when I lost her. That was the end of my story," I said, cupping her chin and tilting it upward. "Until you. My heart is mending because of you."

When our lips met this time, our kiss was tender and slow. It was nothing like the passionate reunion from earlier. I savored each moment, pouring in every emotion and feeling I wasn't yet ready to say. I knew now that until I forgave myself and said good-bye to my ghosts and the memories haunting me, I'd never be able to fully move ahead.

Lailah and I spent the afternoon making up for lost time. We talked and laughed over the selection of books Lailah's mom had brought her.

"*The Baby-Sitter's Club*?" I asked, holding up the worn paperback with the title written on blocks.

"My scatterbrained mom sometimes just picks up what-ever she sees first at the library."

"Make a list. I'll pick up whatever you want."

"Really?" she asked with a mixture of excitement and a little embarrassment.

"Why the blushing?" I asked, skimming my fingers across her cheeks.

She bit her lip before speaking. "There are some books I've been dying to get but they are a bit…"

"What?" I asked.

"Nothing. Just get me some crime novels."

"Are these books you're not asking for sexy books perhaps?" I asked, giving her a lopsided grin.

"Maybe."

"Can we read those parts together?"

Her cheeks flared up from that comment, causing me to laugh. I got my book list. It was a long one.

"Hey, do you want to watch a movie?" I asked, flopping down beside her on the bed.

"Oh my gosh, that reminds me!" she exclaimed.

"What?"

"Have you seen the news?" Her expression was now much more serious.

"No, I usually avoid it."

"You should probably turn on CNN or pull up their website," she suggested, reaching down to pull out her laptop.

That thing was reaching geriatric years, but with the hospital Wi-Fi, it was passable for Internet use. I plucked it out of her hands and flipped it open.

"Why? What should I be looking for?" I asked, typing *CNN* into the search engine.

"You'll see it."

I clicked on the website, and as soon as the site loaded, I saw several headlines—a tropical storm, something about a celebrity—and then my eyes stopped.

"'Cavenaugh Dynasty Headed for Disaster'?" I announced, repeating the headline to myself.

I looked up at Lailah, and she nodded.

"It's all over the news," she said.

I clicked on the link to bring up the full article. A full-color picture of my brother was included, showing him walking through the doors of Cavenaugh Investments. He looked older, and his eyes were downcast as he tried to avoid the cameras and attention.

My eyes quickly skimmed the words, and it didn't take a genius to figure out what was going on. The phrases *poor business decisions*, *family in turmoil*, and *investors not happy* all popped out at me.

"My father's and brother's little scheme to cover up my whereabouts has finally leaked as well as their lack of business skills. How my father managed not to run the business into the ground sooner has never failed to astound me. It was my grandfather's vision, not his." I shook my head, shutting the laptop and setting it aside.

"Are you going to do anything?" she asked softly.

"No. They made the mess, so they can clean it up," I answered. "My place is here now."

CHAPTER TWENTY-ONE
FLYNN RIDER

LAILAH

'd just finished my lackluster lunch of lasagna and broccoli when there was a knock on my door. My heart fluttered in anticipation, wondering if it was Jude about to grace my presence, but then I realized I had no idea when or even if he was going to visit me today. When I'd asked him yesterday, he'd been especially vague, actually sidestepping the conversation altogether.

I gave my okay to enter and felt my jaw hit the floor.

Weighed down by an assortment of glittery gowns, boxes of shoes, and several other bags, my mother and Grace entered my room and nearly collapsed as they dumped things on the end of my bed.

"What the heck?" I said, looking around for some sort of clue. "Are we playing dress-up?"

Grace's eyes lit up, and it was then that I noticed she wasn't dressed for work. Instead, she wore a pair of slim dark jeans, pink ballet flats, and a flowery top. Her hair was pulled back into a large neat bun at the top of her head. I'd never seen her out of scrubs. She looked beautiful and exactly how I would have pictured her—girlie with a touch of class.

"We are here to get you ready," Grace announced.

"Ready for what?" My eyes darted around the room from her to my mom, who was not nearly as excited but still showing more emotion than I usually saw out of her.

"I can't tell you," Grace said.

"Okay."

"It's another one of those crazy ideas your boyfriend thought up," my mom added with a slight smile and a roll of her eyes.

She was warming up to Jude. It was taking a while, but slowly, she was coming around. Maybe by the time we were in our forties, she might work her way up to a hug.

"So, where do we start?"

We started with dresses. Grace had brought a huge selection, all with various styles and colors.

"Where did you get these?" I asked.

"Never you mind that," she answered with a wave of the hand. "Jude asked me to handle the beauty side of things, and I did. Now, which one do you like best?"

I looked through all my choices. Some were sweet, and some were sexy. I chose several to try on, but my eyes kept going to one—a strapless mint green gown that reminded me of Jude's eyes. I saved that one for last. Grace loved everything, and my mother even got teary-eyed from seeing me in something other than sweats and jeans. But when I came out in that last dress, there was silence.

It was stunning. The bodice was simple with a sweetheart shape that gave lift and shape to my otherwise straight body. The part that made it interesting was the lace overlay covering my scar just perfectly, curving around my collarbone, but it was still see-through enough that the sweetheart-style was visible. The dress hugged at the waist and then flared with wisps of fabric cascading elegantly down to the floor.

They both stared up at me.

"It's perfect," Grace finally said.

"It's lovely," my mom chimed in.

"Yay!" Grace exclaimed. "Now, let's choose shoes!"

Those were an easy choice. I went with a flat silver sandal. The dress was long enough, so no one would see my shoes anyway, and since I'd never in my life walked in heels, I didn't want to start now. I actually wanted to get out of this hospital sometime in the near future.

Once that decision was made, we moved on to makeup. Grace had me strip out of my dress and back into my regular clothes. She pulled out this huge toolbox-looking thing that had about fifty-thousand compartments crammed inside.

"Are you sure you don't have an apartment in there?" I asked.

She opened yet another hidden drawer. "No, I'm just very organized when it comes to makeup."

"Obviously."

I was nervous when she began painting on foundation and puffing on powder. I'd never worn makeup, and even though I had no clue what was going on, I knew I didn't want to look like a hooker for it.

"Okay, time for the reveal," she said, holding a mirror out in front of me.

I took a deep breath and looked up at the reflection staring back at me.

"Oh my God, Grace."

"I know," she said.

She'd done an amazing job. It was me, only slightly improved but nothing overstated. There were no harsh black lines or daring eye shadow. I just had subtle highlights here and there to accentuate my cheekbones and eye color.

"Thank you, Grace," my mother said, giving her a hug.

"So, someone please tell me we're going to do something with my hair?" I said, looking into the mirror at my long blonde hair pulled to the side.

"Your mom has actually asked to do your hair," Grace declared with a smile.

I looked over to my mom, who was pulling out a few things from a shopping bag.

"What?" she scoffed. "I do know a thing or two!"

I held up my hands and laughed as she gathered her things and sank down behind me.

Smooth, methodical strokes of the brush moved through my hair, tingling my scalp and relaxing my tense shoulders.

"When I was younger, Grandma used to braid my hair. She could do every kind of braid you can imagine. I'd hold up a mirror and watch her every day as she'd create beautiful patterns in my long hair."

The tips of her fingers brushed my crown, and I felt her grab several strands.

"By the time you were born, her arthritis had taken over, and she wasn't able to do many of the things she'd done before. I regret to say that somehow over the years, I've forgotten about the simple things."

"Mom, you've kept me alive."

"Yes, but what have I cost you? Jude said you keep a list. Everything he's been doing has been to give you a piece of a normal life. I should have done that."

"You're doing it now by braiding my hair and having an afternoon with my friend and me," I said.

Grace smiled from the chair.

"It's never too late."

"He really does care for you, doesn't he?" Mom softly tugged and smoothed strands of my hair, putting them in place.

"He's her Flynn Rider," Grace said in a dreamy voice.

"What?" my mother and I said simultaneously.

"Remember when I said you were Rapunzel, sitting up in your tower, just waiting for your prince? Well, he's your Flynn," she said with a grin. "And he found you."

Who knew being a girl could take up so much time?

The three of us spent the entire afternoon primping and preparing for an evening I didn't know a thing about.

But I knew I wasn't going solo.

After my hair had been braided into an intricate updo that even Katniss Everdeen would envy, both my mother and Grace pulled out dresses of their own, and they proceeded to get ready. My mother was understated in a simple black cocktail dress. It flattered her small figure and brought life back to her cheeks.

"Mom, you look hot," I said, grinning.

"Oh, stop. It's just something I picked up on sale."

"It's beautiful."

Grace wore sapphire blue, and the dress she'd chosen was gorgeous. Strapless with a fitted bodice, it flared at the waist. It was short and showed off her toned legs and monstrous high heels.

"How in the world do you walk in those things?" I asked, eyeing them warily.

"Just a bit of practice. Besides, shoes like these weren't meant to be walked in. They're just meant to be admired," she said with a wink.

By five o'clock, all three of us were dressed and ready…for something.

"Okay," I said, looking at them. "What do we do now?" I asked.

They both just turned to me, smiling, and then the knock came.

"Right on time," Grace sang, skipping to the door in her stilettos.

She cracked it open, and I heard murmuring. She turned around and motioned with her head to my mom to join her. Within seconds, they were both exiting through the door with a few winks and grins, leaving me alone in the room.

Another knock came, and before I could answer, it slowly swung open, and Jude appeared.

"Holy shit," he whispered, stopping dead in his tracks.

He'd dressed up for the secret occasion as well. Until this moment, I'd never seen Jude in anything other than jeans and scrubs. Dressed in head-to-toe black, he oozed sexiness without even trying. He'd also cut his hair. No longer shaggy and overgrown, his hair was now cropped short but left purposely messy in the front.

"You're breathtaking," he said as his eyes drank in every detail.

"So are you."

He stepped forward, closing the distance between us, and he cupped my cheek tenderly. Bending down, his lips brushed mine ever so briefly. "I couldn't let another second go by before I did that." He smiled against my cheek.

"Are you ever going to tell me what we're doing?"

His hands curved around my waist, and I felt his smile grow wider. He pulled back, and I saw the excitement and anticipation in his eyes.

"Not yet. First, we are going to eat dinner."

"Like this?" I asked, looking down at our formal attire.

"Don't worry. No trays for you tonight." He ran back to the door, opening it briefly to reach for something on the other side. He came back with a picnic basket. "We're having a picnic," he declared.

"Number eighty-two." I remembered a night not too long ago when I'd told him a few new dreams and wishes from my list, which included having a picnic.

"I'm trying to knock a couple off that list tonight."

He'd thought of everything, and he'd brought enough food to feed the entire floor. We sat on my bed, enjoying fruit, gourmet sandwiches, and even pudding.

"This is much better than snack packs," I commented, dipping my spoon into the container we were sharing.

"You don't like my snack packs?" he joked, looking wounded.

"No, I love your snack packs. This is just different. It's like what a snack pack could be, if it wanted to be."

He stared at me blankly. "Why do I think that had nothing to do with desserts?"

"I'm sorry. I just can't stop thinking about you and the stuff going on with your family. Are you really not going to do anything?"

"No," he said firmly.

"Do you miss it?"

"What?"

"That part of your life and using that part of yourself—the analytic, brainy side that can't possibly be happy with checking bedpans and taking vitals all day."

"Sometimes, I guess," he answered honestly. "I was good at it, but money always came first. I can't go back to that."

"Don't you think they'd listen to you? Especially now?" I asked.

He stared off into the distance and finally shook his head. "I have no desire to go back," he said, looking back at me. "I have everything I need right here."

"No peeking!" Jude laughed as he pulled me out of the wheelchair the hospital had insisted I use.

The mint green fabric of my dress had been tucked neatly underneath me as the wheels creaked along the worn linoleum. We'd gone down several floors in the elevator and passed through many different hallways—all the while, with Jude's large hands firmly planted over my eyes.

"I don't think I could if I tried!"

"Good. Now, just a little bit further. We're almost there. Okay, I'm going to take my hands away. Don't open your eyes yet."

I heard a door swing open, and the booming sound of music immediately poured out.

"Okay, stand up, and take my hand, but keep your eyes closed." His firm grip closed around mine as he guided me, and then his arms reached around my waist from behind. "Now, open your eyes," he whispered in my ear.

My eyelids fluttered open, and I immediately noticed we were in a low-lit room. Multicolored balloons and streamers lined the ceiling. A large group of people were dancing in the center of the room, and tables were off to the side with drinks and food.

"What is this?" I asked.

"It's your prom," he said, pointing to a banner near the ceiling.

The Someday Prom, the banner boasted in large loopy script.

Emotions so deep that I couldn't describe them poured through me. I turned around and flung myself into his arms as tears made their way down my cheeks. "Thank you."

I didn't care if it all ended that very moment. We could never even make it to the dance floor, and I didn't think I would ever feel happier.

In all my days of sitting in that hospital bed—wondering why me, why had I been selected to have this burden, to be given this life—I never expected such amazing things were going to happen to me.

"How did you manage to do this? I don't know what to say," I said, looking around. I started to recognize several nurses and staff from the cardiology unit.

"Don't cry," he said, giving a small smile, as he gently wiped away the tears. "Dance with me?"

I nodded, and he pulled me to the small group of people in the center. I recognized Grace with a guy who must have been her fiancé. She gave me a wink as she placed her head on his broad shoulder.

I went into Jude's embrace and let him lead us as a new song began. John Legend's "All of Me" played as we swayed back and forth, and I listened to Jude hum the melody in my ear.

"Have I mentioned that you look beautiful today?" he said softly.

"Jude," I said, turning away, as I felt the blush beginning to burn.

He didn't need to do this.

"No, look at me," he demanded, turning my chin up until

my eyes met his sizzling gaze. "You are stunning. I don't say this because I pity you or want you to feel normal. I say this because it's the truth. If I saw you anywhere else, I would think the exact same thing."

He kissed me, and I melted into his embrace.

"You make me feel beautiful," I murmured against his lips.

"That's because you are."

I rested my head on his shoulder as he continued humming. We were lost in each other and the moment.

"I hope you won't mind if an old man tries to cut in?" I heard from behind, a male voice bringing me back to reality.

I looked up to see a finger tapping Jude's shoulder and a face I didn't recognize, but Jude apparently did.

"Nash," he said with a grin. Jude greeted the man with a handshake that turned into a big hug that included the big man picking Jude up off the ground.

"I missed you and our quiet talks, Jude," the man said after setting Jude back on the ground.

"You, too, Nash. The cardiology unit hasn't been the same without you." He laughed. Looking over at me, he grabbed my waist again. "Nash, I don't think you ever got the chance to formally meet this one before you were discharged. This is my Lailah," he said, giving me a squeeze.

My Lailah.

I had a ridiculous amount of butterflies in my stomach over the addition of that one word to my name.

I shook hands with the infamous author, and he took Jude's place on the dance floor. I saw him walk over to the drink table to talk to Dr. Marcus, who was sipping punch. He was nicely dressed in a suit and tie.

"You've changed him," Nash said with a grin. "He's not broken anymore."

"He did that on his own," I said as we moved back and forth to a song I didn't recognize.

"Maybe so, but you gave him a reason."

He didn't press for any more conversation after that, but he did insist on teaching me how to *really* dance. I had visions of rose stems in my mouth with my leg up in the air, but he kept it tame and just turned me in a slow circle before doing a little dip. I couldn't help but laugh. The old man was a charmer. When the song ended, he thanked me for the dance and said he had a little surprise for me. Disappearing out the door, he reappeared seconds later with a small cherub by his side.

Abigail.

"Lailah!" she shouted, running up to me with outstretched arms.

I bent down as she came into my embrace.

"I missed you!" she exclaimed.

"I missed you, too."

"I've been writing almost every day. I wrote so much that Papa had to buy me another diary, and this time, he let me get one that's pink," she said with a grin.

"Good." I laughed. "Make sure you get one with sparkles and rhinestones on it next time."

She giggled, and I pulled her over to the snack table for a healthy dose of sugar. We joined Jude around the table of goodies and stacked our plates high with brownies and sugar cookies. Jude led me over to a table where he made me sit down and rest.

"I don't want you to overdo it," he said, pulling my legs into his lap.

He pulled my shoes off and began rubbing my feet as I dived into a chocolate brownie.

"Thank you."

I'd polished off an additional cookie or two in record time when Dr. Marcus joined us at our table.

"Nice party," he said. "Didn't think you could actually pull this all off, J-Man."

Jude smirked. "I can be very persuasive."

"I see that, and it turned out great. It's a perfect way to say good-bye to Lailah." He gave a knowing grin.

My eyes widened, wondering what Dr. Marcus was talking about.

Jude and I looked at each other in confusion before our eyes settled back on Dr. Marcus.

"Lailah is being discharged tomorrow."

"Oh my God, are you serious?" I said in one quick relieved breath.

He nodded. "I should have sent you home a week ago, but I was being overly protective. That sickness you came down with scared me, and I just hated the idea of not having you here, but there is no reason for you to stay. We are here if something happens, and if not, we'll just wait for more news regarding the transplant."

I looked back at Jude, and his eyes were full of excitement and anticipation. I jumped into his arms, laughing and crying, as Marcus made his exit.

"I'm going home."

"No, you're coming home with me," Jude said.

"What?" I laughed, pulling back to see the seriousness on his face.

"What are we waiting for, Lailah? Call it a visit or an extended stay. I don't care. All I know is that I want you with me."

My hands came to his face, and I kissed him. "Yes. I'll go anywhere with you."

"Good. Now, let's go find your mom. I want to get the beatdown over with, so we can start packing. I know she's not going to take this well."

"That's the understatement of the year."

I looked around, but I didn't see her. I'd seen her standing in the corner, talking with Grace and her fiancé earlier, but she was gone now.

"Maybe she took a breather," I suggested. "The hallway might be a good place to tell her anyway." I grinned.

"Yeah, that way no one can hear me scream," he joked.

I giggled as we walked out into the hallway and found it deserted. Marching to the end, I turned and heard movement, and I instinctively followed the noise. In a dark corner, two silhouettes shared a passionate embrace. I moved closer, and a gasp escaped my mouth as recognition washed over me.

"Lailah," my mother cried, instantly pulling away from Dr. Marcus as if he were on fire. "I'm sorry. This was a mistake."

She took a step forward, but I held out my hand in an attempt to halt her. I couldn't help the slight laugh that escaped me from finding my mother in a compromising position, considering all the illicit behavior Jude and I had engaged in over the last week or so.

"Please, Mom, don't be sorry. If you want to date my doctor, you shouldn't feel like you have to sneak around hospital hallways and hide it from me. Allow yourself to be happy, Mom," I said with a warm smile. I was suddenly very proud of my maturity.

She and Dr. Marcus gave each other a brief glance filled with emotions I couldn't quite decipher. They both looked hurt and angry and deeply filled with regret, and I could only wonder why. I turned around and took the hand of a very silent Jude, who had his gaze fixed on Dr. Marcus.

"Molly, I can't keep doing this—the back and forth between us and the lying. We need to tell her," Dr. Marcus said with an edge to his voice.

"Please, Marcus, don't," a tiny voice pleaded.

"I'm your uncle, Lailah," he whispered.

I spun around and saw hurt and regret in the eyes of the man who had taken care of me since the day I was born.

"Your father was my brother. We should have told her a long time ago, Molly."

I turned to my mother, waiting for her to dispute it or to offer some other alternative for why they both felt the need to lie to me throughout my entire life. But she didn't say a word. She just looked at me like she'd been mortally wounded.

"Why?" I asked them both. "Why didn't you ever tell me?"

"I wanted to, but it wasn't my secret to tell. But I'm tired of being just a doctor to you Lailah," Marcus said. "And your mother has her reasons. Don't be angry with her. She went through hell and back with my sorry excuse of a brother. The fact that she even allowed me to be a part of your life was more than I could have ever asked."

I shook my head, trying to expel the words and images out of my head.

It didn't work.

"No, I can't handle this right now. I'm being discharged tomorrow. In the morning, I'm going to pack, and I will be leaving—with Jude. Please give him all my discharge paperwork. Mom, I'll come home when I'm ready to talk."

Her echoed cries were the last thing I heard as I left that hallway.

Sometimes, being a grown-up sucked.

CHAPTER TWENTY-TWO
YERTLE THE TURTLE

JUDE

Sleep completely eluded me as I waited for the minutes to pass by until morning came.

I should have told her.

I should have said something the second after it had happened. But I hadn't. I'd walked away from Marcus and her crying mother, holding Lailah's hand as she'd softly sobbed. Then, I'd comforted her as we made our way back to the cardiology floor. I'd helped her take down her hair and wash away what was left of her makeup. She'd changed out of her dress, and I'd held her as she fell asleep.

I never said a word.

I'd known Marcus was her uncle. I had known, and I hadn't told her. I'd kept his secret because, like Marcus, it wasn't mine to tell. Too many cards had been stacked up in this crazy lie, and I hadn't wanted to be the one to bring it to a tumbling crash.

But now, I was stuck in it, and I had to find a way to tell Lailah.

The first rays of sunlight began to stream through my window, and I sat up. I looked around the sparse room, wondering if I would have her here with me tonight or if I'd be alone again.

Only one way to find out.

I jumped out of bed and headed for the shower.

Twenty minutes later, I was throwing a T-shirt on and grabbing an apple as I headed out the door.

It was early, but I knew Lailah would be up with the sun, packing and getting ready to leave. I wanted to be there, helping her. It didn't take long to drive to the hospital and park. A short elevator ride later, and I was at her door. It was open today, and I saw her before she noticed me. Her long blonde hair was loose and falling forward, still wavy from the braids her mother had done. As she folded a shirt and placed it in a pile, I felt like I'd been slapped with déjà vu. On the eve of her last discharge, I'd walked in and watched her do the exact same thing. Finding out she was leaving that day had left me feeling frightened and happy all at the same time. I'd been frightened because she was leaving me and happy because she was finally getting to go home.

Today, I felt all of that and more.

Please don't change your mind. Please come home with me, I silently begged as I stepped forward, announcing my arrival.

She turned and smiled. "You're here early."

"I figured you would be up, so I thought you might want some help packing."

"I do, thanks. Can you get that bag over there?" she asked, pointing to a duffel bag next to the bed.

I grabbed it and placed it on the bed beside her.

"I have to tell you something," I said, my hesitance weighing down every word.

She turned to me with nervousness lining her features. "What?"

"I knew Marcus was your uncle," I admitted.

"How?" She sat on the edge of the bed with the shirt she was folding still balled together in her hands.

"I guessed from the way he'd protect you, how he talked

about you and your mother. He loves the both of you much more than a doctor loves his patients."

"Why didn't you tell me?" she asked, looking up.

"Honestly, would you really want that information to come from me? It wasn't my place to say. I hated knowing it to begin with, but I do know that Marcus and your mother didn't mean to hurt you."

I sat down next to her and took her hand.

"Then, why keep it a secret? I don't understand."

"Marcus said your mother wanted your father erased from her existence. I guess having an uncle around you would only make life more complicated. It was easier if Marcus was just—"

"Dr. Marcus," she finished.

"You need to talk to her," I encouraged.

"I will…soon. I just need some space."

"Well, I can definitely help with that. Come on, let's get you packed."

I pulled her off the bed, and she gripped my shoulders as she rested her head on my chest.

"I was so scared you were going to leave this hospital without me," I confessed.

She looked up at me, confused. "Why? Because of that? You were put in an incredibly tough spot, Jude. I don't fault you for that. But it's over now. No more secrets. So, let's get going already!"

Her beaming smile destroyed me.

No more secrets.

My raspy and pleading voice, the sound of my cries as I'd begged them not to do it, not to take her away from me—it all swiftly came back, making my head spin.

I was the biggest secret of them all.

"Here are your discharge papers," Dr. Marcus said, holding his hand out to a wary-looking Lailah.

She'd been still and eerily quiet since the moment he'd walked in with instructions on her home care.

"We've done this many times before, so I feel like I'm repeating myself. I'm just going to tell you to be careful, Lailah. Take care of yourself. Don't be overly ambitious and find yourself back in this room. You might not believe me, considering how protective your mother and I have been over the years, but I really do want you to have a life outside of here."

She looked up at him from her position on the bed. Her legs were crossed, and I could see the wheels turning in her head as she considered what to say in response.

"Thank you…" she responded. "I don't even know what to call you anymore."

"How about Marcus? Can we start with that?"

She nodded, and I saw the briefest smile pass between her lips before she sobered once again.

"What exactly is going on between you and my mother?"

Marcus let out a lingering sigh as he leaned up against the wall. He looked tired. His salt-and-pepper hair that usually made him look suave and sophisticated now only served to accentuate the lines and dark circles under his eyes.

"The same thing that has been going on between us for twenty-two years. I get too close, and she pushes me away. She refuses to acknowledge that there's anything between us, and I'm foolish enough to keep trying to convince her otherwise."

"You love her," she said softly, looking up at the man who could have been her father if things had been different, if life had been different.

"Every day since the first day I laid eyes on her," he said with such conviction that it made my heart constrict in pain for him.

The CNA arrived, a guy I knew from the day shift, to help escort Lailah to the parking lot, and she stood, facing Marcus with uncertainty.

Finally, she stepped forward and wrapped her arms tightly around his neck. "Don't give up on her, Marcus."

Heavy with emotion, his eyes squeezed shut as he held the girl he'd loved as his own. "I'll never give up—on either of you."

I gathered up Lailah's belongings and helped her settle into the wheelchair. We said brief good-byes to Marcus, promising to check in once a week, and then we headed for the door.

"Jude?" Marcus called on our way out.

I turned and found him standing in the same spot by the bed, watching us leave.

"Take care of our girl."

"I'll guard her with my life," I vowed.

"I know you will. Take care, J-Man."

I caught up with Lailah, who was halfway down the hallway with the CNA, chatting about the beautiful weather. We made our way downstairs, and within three minutes, we were stepping outside.

I thanked the guy, glancing down at his name tag to catch his name, and I helped Lailah up from the wheelchair. "We got it from here, Adam," I said before turning to Lailah with a wink.

She looked around, closed her eyes, and took a deep breath of fresh air as it breezed past her.

"I'm free!" she squealed.

"Well then, why are we standing around and wasting time? Let's get the hell out of here!" I laughed, grabbing her hand and tugging her in the direction of my car.

"I'm sorry it's not that great-looking, but it runs," I said, regarding the less than stellar state of my car, which had probably seen more birthdays than she had.

"It's green!" she exclaimed.

I threw her bags into the trunk. "Yep, split-pea, baby-shit green."

"Eww…gross. Why did you have to ruin split-pea soup for me?" She laughed as we got in.

"Well, that is a color!"

"I think we should name it," she declared.

I turned the key. "The color? I thought I just did." I pulled out of the parking spot and drove the short distance out of the hospital.

We were officially free.

"No." She laughed. "The car. Cars that are baby-shit green need to have a name."

I turned my head with a look of mock surprise and shock. "Did I just hear you curse? I don't think I've ever heard a bad word leave those pretty little lips of yours before in my life. Two seconds out of the hospital, and you're already swearing like a sailor! I think I'm having a bad effect on you."

She stuck out her tongue and laughed. "I've cursed before—in my head and maybe once or twice out loud," she said, grinning. "You're changing the subject. From this day forward, I hereby do so-eth—"

"Do so-eth?" I couldn't help but ask.

She was literally vibrating with excitement. Being out of the hospital had awoken her spirit and had breathed fresh new life into her lungs.

"Shut up! It's my fancy car dubbing speech. I'm supposed to sound like Shakespeare."

"Oh, sorry," I faked a cough as we turned west. "Go on. You do so-eth?"

"I hereby name this car, um…" She looked around, searching, and finally her eyes grew wide. "Yertle the Turtle!"

She was so proud of herself that she didn't even notice where we were when I pulled the car to a stop.

"Very clever, Sam I Am." I laughed. "But Yertle the Turtle was blue."

"He was not!"

"He was," I urged. "In the book illustrations, he's blue."

She looked over at me with her arms folded over her chest. "How the heck do you even know that?"

"My mom used to read to us a lot when I was little." I

shrugged. "And I'm smart," I added with a grin, tapping on my temple.

"Well, whatever. We're calling it Yertle, even if it isn't blue. Now, where are we? And what are we doing?" she asked, looking up. She gasped when her eyes took in the panoramic view of the ocean.

"We're going to put your toes in the ocean."

CHAPTER TWENTY-THREE
COMING HOME

LAILAH

I hadn't lived my life completely in a box.

Living in Southern California my entire life, I had seen the ocean from time to time as we drove around the city. But sitting there in Jude's car, seeing the turquoise water sparkle endlessly before me, I felt like I was seeing it for the first time. My gaze wandered down to the long stretch of sand standing between me and the gentle waves lapping at the coast.

I turned to him. "How? I don't know if I can make it through all that thick sand without having breathing problems or getting too tired," I admitted, hating my limitations and weakness.

"I'm going to carry you," he simply stated.

"The entire way? In the sand?"

"Yep. Now, come on, let's go!"

He pushed open his door and jumped out, and I was left staring at an empty seat. Moments later, he was opening my car door, grinning.

"The water isn't going to make it all the way up here." He held out his hand.

I reached out and took it.

"But that's a long way to carry me, Jude," I said.

He gave me a dubious, amused expression. "You weigh about as much as a box of Cracker Jacks, and in case you didn't notice during all those times when you had your hands shoved up my shirt, I'm in good shape."

His wink that followed was what sent my cheeks aflame, and I couldn't contain the laughter that sprang forth when he lifted me into his arms.

"See? Piece of cake. Now, if you're done complaining, I think we have something to do."

I nodded excitedly, wrapping my hands around his neck, as he cradled me, and we took off down toward the sand.

"Where is everyone? I thought California beaches were always packed," I said, looking around at the very empty beach.

Only a few surfers dotted the shoreline, carrying boards to and from the beach.

"It's early still. The beach will start to fill up in the next hour or two, which is why I wanted to come now. I thought it would be nicer to be here without a thousand people running around."

Gazing up and down the long beach, I smiled. "Yeah, it's peaceful now. I like it."

The sand changed from light to dark as the waves grew closer.

"Can I walk the rest of the way?" I asked, eager to feel the damp sand between my toes.

"Yeah," he said with warm tenderness echoing in his voice.

I kicked off my flip-flops just as he began to slowly lower me to the ground. Our eyes met the second my feet hit the cool sand. It was gritty and wet, and it felt completely wonderful between my toes. Our fingers laced together as a crooked smile tugged at the corner of his mouth. I turned toward the horizon, and we walked the last few steps to the water's edge. The icy water rushed over my toes, and I gasped.

"It's cold!" I yelped.

Jude's deep laughter filled the air. "Why do you think the surfers are in wet suits? You'll get used to it," he promised. "We can walk for just a little bit."

Hand in hand, we walked down the beach, talking and laughing, as others passed by. It was the most normal morning I'd ever had, yet it felt extraordinary and exhilarating. It was a feeling I never wanted to end.

"I didn't think this would happen," I admitted.

We came to a stop not too far from where we'd started.

"I never thought I'd have a day like this, a day where I wouldn't have to think about what others were doing while I was stuck at home."

"We'll have a lot more days like this," he promised, tilting my chin.

He captured my lips. The kiss started sweet and delicate as our mouths brushed lightly against each other. As his fingers found their way into my hair, pulling me closer, while he fisted strands of my blonde waves in his palms, it turned into anything but sweet.

"We need to get off this beach," I urged, pulling away breathlessly.

"Yes, good idea," he agreed.

He grabbed me at the knees, and I was tossed up into his arms. We reached the car, and he set me down.

"Where to now?" I asked.

"We're going home," he answered, his eyes blazing with fire.

And my belly clenched in anticipation.

We drove several miles and pulled into an older apartment building lined with palm trees and a faded wooden sign. Jude pulled into a marked spot, which I assumed was his, and he shut off the engine.

"Stay here, and I'll get your door," he offered before disappearing out the driver's side.

I heard the trunk pop open, and moments later, he was at my door. I took his hand and stepped out, taking a moment to look around. Even though the building was showing its age, it was well maintained, obviously by a dutiful manager or owner.

Our apartment was similar in style and had much of the same feel. The owner had inherited it from his father and strived to make sure his family's legacy lived on. He didn't have much, but he was a loving landlord, and he was always there to help when something had gone wrong. Our appliances weren't brand-new, and our carpet had a few years of age, but everything worked perfectly. I was fairly certain he was undercharging us as well, which was the reason my mom had stayed for the last fifteen years.

Jude walked us over to a flight of stairs and stopped. "Sorry, second floor, no elevator."

"It's okay, Jude. I can manage a few stairs," I said, taking the first one as I pulled him along.

He followed as we made our way up. A cool breeze from the ocean tickled my neck as our feet found the final step, and he turned to the right to take us along the open hallway. Passing by three or four other doors, we came to a stop, and he fished out a key before opening the door.

I peeked inside, seeing a small love seat and kitchen table, as he dropped my bags on the floor in front of me. I'd just crossed the threshold and heard the door shut when he pushed me against it, and his mouth closed over mine. My gasp of surprise quickly turned into a longing moan as his hand skimmed up my bare thigh.

"You have no idea how long I've waited to have you to myself without anyone else around. No distractions," his husky voice rumbled. "No interruptions."

My belly tightened, and my legs quivered from hearing him speak. Just his voice alone had me nearly panting. "And now, you have me," I answered, not believing the bold words that had just escaped my shy, innocent lips.

His lips curved upward as he repeated, "Now, I have you."

His mouth slammed against mine, and I lost myself in his touch. He pulled my thigh around his waist, fingering the delicate edge of my panties running along the curve of my butt under my shorts. Every nerve ending in my body was on high alert as I felt his touch against my skin. His free hand curved around the back of my head, angling it, as his tongue thrust deeper and harder.

A tiny beeping sound behind my ear startled me like a bucket of cold water, and my eyes flew open. I felt the warmth of Jude's hand leave my neck, and then he held it in front of him, looking at a watch. Curious, I looked up at him, waiting for an explanation for the beeping.

"Time for lunch and your pills," he said, pushing a button on the side to turn off the high-pitched noise.

"You set an alarm?" I asked.

"Yep, I have alarms set for each one of your pill times and every meal. I might have put one in there for a once-a-day vitals check."

"You are pretty serious about this." I laughed.

"Nothing will ever be more important than taking care of you. Ever," he said.

Oh…

Well, I couldn't think up much of a cheeky response to that.

I love you. Will you marry me? Yeah, that would probably be a bit too soon.

"Now, stop distracting me with your womanly ways, and let's get you fed and medicated."

He kissed me briefly on the cheek and slapped my butt, which caused me to yelp. Picking up my bags where he'd left them in the middle of the entryway, he started down a hallway, and I followed. There were two doors, which I presumed were the bedroom and bathroom.

He stopped in front of one and turned. "You don't have to sleep with me. You can take the bed, and I'll sleep on the floor or the couch. I don't want to rush you," he said hesitantly.

I took a step forward and then another until I brushed up against him. My fingers moved around his stomach, up his chest, and to his shoulder where the strap to my bag was resting. Sliding my fingers underneath, I lifted it and placed it on my shoulder.

"I'm sleeping with you."

"Thank God," he answered, a relieved breath of air escaping his lungs.

I walked past him, grinning, and entered the bedroom.

Like the few other places of the apartment I'd seen, the bedroom was sparse in its decoration. It fit what I knew of Jude. Alone and lonely for so long, I didn't expect to walk into something out of a Pottery Barn catalog. His room was neat and tidy with no dirty piles of clothes or trash lying around. His bed was made, and he had a small dresser in the corner.

I set my duffel bag on the dark blue comforter and zipped open the top to pull out the giant Ziploc of pill bottles.

"Old people have nothing on me," I joked, opening the top to sort through the different bottles.

He settled down on the bed and watched me. "If they keep you here, in my arms, it doesn't matter."

I found the three bottles I needed for lunch and turned to face him. His hands moved up my legs as I slid into his lap. I loved the feel of his arms around me.

"That's all I want," I said. "To stay in your arms forever."

His arms tightened, and conviction laced his words as he spoke, "You will, I promise."

I only hoped he was right.

———

The alarm on his watch went off two more times throughout the afternoon, and I couldn't help but laugh at his dedication.

"Did you steal my hospital chart?" I asked when the second alarm went off.

"I didn't have to steal it," he scoffed. "I'm a hospital official. I just went in and looked." A grin spread across his face.

"Well, you're not going to wear that watch all the time, are you?" I asked, sinking down into his lap on the couch.

"No," he said softly. "I think I could ditch it at bedtime."

The tip of his nose skimmed the curve of my neck, making me shiver. My lips parted, and my eyes fluttered closed. His hands closed around my waist and squeezed. Then, he lifted me up onto my feet. I opened my eyes to meet his cocky grin.

"Dinner first," he said.

My mouth curved into a pout.

He laughed, tapping on his watch. "Okay, okay...stupid watch."

He grabbed my hand and pulled me in the direction of the kitchen.

"I hope you don't mind, but I thought we'd do another meal in. We can go out tomorrow, but I'm not ready to share you yet."

Yes, please.

"Sounds good," I answered, watching the way his butt moved as he walked ahead of me. I definitely wasn't ready to share him either.

Could I just hold him hostage in here forever?

"Do you want to help me make dinner?"

"Yes, absolutely. Are we making pizza again?" I asked, grinning.

I remembered him saying he'd had to get directions on how to make it, so I was curious on what he was going to cook up tonight.

"Nope, no pizza. We are making baked chicken, mashed potatoes, and green beans."

"Did you go to chef school while I was in the hospital?" I asked, sitting down on a stool he'd placed in the kitchen for me.

After pulling several things out of the fridge, he turned to me. "Asking you to stay with me wasn't a rash decision. I'd been planning it, hoping, and praying for it. I knew you'd get out of that hospital one day, and I hoped that when you did, you'd come home with me, so I wanted to be prepared," he admitted.

"You learned how to cook for me?"

"I just did some Internet browsing. It wasn't that hard. I looked up basic recipes, bought groceries for a change, and tried a few things."

I stood up, took the things he had in his hands, and set them down on the small counter. "You learned how to cook for me."

"Yeah, I guess I kind of did." He smiled.

"I don't know what to do with that," I said in bewilderment.

"Help me." He laughed.

"You got it!"

He made me sit the entire time, but I managed to help wash potatoes and chop them up. Once again, we made a good team, working in tandem as we talked and laughed. A day hadn't gone by where I didn't learn something new about him, and vice versa. Every little new thing I'd learned was like falling in love with him all over again.

DINNER WAS FANTASTIC, AND I THOUGHT EVEN JUDE WAS pleasantly surprised. I offered to help clean up, and he adamantly turned me down. He picked me up and settled me onto the couch to rest. I watched TV until I heard the dishwasher start running, and then I felt his fingers slide up my legs.

"Do you want to watch a movie?" he asked.

"No," I answered, shutting the TV off.

I placed the remote on the floor and gently moved my feet before coming up onto my knees. I crawled over to where he was sitting. He silently watched as I moved over him. I slowly straddled his waist while his hands found my bare skin.

"Are you sure, Lailah?" he asked, his voice heavy with emotion.

"Yes."

The second the word was spoken, his mouth came down on mine—devouring, licking, and tasting me. With his hand around my waist, he stood, and I coiled my legs around him. Our kissing briefly faltered as he stopped along the way to his bedroom to press me against the hallway wall to remove his shirt.

After he stumbled us into the bedroom, he placed me down on the bed. It was the first time I'd seen him completely shirtless, and I took it all in. The dark scrolling pattern going up his forearm continued over his massive bicep and went around his shoulder. I wanted to trace it with my fingers and lick it with my tongue.

"You need to stop looking at me like that," he warned, his expression hooded.

"Like what?"

"Like you want to eat me."

"I kind of do," I admitted, my hands snaking up his chiseled torso.

"Jesus, Lailah," he growled as he hovered above me on his knees. "You're going to kill me."

Fingers danced along the edge of my shirt, lifting it slightly, and he bent down to kiss the exposed skin. His hands slid underneath the fabric and skimmed up the sides of my body with the shirt. I helped, lifting slightly, so he could remove it the rest of the way.

"I need to see all of you," he said as his eyes hungrily took in my simple cotton bra.

There was no staring at the large red scar running down my chest before disappearing into my bra. There were no gasps or dodgy eyes. He looked at me like I was a woman. I wasn't broken and weak in his eyes. I was beautiful, sexy, and sensual.

He removed my shorts, sliding them down my legs, as he placed greedy kisses along my thighs and calves. His eyes wandered up my body, and he watched me as I reached behind and unhooked my bra.

"You're exquisite," he whispered. Leaning forward, he ran his hands over my thighs, teasing the sensitive flesh, then over my hip bones, and across my rib cage until he was palming my breasts. When he pinched my nipple, I moaned, squeezing my thighs together to prolong the pleasure.

He gave me a wicked grin, hooking his fingers into the waistband of my panties, and he slowly dragged them down, removing the last piece of clothing from my body. They fell onto the floor, and his hands drew a lazy path up the inside of my thighs, parting my legs, so he could move in between.

"I don't want to hurt you, so we're going to go slow," he said.

His lips closed over the tight bud of my nipple. His tongue made circles over my rosy flesh, and I gasped out loud when his fingers skimmed my sensitive core.

"Oh God!" I cried as his thumb rubbed my clit.

"Shit, touching isn't enough. I need to taste you again," he growled against me.

He crawled down my body, kissing a wet path as he went. The second his tongue touched my slick folds, I instinctively pushed against him, needing more.

"That's it, angel. Take what you need."

I heard him groan as his mouth licked and sucked at my core, and I writhed and moved against him. Tightening in my belly and tingling up my spine like I'd never experienced before intensified until I was pawing at the sheets and crying out his name. His hands clamped down on my thighs, making me helpless, and then he sucked down hard on my clit. I saw stars, and I might have traveled to another universe.

He crawled up my body and tenderly brushed the hair from my face, and then he bent down to kiss me. "Ideally, I'd love to do that about two more times to make sure you're really ready, but I'm afraid that might kill you in the process," he said with a small grin.

"I'm ready," I answered.

His grin disappeared, and he became more serious as he stared into my eyes. "What's your number one?" he asked as his hand drew shapes down my arm.

"You've already fulfilled it," I answered, evading the question.

"What is it, Lailah?"

"To fall in love," I finally answered, looking up at his eyes with a questioning expression.

Wordlessly, his lips crashed down onto mine, branding me with his kiss. I felt his body lift as he shed his clothes. My hands curled around the curve of his butt and pulled him back down. Skin on skin, his soft green gaze sliced through me, and I knew the depth of his love even without the declaration.

He loves me.

I felt him hard and ready against me, and my heart raced in anticipation.

"I need you to tell me if I'm hurting you. If you feel weak or—"

"Jude," I said, gripping his arm, "I'm not going to break. Please, make love to me."

His eyes softened and warmed. "Always," he vowed.

Reaching into the drawer by the bed, he grabbed one of the condoms he'd bought as a precaution. I had a birth control implant in my arm for years, but considering pregnancy was basically a death sentence for me, he wasn't taking any chances. I watched as he broke the wrapper open with his teeth and pulled the condom out. The whole process kind of fascinated me. I couldn't help myself from reaching out to help him, and I started to put it on. His strangled gasp startled me, and I quickly pulled away.

"Having you touch me is like tugging on a pin of a grenade. I'm about to explode," he said, taking my hand back to his cock.

I wrapped my small fingers around his large girth and watched as his eyes closed, and his head fell back.

"Stroke it," he commanded.

I moved my fisted hand up his bare shaft and back down again. He groaned, and his eyes flew open.

"I need to be inside you." Taking over, he quickly finished sheathing himself with the condom and pushed me back onto the mattress.

Our eyes collided as I felt the tip of him hit my wet core.

"Say it, Lailah. I want to hear the words."

He pushed in slightly, and I felt my body tighten around him.

"I love you," I said.

He moved slowly, inch by inch. "Again," he demanded.

I felt him enter me completely. There was a slight pain, but when he pulled back, slowly moving inside me, it quickly changed from pain to pleasure.

"I love you," I moaned.

His head fell, and he kissed my neck as he pushed my knee forward. It changed the pleasurable feeling to intense, smoking-hot bliss. I cried out, gripping his shoulders, as he began to thrust slow and deep into me.

His body was magnificent, even more so when it was making love to me. He moved with grace and raw masculine power. Every thrust was exotic and thrilling to watch. I ran my hands everywhere—over the curves of his butt, the deep V of his hips, and around the wide expanse of his shoulders.

His mouth returned to mine, his tongue moving in the same rhythm as his body. A hand snaked between us and went to the sensitive spot between my thighs, pressing down, as he moved against me. Every time he slammed into my willing body, his thumb hit my throbbing clit.

"Oh God, I'm going to…" I cried, feeling everything in my body tighten.

He moved faster, harder, and our bodies began slapping together in a fast-paced tempo. I climaxed, and my body tightened around Jude just as I felt him go rigid above me. Groaning, he kissed me furiously.

Some time later, he got up and went into the bathroom to get rid of the condom. When he returned, he collapsed onto the bed and tucked me into his side. I wrapped my legs around his and kissed his chest. We cuddled while talking, laughing, and kissing into the late hours.

"I want to take you somewhere tomorrow," he said.

I started to feel sleep taking me under.

"Okay," I answered with a yawn.

His fingers gently stroked my hair, and his warm lips on my forehead were the last things I remembered before I fell asleep.

CHAPTER TWENTY-FOUR
TIME TO SAY GOOD-BYE

JUDE

Sleep had never come easily to me in this place. Ever since the night I had rushed into the ER, cuts and bruises scattered across my body as I'd screamed Megan's name, the ability to drift out of consciousness and find peace had eluded me.

If I was being honest with myself, sleep and I hadn't been friends for quite a long time before the accident. I couldn't count the number of sunsets I'd watched blaze into the horizon, morning after morning, as I had counted down the days until graduation. It had felt like doomsday. The clock had been ticking, and freedom would soon be over. Like most of our friends, Megan had been thrilled. After four years, we had almost been done. All our hard work had paid off, and after crossing that stage with a fancy degree in hand, we would be set to go out and tackle the world—together.

Late at night, I would hold her as she slept. I'd watch the way the moonlight hit her dark chestnut hair and the way a small smile formed on her lips as she dreamed. I would watch her, and I'd worry. I'd worry about everything I'd so neatly kept from her over the years. As far as she had known, I was going to work for my dad. It had been what most of our friends were doing as well, so it should have been no big deal. Except, I wouldn't have been going to work for my dad. I would have been handing my freedom over to him on a silver fucking platter. He'd shown me the status of the company, and we hadn't been doing well. They had been counting on me to turn things around, and it wouldn't have happened overnight.

My life had been about to change drastically, and I hadn't even told her.

Would she have hated me? Would she have resented me for bringing her blind into a situation?

I had planned on telling her everything after our trip to Hawaii, but I'd never gotten the chance.

She'd died, believing our life would have been perfect, and God willing, I would have given everything to make it so.

Am I making the same mistake with Lailah by withholding the truth about Megan's accident?

As the first light from morning cast its rays through the bedroom window, I looked down at the angel sleeping in my arms. Her long blonde strands fell across her body like a golden silk sheet, and I couldn't stop myself from bending down to kiss her bare skin.

Her eyes fluttered open, and she smiled.

"Good morning," she said softly, her voice still groggy from sleep.

"Morning," I replied. "Sorry, I didn't mean to wake you."

"You can wake me like that anytime." She grinned shyly, stretching her body in an innocent way that looked anything but. Her arms went above her head, which accentuated her bare breasts and hips. She arched her back and lifted her knees while she let out a small sigh.

"What?" she asked as she curled back into me.

"That was the sexiest thing I think I've ever seen."

"What was? Me stretching?" she asked. "You're insane."

Reaching out, I placed my hand on top of hers and guided it across my stomach and down to the apex of my thighs, letting her fingers brush against my sensitive skin under the sheets. When fingertips reached my hard and ready cock, she gasped.

"Does that feel insane to you?" I asked.

I didn't expect her to answer my question by touching me nor had I anticipated her eager small hands to boldly reach out and grip my shaft.

"Shit!" I cursed through my teeth.

Her hand stilled, and she looked up at me. "Was that wrong? Am I supposed to grip it harder...or softer? I'm sorry. I suck at this, don't I?"

Her hand was still gripping me, and I was going to pass out soon if she didn't start moving her palm again.

"You know I love it when you babble. It's damn cute. So, please don't get mad at me when I say this, babe," I said before pausing. I waited until she met my gaze. "Shut up, and for the love of God, please keep going."

Red stained her cheeks, and a sly grin spread across her face. "Like this?" she asked as her blessed hand moved back up my dick and slid back down.

My head fell back as I groaned. "Yes," I answered.

I was so completely taken by the feeling of her hand moving up and down my cock to notice that she was moving, shifting around, until her body was facing me. I felt her knees brush against my thighs as she straddled me, and I looked up.

"Those books you got me in the library," she started, rubbing a slow circle with her thumb on my sensitive tip. "They were very educational in certain areas of study...and I'd like to, um...try something," she said, the blush spreading further down her neck.

"I thought we were going to read those books together," I joked, positioning myself up on my elbows so that I could watch her stroke me.

"Maybe later," she replied. "But I wanted to read a couple first by myself."

"Why?" I asked.

She leaned forward, her eyes still trained on me. "So I could learn to do things like this," she answered.

She bent forward, and I watched her tongue dart out before licking my shaft from root to tip.

"Holy fuck!" I shouted as her warm, wet mouth closed over my cock.

Eyes the color of ocean water met mine as her mouth moved up and down, her cheeks hollowing as she sucked and licked. There was no hesitation, no second-guessing or doubting herself. She was fierce and confident as she loved me. I watched every single second, and it was sexy as hell.

"I need to be inside you, Lailah," I managed to say.

One last lick, and she was crawling up my body, scattering kisses up my torso and chest. Her hair fell forward as soft pink lips found mine, and a beautiful sun-kissed cocoon of golden strands surrounded us.

I reached into the drawer next to the bed and grabbed a condom from the box I'd bought. This was something I would never forget. I'd read Lailah's chart backward and forward. I knew the risks if we ever forgot this simple step. Other men could risk an accidental pregnancy with their girlfriends but not me, not when it could kill her.

Reaching down between us, I slid on the condom and then brushed my fingers along the inside of her thighs. She was already wet and ready for me.

"Are you sore?" I asked, softly rubbing my thumb over her clit.

"No," she answered softly, the blush slowly returning to her cheeks.

She'd just given me a blow job—her first, no less— that had damn near killed me, and she was now blushing over the mere mention of us making love last night.

The pads of my fingers danced across her pink cheekbones. "Never lose this. I love the way you look when you blush," I said, gazing up at her.

I positioned myself and joined our two bodies together once again. Her look of pure rapture would stay with me until the day I died. Her eyes unfocused as she pushed back against me.

"That's it, angel," I coaxed.

Her hips began to grind back and forth against me. My hands ghosted up her thighs and wrapped around her waist as I sat up. I wanted to touch her everywhere, all at once, and brand myself to every inch of her skin. Being inside her, feeling her wrapped tightly around me as she wound her body around mine, felt like coming home. She was the solace I hadn't realized I was searching for. She gave me strength and peace and a reason to watch the sun rise again.

She continued to ride me as I met her thrust for thrust while I gripped her shoulders and slammed into her with wild abandon. Always conscious of her health and how quickly she could get tired, I grabbed her and flipped us, so she was on her back against the mattress. Eyes locked, she wrapped her legs around me as we moved together. She moaned and cried out as my thumb grazed the sensitive flesh of her clit.

"Oh God, I'm going to come!" she screamed seconds before she tightened around my cock. She broke apart, shaking and crying out my name.

It was like music to my fucking ears.

Every thrust I made while she climaxed sent me spiraling closer and closer to my own release. As the orgasm took over her body, she squeezed my cock like a vise until I lost control, slamming into her. Fireworks exploded as my body came so hard that I collapsed down beside her.

Lying on my side, I lightly kissed the smooth curve of her shoulder before reaching up to briefly touch my lips to hers.

"You said you wanted to take me somewhere today," she said.

I smiled. "Yes, I do. But first, I think we need to make a trip to the library."

Her eyes widened as her lips rounded with humored shock. A pillow was launched at my face seconds later.

Probably deserved that.

"Why are we back at the hospital?" Lailah asked as we pulled into the familiar parking lot.

"This is where I wanted to take you," I answered before stepping out of the car.

I went around the front to grab her door.

"You know I've been here a few times before, right?"

She smiled as I took her hand, and we headed toward the entrance.

"Yes, smart-ass, I know that, but you haven't been to where I'm taking you." I brought our joined hands to my lips, and I kissed each knuckle.

As we approached the double doors, I stopped and turned toward her. "This is something I need to do…" I started before taking a long deep breath. "To move forward. I want you to be with me."

Her expression turned tender, and she nodded. "Of course. I don't want to be anywhere else," she answered.

She silently followed behind me as we made our way through the hospital and down to the lonely long hallway I'd claimed as my own. When we reached the wide wooden beach, I stopped and turned to face the closed door of my past.

"This was where she left me," I said, "where she took her last breath."

The doctors, her parents—they were all wrong.

They didn't understand, they didn't realize how strong she was, how strong we were.

She would fight.

She would fight for us.

Because if she wasn't here, I wouldn't know how to go on. I couldn't face this life without her.

"Son, it's time to say good-bye," Megan's father said through choked tears as his hand rested on my shoulder.

I looked up to see red-rimmed eyes staring down at me. His eyes reminded me so much of his daughter.

"No," I whispered, my head shaking back and forth, as tears poured down my face.

She wasn't dying.

She couldn't.

We had to get married.

I looked down to her empty ring finger where I'd placed her engagement ring not two weeks earlier. The paramedics had cut it from her hand in preparation for surgery, and it had never been returned.

This couldn't be happening. Any second now, I'd wake up, and Megan would be lying in my arms. She'd be happy and whole, and all of this would be nothing more than a terrible nightmare.

But deep down, I knew there was no waking up from this.

"We're going to give you a few minutes alone with her," Megan's mother said before a door clicked.

I looked around the sparse room. It beeped and hummed as Megan slept before me. Her head was wrapped in white bandages, and bruises and scrapes covered her perfect skin.

Gently taking her hand, I traced the lines of her palm and watched her features for some sort of response. But like the hundreds of times before, there was nothing.

"Please come back to me," I begged. "I can't do this. I don't know how to say good-bye to you."

My head fell forward, and I kissed our joined hands.

Loud beeping and alarms jolted me upright, and I watched as nurses poured into the room, trying to push me out of the way.

Megan's parents rushed in, and I watched as her mother collapsed to the floor, crying out in agony.

With my hand still clutched in hers, everything happened in a blur, and soon, the nurses and doctors slowed before turning toward us with blank expressions.

"I'm sorry. She's gone," the doctor announced.

"I never got to say good-bye," I said, turning toward Lailah as she took my hand. "I think I've been refusing to do so ever since. I can't tell you the number of hours I've spent in this hallway, staring at that door while sitting on this bench. I wasted years here." A strangled laugh escaped my lips. "God, she would kick my ass if she knew how I ended up."

"You're not that person anymore," Lailah reminded me. "She would be proud of the man you are today, and the journey you took to get here."

Reaching up, I caressed the soft skin of her cheek. "It brought me to you. But now, it's time I say good-bye," I said, turning toward the bench. "I lost contact with Megan's parents after I refused to attend the funeral. I wasn't in a good place back then, and the only way I knew how to cope was by pushing everyone I knew away. They didn't deserve that. They were always so good to me. They had this bench put in place when they found out I was still here. I guess they thought it might help me mourn in some way. I'm not even sure I understood the meaning of the word until recently."

She took a seat, and I watched her fingers trace the golden edge of the plaque that had been placed the day before.

"*Life: It goes on.* It's a Robert Frost quote," she said as her fingertips brushed across the elegant script.

I joined her on the bench and smiled. "Yeah, she loved that quote. She had it taped on the visor of her car as a little reminder to keep going when things got tough. She was a constant force of positive energy, and she never would have wanted me to let life pass me by while I sat in this hallway, waiting for her to come back."

"Thank you for sharing this with me," she said, skimming her hand over the shiny brass one last time. "Thank you for sharing her with me. But like you said, it's time for you to say good-bye, and I think that is something that should only be shared between the two of you. Pour out your soul, Jude. I'll be waiting outside."

She kissed my cheek briefly, and I watched her disappear down the hallway.

I didn't know how much time had passed as I sat there. I stared at that closed door—thinking, breathing, waiting for the words to come. People shuffled past as I tried to find the right way to say good-bye to the woman and the life I'd been holding on to for far too long.

"I would have given you everything, Megan. You would have been my world, my wife, and my reason for existing. There wouldn't have been a single moment I would have regretted," I whispered into my palms as I cradled my head.

"But life had a different plan for us, for me. And now, I have to say good-bye," my voice cracked as I said the words. "I met a girl. She pulled me out of the darkness, and I can't stay here anymore. I can't stay here with you and love her at the same time. She deserves all of me, and I want to give her everything. So, please believe me when I say I love you. I love you enough to remember you for the woman you were and for the beautiful life we shared. I love you enough to let you go, so I can live the life you'd want me to have. Every minute I have on this earth is even more precious because of the time I spent with you."

I stood, taking one final look at the plaque I had placed in her memory. Kissing the pads of my fingers, I placed them against the cool metal on the back of the bench.

"Life—it really does go on, and I'm going to live mine now. Good-bye, Megan."

Every step down that hallway felt final, another footfall into my future. My eyes dried as I moved up in the elevator. As I turned toward the exit, I saw her sitting on the concrete bench, waiting for me.

God, she's beautiful.

Our eyes met as she stood, and I strode out the double doors.

I pulled her into my arms. "I love you, Lailah," I said breathlessly. "I've loved you longer than I can remember, but

I couldn't ever find a way to say it until now. Now, I want to say it over and over—"

"Stop babbling"—she grinned—"and kiss me."

I pressed my lips to hers as I gently lifted her off the ground and spun us around. Her laughter and squeals quickly filled the air.

"Come on, let's go home," I said, letting her feet touch the ground once again.

"I like the sound of that."

"Yeah, me, too."

CHAPTER TWENTY-FIVE
DATE NIGHT

LAILAH

"Let's go shopping," Jude said one lazy afternoon while we were lying on the couch, watching a movie.

"Shopping?" I said, pausing the movie. I looked up at him from my very comfortable position in his lap. "Why? We just went grocery shopping yesterday."

"I want to buy you a dress and take you out to dinner," he answered before bending his head down to kiss my forehead.

"You don't have to do that. You've already done enough."

It had been over a week since I moved into Jude's small apartment. It'd been a week since I spoke to my mother. As much as I loved my new living arrangement, I couldn't help but feel guilty about a number of things. A twist of regret and longing would hit me every time I thought of my mom, and I wondered how much damage I had done to our relationship after walking away from her that night. But as terrible as I felt, I couldn't bring myself to pick up the phone and call her. I needed to apologize, but my damn pride was getting in the way.

Why does she always feel the need to protect and shelter me so much?

The more I thought about it, the more I began to realize that it might not be me she was protecting after all, but rather herself.

Living with Jude had also brought out the guilt of not being able to contribute anything financially. I hated that feeling. I was twenty-two years old, and I'd never had a job or gone to college. I didn't have a single dollar to my name. I felt like a freeloader. Jude might have been born to wealth, but he wasn't living a lavish lifestyle anymore. He didn't have money to throw around, and part of me worried how he could afford another person in his life.

"I want to. Besides, you can't tell me going out on a date isn't on that list." A sly grin spread across his face.

"Well, considering I showed you the entire list in bed last night, I'd say you already know the answer to that question."

His grin widened. "Yeah, I do, which is why we're going shopping. Come on, get up. Let's go!"

"Okay, okay!" I laughed, rising from the couch. "I should have never shown you that notebook," I grumbled.

I felt his hot breath on my ear as he spoke, "I remember I was very persuasive, and I wanted to make sure a certain number was thoroughly crossed out."

He turned me slowly around, so we were face-to-face. His hands slid down my back.

"I think we've done a pretty good job on that one over the last week." I grinned.

"Just trying to make you feel as normal as possible." The dimple in his cheek appeared. "A hot young thing like you? How could I possibly be around you all the time and not want to be fucking you every single second of the day?"

His bold words left me breathless.

"See?" he said. "I'm just keeping it real."

"Uh-huh," I managed to say.

A slap to my backside brought me out of my lusty trance.

"Come on," he laughed.

He grabbed the keys off the counter, and we headed out, immediately feeling the warm summer breeze blowing past us as we exited the apartment. Southern California had been having a bit of a heat wave over the last week. Rather than being greeted by the comforting cool ocean breeze that was one of the advantages of living so close to the coast, we were all being bogged down by the stifling heat.

"So hot," I said as we got into the blazing hot car.

"Let me turn the air on. At least that works in this pile of—"

"Hey! Be nice to Yertle! He will hear you!" I said, rubbing the worn dash lovingly.

Jude shook his head as we pulled out into traffic. "I have no idea why you love this car so much."

"It's yours. Why wouldn't I love it?"

He didn't answer, but I saw the corner of his mouth curve into a small smile.

Several minutes later, we arrived in a popular area in Santa Monica that was well known for little boutiques and great restaurants. He didn't bother asking me where I wanted to go. He knew I'd say some place cheap like Old Navy, or I'd ask if there was a Target around. He was so right. I was already scamming the area for the big red bull's-eye.

About a block down, he pulled us into a fairly large store. It didn't have that stuffy, cramped feeling many others had as we'd walked past them, and I wasn't bombarded by sales-clerks the minute I'd walked in, which was a plus in my mind. They also had a clearance rack.

Score.

"Really? You go straight for the sales?"

"You can't blame me for being thrifty. Besides, it doesn't matter if it's fifty percent off and looks like this." I held up the dress I'd spotted at the door, and I watched his eyes bug out of his head.

"Try it on—now," he demanded.

I searched for the dressing room and made a beeline to the entrance. Eye contact was made with the store clerk, and she ushered me to go ahead. Jude took a seat just out front. I pulled the curtain back, lifted my shirt, and slid my shorts down my legs.

"Nice," I heard from beyond the curtain.

I snorted out a laugh and shook my head as I unzipped the dress from the hanger. It covered my scar perfectly, and it tied in a bow just at the nape of my neck. Nearly backless, the vibrant summery pattern gathered at my waist and flared out in an asymmetrical pattern. It felt light and airy against my skin, and it did amazing things to my slight figure.

I took a deep breath and turned, facing the curtain. I slowly pulled it back, revealing myself to Jude. His gaze lifted, and I watched his surprised expression change into raw hunger.

"I think the zipper isn't up all the way in the back," he said, swiftly rising from his chair.

I looked down immediately and turned to check.

"What? Yes, it is. Oh—"

The curtain was yanked shut, and his mouth slammed down on mine. He pressed me up against the cold mirror, and anxious hands slid under my dress. I grabbed fistfuls of his hair, pulling him closer, as his tongue moved against mine, over and over, relentlessly,

"Is everything okay in there?" the clerk hollered from outside the curtain.

My hands froze, and our frenzied kisses slowed. A wicked grin appeared on Jude's face seconds before he reached up and snapped the tag from the dress.

"Go pay for it," he said, handing me his wallet. "I'm going to grab your clothes, and I'll be out…in a minute."

I looked down to the impressive bulge in his pants, and I had to bite my bottom lip to keep from laughing before I left to pay the weary-eyed cashier.

"Oh my God, we almost had sex in a dressing room!" I

giggled into his shoulder as we walked arm in arm down the street minutes later.

"I was perfectly in control. I don't know what your problem was."

I playfully smacked his chest as we continued our goofy banter down the block. We stopped at a quiet little Italian restaurant. There was a bit of a wait, so we headed to the bar and took a seat.

"You can order something if you want," I said, motioning to the bartender on the other side of the bar.

"I don't need anything."

I placed my hand on his. "Just because I have limitations doesn't mean you have to."

"It's not that," he answered. "I haven't had a drink since the night of the accident. I just can't."

Nodding, I smiled warmly. "So, water for both of us?"

His eyes crinkled together. "I think I'll be daring and go with a Coke."

"Oh, crazy."

We ordered our drinks, and after twenty minutes, Jude began to get impatient.

"I'm going to go check on our table. I'll be right back." His hand brushed across my back, and then he vanished into the crowd.

I was left swirling the ice in my cup, waiting for him to return.

People sat around the bar, laughing and joking, oblivious to how lucky they were to have moments like this. They were completely unaware of how incredibly blessed they were for the normalcy they had in their lives.

Then again, I was finally having my chance as well.

I was finally the lucky one.

"You look awfully lonely, sitting there, all by yourself," a deep voice said from behind me.

Smiling, I thought Jude was playing a trick on me, but I turned to find an older broad-shouldered man standing behind me. His neatly trimmed dark hair and dazzling white smile startled me, and I wondered for a moment if he was actually speaking to someone else.

"Excuse me?" I replied softly.

"I said, you look awfully lonely. Can I buy you a drink and join you?"

"Uh…I am actually—"

"She's spoken for," Jude's baritone voice filled the air as his possessive hand slid across my shoulder.

The man looked immediately put out, and his gaze narrowed in on Jude. "Well, I think she probably has a say in that, doesn't she?" he said smugly, looking down at me like he expected me to shove Jude and throw myself at him instead.

"I'm definitely spoken for. Thanks," I answered, turning to Jude and forgetting all about the man with the bleach-white smile.

Jude's hands cupped my face, and he shook his head. "Five seconds. I leave you alone for five seconds, and they're on you like vultures."

"I got hit on!" I exclaimed with a slight high-pitched thrill in my voice.

He rolled his eyes. "That was one thing on your list I really could have left undone. Or better yet, I could have just done it myself. In fact, let's just say I did it first and forget this ever happened."

"Aw, poor Jude," I said before sticking my lip out in a fake pout.

He shot forward and bit my lip before sucking it into his mouth for a dizzy kiss. "Mine," he growled. "Let's go eat."

M'kay.

"You invited my mother over?" I repeated for the second time since he'd announced it.

We'd just finished our amazing dinner, and we'd hopped into the car when he dropped the mom bomb on me.

"Angel"—he turned to me after starting the ignition—

"Grace can't stay with you tonight, and you know I can't leave you alone while I'm at work."

I might have rolled my eyes as he backed out of the parking space.

"I called her this morning, and she really misses you."

Guilt? Party of one!

"Well, she hasn't bothered calling," I said gruffly, crossing my arms over my chest.

"She said she wanted to give you the space you requested, but it's been killing her. I think she's been sneaking updates through Marcus."

"That just figures," I grumbled.

He gave me a warm smile as he made a right turn at a stoplight.

"Oh, fine!" I said, caving to his silent torture.

"I know you want to see her."

"Yeah, I do," I admitted.

"Good. It's only a few hours. I managed to get a short shift tonight, so I'll be home by midnight."

I nodded as I watched while he killed the engine and opened the door. I looked around and noticed my mother's car a few spots over. The driver's side door opened, and she appeared.

"Hi, Lailah," she greeted me.

We walked up the stairs to Jude's apartment. We stopped at the door, and she awkwardly wrung her hands together, uncertain what to do next.

"Hi, Mom," I answered, stepping forward to wrap my arms around her.

She melted, her hands moving around my back, snug and sure. "I missed you," she said, pulling back to take a look at me. "You look beautiful."

"Thank you. Why don't you come in?" I offered.

She nodded as Jude unlocked the door, and we stepped forward. I watched as she appraised the apartment. Over the last week, I'd managed to make it look a little less dismal. A few pillows and blankets on the couch, and the lack of boxes definitely helped.

I offered her a spot on the couch and turned to Jude.

"I've got to get to work, but I wanted to give your mom this," he said, handing off a plastic bag and a piece of notepaper. He turned to my mother. "Her meds are in there, and I wrote down what she needs to take and when just in case it's changed since the last time she was home."

I thought my mother's respect for Jude tripled in that moment as she looked down at the clear bag and silently nodded.

"Thank you," she replied.

"You got it."

I turned to him, and he gave me a quick peck on the cheek.

"I have a change of clothes at work, so I'm going to go. You two have a good night," he said with a smile before heading out the door.

I joined my mom in the living room and watched in curiosity as she quietly gazed down at Jude's handwritten note regarding my meds.

"He's really anal." She let out a short laugh as a single tear ran down her cheek.

"Just like you," I answered before watching her face crumble. "Mom?" I said, moving closer to her. "What is it?"

"It's nothing, nothing I can't fix."

She was lying. Her features were giving away that much. She'd obviously been doing everything in her power to keep it all together. She was like a jar of sand. It looked so strong on the outside, but just a tap in the right spot, and everything fell apart.

"Mom, please. You've spent your life hiding things from me because you thought you were protecting me. Look where it's gotten us. Tell me," I pleaded.

Her eyes met mine, and I saw complete devastation.

"Your transplant was denied."

I couldn't breathe. The air around me felt too heavy, too gritty, to possibly grasp and swallow down my shallow windpipe. My eyes frantically went to the door where Jude had just left through, and I suddenly wanted to rip it wide open and scream his name to come back.

I need him.

I need him to…what?

Tell me it's going to be okay? Because it's not.

None of this is okay.

I looked back at my mom, wide-eyed, with tears running down my face as she waited for me to say something.

"Denied?" I repeated just to make sure I heard the word from my own lips.

She nodded. "But we're going to appeal it. They can't do this. They can't. We will fight. They don't understand what we've been through, what you've been through. I'll explain. I'll explain everything. I'll make them see. Marcus will explain, and we will get them to change their minds."

All her words sounded like white noise. A buzzing in my ears just kept getting louder, stronger, and sharper.

I needed it to stop.

I needed it all to stop.

I wrapped my arms around her and let her sob as she repeated over and over that she would find a way to save me.

I didn't listen. I didn't hear any of it.

I was done being saved.

CHAPTER TWENTY-SIX
DECISIONS, DECISIONS...

JUDE

Leaving Lailah at night was my least favorite part of our new living arrangement. I'd briefly thought about putting in a request for the day shift, but with her mom and Grace available at night, it made more sense for me to continue working the night shift.

I still hated it.

I hated not falling asleep with her at night, and I hated knowing she was sleeping alone in our bed.

I raced up the steps of our apartment building and smiled, thinking of how quickly everything had become *ours*.

Barely two weeks together, and she had ingrained herself to me, body and soul. Even the idea of sending her to her mother's for a night sounded so horrible that I'd actually asked the woman to stay here instead just so I wouldn't have to sleep a night without Lailah.

I quietly unlocked the deadbolt and stepped inside. Molly was asleep on the couch, and after a few nudges, she came awake.

"Hey, I'm home. You can stay here if you want though," I offered.

She rubbed her eyes, which looked red and puffy, as she yawned. "No, I'm going to go home. You two need some time alone, I think," she said, placing a tender hand on my shoulder.

I looked down at the gesture with a curious gaze. *Okeydokey.*

She saw herself out, and I locked the door behind her, shaking my head at her odd behavior.

Maybe she was just tired. Maybe she decided she finally liked me.

Probably not.

I *was* sleeping with her daughter after all.

Tugging my shirt over my head, I snuck into the bedroom and stopped when I saw Lailah was awake, sitting upright in bed.

"Hey," I said. "What are you doing up? It's late."

"Couldn't sleep," she answered vacantly.

Joining her on the bed, I slipped under the covers and cupped her chin. "Everything okay between you and your mom? She seemed a little off when she left a few minutes ago."

"Yeah…no," she answered, her utter calm never wavering. "I'm always this problem that needs to be fixed. Why can't I just be her daughter?"

"Angel, please, you're freaking me out."

"My transplant was denied," she finally said.

"Lailah, no." My voice cracked.

I pulled her into my arms, and she willingly came. I tried pushing down the rising panic I felt with her sudden announcement.

"We'll figure it out, okay?" I said. "This isn't over. I'm sure there is a way to appeal it."

"I don't want to appeal it," she said quietly against my chest.

My heartbeat faltered at her words, and I pushed back

against her until I saw those baby-blue irises. "What do you mean, you don't want to appeal it?"

"I'm tired of fighting, Jude," she huffed. "They denied me once. Why would they suddenly approve me? This new insurance company isn't like my old one. They don't want to fork over the cash. How many more months am I going to agonize over an appeal just to see it denied again? I can't take it anymore."

"You're giving up?" I whispered, completely stunned.

"It's not giving up. It's just accepting what is."

I stepped away from the bed, the anger rising so fiercely that I wanted to punch the wall in. "And what exactly are you accepting? That you're dying?" I yelled, turning back toward her.

She visibly flinched. "I just want to enjoy the time I have left, Jude."

My head began furiously shaking back and forth. "No, no, I don't accept that."

"It's not your decision."

Tears stung my eyes. "This is all my fucking fault."

Her tender touch brushed against my bare shoulder. "This isn't your fault. You had nothing to do with this, Jude," she said.

"I had everything to do with this," I replied, pulling away from her. "I'm the reason you didn't get that first transplant, Lailah. I'm the reason you're still here, waiting for one."

Her head turned to the side. "I don't understand."

"Megan," I answered. "Megan was supposed to be your heart. You said it happened three years ago on Memorial Day weekend. That was when the accident happened. Megan's parents wanted to donate her organs—or the ones that weren't damaged. She was severely brain damaged, but her heart was in perfect condition."

"No, it's not possible," she said, her voice distant.

"Yes, it is. They knew she was gone, but I didn't. I begged and pleaded with them to reconsider. I told them they were killing her. I said I could bring her back. I did everything I could to change their minds. It worked, Lailah. I'm the reason you didn't get that transplant."

I didn't know how long she sat there, staring at the stitching of the comforter, as I waited for her to say something, anything.

"Please, Lailah, yell at me, scream at me, tell me to get the hell out. Do something, anything but give me silence," I begged.

Her eyes met mine, and they nearly cut me in two.

"When you came to my room, did you know who I was?"

Falling down on my knees in front of her, I took her hand. "God, no, I had no idea. I didn't put it all together until later."

"Was I some sort of project? A way to get rid of your guilt?" she mumbled.

"Jesus, Lailah," I cursed as my head fell to the mattress. "No...maybe...I don't know." I lifted my head. "At first, yes. Maybe I felt responsible and acted out of guilt, trying to make amends for what I'd done...but not anymore," I said. "Not anymore."

Her long hair moved back and forth as her head shook against her palms. "I don't know what to think anymore."

Crawling up beside her, I took her hands in mine, holding them against my beating chest. "Know that I love you. Know that this is real—what I feel for you. Know that you must fight for it. Fight for us, Lailah. Don't give up."

"It's not giving up to want to spend the rest of my life with you," she said softly. "Regardless of how we met or what brought us to this moment, I want to spend every minute I've been given with you, Jude. That's not giving up. That's living."

"It is giving up when that life is being cut short! Don't you get it, Lailah? Don't you see? You're my fucking life. I might have survived Megan's death, but if you leave me, it will obliterate me. Life—it doesn't go on without you."

Tears poured down her cheeks as she met me halfway. Our kiss became frenzied and lacked any sort of finesse. It was raw and powerful. As our clothes hit the floor and our bodies became one, I looked into her eyes, into her soul, and I begged her to stay with me, begged her not to leave me in ruins.

I didn't know why I awoke, but a few hours before dawn, I came to with an overwhelming feeling of dread. Looking around the room, I felt around the bed until I found Lailah's sleeping form. She was lying still, a little too still. Her breaths were shallow and short.

"Lailah," I said, shaking her.

Her eyes slowly opened, and that was when I began to panic.

"I don't feel good," she said, clutching her chest.

"Where's your oxygen tank?" I asked, jumping out of bed to flip on the overhead light.

Her tank was in the corner, and I quickly set it up, positioning the mask over her head.

"My heartbeat is erratic," she said through the plastic covering her mouth.

"I'm calling Marcus," I announced, grabbing my phone from the nightstand.

Five seconds later, she passed out.

"Shit! Lailah!" I yelled, punching 911 into my cell.

I stayed calm and collected, my training kicking in, as I cradled her in my arms. She was thankfully breathing, but it was slight and not nearly enough.

"Come on, angel, stay with me," I pleaded before kissing her pale lips.

I waited for the paramedics to come. Within minutes, the ambulance arrived, and we were being transported to the hospital. I held her hand the entire way as they started her IV and took vitals.

Marcus met us at the entrance of the ER, having rushed in after my panicked call. They let me follow her back into a room, but I was quickly left alone when they wheeled her away for tests.

Hurried footsteps came toward the door, and I looked up to see Molly standing there, breathless.

"Where is she?"

"They just took her back for some tests."

She nodded, stepping forward to take the empty seat next to me. I was honestly surprised that I wasn't being bitched out. I fully expected to be blamed for this entire event. Looking back on the evening, I worried I might have pushed her too much—dinner and shopping, the lack of sleep, all combined with the way we'd torn into each other just hours earlier.

"What happened?" Molly asked quietly.

"I woke up, and I just felt petrified. I looked over and heard her shallow breathing. I woke her up, and as I was calling Marcus, she passed out."

She shook her head and dropped it into her hands. "It's my fault, telling her about the transplant. It was too much stress. I never should have told her."

"No, she deserved to know."

"It's just so hard not to protect her from everything," she said softly.

"I know," I answered.

We sat there in silence, waiting for her to return. The cheap plastic clock slowly ticked by the seconds on the wall, reminding us exactly where we were and why we were here.

"I wanted to hate you," Molly said suddenly.

I turned to her and watched her brows furrow together.

"When you first showed up, so young and slick-looking, I thought you would break her heart. No one could possibly understand the cost of loving a girl like Lailah. Yet, you stayed, and I realized something yesterday. You just want the same exact thing I do."

"And what is that?" I asked.

"To keep her here, no matter the cost."

I placed my hand on hers. "We're not going to lose her. No matter what, I promise you that."

She opened her mouth to respond, but the door swished open, and a woman appeared, wheeling Lailah behind her.

"Hey," she said weakly.

That one word was like a precious blessing from heaven. She was awake.

"Hey back," I answered, rising from my chair to take her hand. "How are you?"

"I'm okay. Been better, but I've been a ton worse, too. Marcus said I probably just overdid it—maybe a bit too much salt for dinner and lack of sleep—but he's running some tests just in case."

Squeezing my eyes shut, I shook my head. "I'm so sorry. It's my fault. We should have stayed in."

"We're not playing the blame game, Jude. This is how it goes with me. Sometimes, I have bad days, and yesterday was just one of those. It's going to happen more often since…"

My head jerked up as my eyes widened.

She couldn't possibly still be considering it—not after last night, not after I'd spilled my soul. Looking over at Molly, she glanced at Lailah and then to me. Her head tilted to the side as she tried to figure out what was going on.

"Jude, could you give my mother and me a minute?" she asked.

My gaze wandered back and forth between her and Molly, I finally settled back on Lailah and gave her one final silent plea. *Please don't do this*, I begged with my eyes.

I drifted out of the room in a daze and walked to the other side of the hallway where I let my body slide down the wall until I hit the floor. Staring at the closed door, I waited, wondering what she was saying, what she had decided.

Three minutes later, I had my answer.

Loud wailing sobs echoed through the hallway as Molly had been delivered the devastating news of Lailah's decision to forgo any further attempts at an appeal.

Sitting on the floor in a lonely hospital hallway with my back pressed against the wall, I felt my life ending—for a second time.

Irony is a bitch.

She can't do this. Screw her and her sense of independence. I made a promise to keep her alive, no matter the cost.

No matter the cost.

Jumping up, I reached into my side pocket. Pulling out my cell, I dialed the one number I never thought I'd need again.

It rang three times before the bastard picked up.

"Hello?" the familiar deep voice answered.

"Roman, it's me."

"Jude?"

"The prodigal son returns," I replied through clenched teeth.

"Does this phone call mean you're ready to come crawling back?"

I could hear the sneer crystal clear over the airwaves.

"I've seen the news, jackass. Don't act like you don't need me."

"Listen, little brother, you left us high and dry. Dad's mind has gone to shit in the last two years—early onset dementia. The board members are calling for my head, so please excuse me for not groveling at your fucking feet."

"Dad is sick?" I said.

"Yeah, asshole. You would know this if you bothered checking on your family."

"Why isn't it in the news?" I asked.

"Because I've kept it out of the news," he spit.

Of course he did.

"Look, I'm sorry I didn't call and check on things. I was fucked-up, but I'm ready to come back."

"Don't do us any favors, Jude. I don't need a visit. I need someone who is willing to go the distance. If you've seen the news, you've only seen half of it."

I took a deep breath. "I'll come back—for good. But I have stipulations."

"I'm listening," he answered.

"We're going to run things my way this time. What I say goes. Do you understand?"

"If you can save this company and keep everyone employed, I'll fucking make your coffee in the morning, brother."

His concern for the employees surprised me. Maybe my brother had actually grown since I left.

"And I want access to all my accounts—immediately. No questions asked," I said.

"Done."

"Good," I breathed out in relief as I braced myself against the wall currently holding me up. "I'll see you in a few days."

"You're making the right decision, Jude," he said.

I hit End, severing the call before I had the chance to change my mind.

There was no right or wrong decision here. Either way, I was fucked.

Lailah would live. I'd just guaranteed that.

I just wouldn't be here to see it.

"She can't know," I pressed as Marcus and I sat in the dark cafeteria.

"All this time," he said, looking at me in a completely different way. "I should have known. You never belonged here."

"I was exactly where I was supposed to be," I answered.

He nodded, pain etching his tired features. "She'll never believe it. The insurance company would never grant an appeal, not now. She knows that. Why do you think she's given up?"

"Make her believe it, Marcus. I don't care what you do. Lie, call it an act of God, say you called in a personal favor. I don't give a flying fuck. Make her believe the impossible happened. And Molly—"

"I'll take care of Molly," he said. "She's stubborn as a mule, but when it comes down to it, she'll do what it takes to save her daughter."

He placed his coffee on the table and looked up at me. "Why don't you just tell her?"

"She'd never let me go through with it. I saw the conviction in her eyes last night, Marcus. She's made peace with it and accepted her fate. I can't allow that."

"What if you destroy her in the process?"

"You and Molly will be here to pick up the pieces," I choked out. "And she'll be alive."

"You know we can't stop her from going after you once she's recovered."

I shook my head, my stomach churning in disgust. "You won't need to. After tomorrow, she won't want to see me ever again."

CHAPTER TWENTY-SEVEN
THE AFTERMATH

LAILAH

Telling my mom had been harder than I thought.

Seeing her break down in front of me, knowing I'd caused it, had nearly torn me in half. I'd been her world for as long as she could remember.

Keeping me alive had become her life.

And I'd basically just thrown that in her face and said, *No, thanks.*

I knew they all thought I was giving up, and in a way, I guessed I was.

But it was my choice.

Mine.

I was done being coddled and given half-truths. I was a grown woman, and it was time I started acting like one. If I had only a limited time left on this earth, I would choose how to spend it.

Me.

Not anyone else.

In the short time I'd known Jude, he'd given me a taste of what life could be like if things had been different, if I had been born normal. It was bittersweet, knowing what kind of life we could have had, and my soul ached, knowing it was something we'd never have. But growing up abnormal, apart from society, I knew I had to be thankful for the time I had been given.

And I wanted to spend that remaining time with Jude, not fighting for something that was never meant to be.

A knock on the door pulled my attention upward, and I watched as Jude walked in, reminding me of all the times he'd done so in the past. I had been moved upstairs, back into the cardiology unit, and even though I was in a different room than I had been previously, it still brought back fond memories to see him enter.

The day had passed in a blur, and I'd slept most of it away. The moonlight now lit up the room, casting a warm glow on his tanned skin.

"Just couldn't stay away," he said, pulling a chair up to the bed. His mood was heavy even though his words were light and joking.

"Well, they do have pudding here," I joked, attempting to pull a smile from his lips. "Marcus said all my tests came back fine, so I should be good to go in a day."

"Good."

His fingers laced with mine, and I watched his brows furrow together.

"Talk to me, Jude. I know you're upset about what I decided, but I—"

He rose from his chair and crawled next to me on the bed.

"I don't want to talk right now," he whispered, lifting the hem of his shirt over his head and dropping it to the floor.

My hands eagerly reached out to touch him, moving over his chiseled lines and defined muscles. "What if someone walks in on us?" I asked, my gaze slowly rising to meet his.

"I sent your mom home for the evening, and Marcus is on his break. As for anyone else, I just really don't fucking care."

His daring words excited me, and I moved to quickly shed my clothes, but his hand steadied me.

"No, let me," he said.

As if we had all the time in the world, he took care in removing each piece of clothing, watching in utter fascination as each tiny part of me was revealed.

"I could spend a lifetime staring at you," he breathed against my skin.

His lips kissed every inch of me until I was moving uncontrollably against him. He pulled a condom from his wallet and shed the rest of his clothes. Pulling the blanket over us, he gently settled himself over me. Every touch felt deliberate—like he was memorizing each curve and valley with his palm, like he was already losing me.

"Hey," I said, turning his chin upward. "I'm still here. Be here with me."

He didn't say anything. Instead, he answered with a torturous long kiss that I felt down to my toes. My fingers dived into his hair, and I pulled him closer, needing more.

"Slow," he said against the crook of my neck. "I need slow tonight."

It was so different from the frenzied, passionate love-making we'd done the night before. He'd been nearly frantic, overcome by emotions and anger. Tonight, I still felt the emotions in him, swirling under the surface, but they were different.

As he cradled my face, looking into my eyes with such love and devotion, I struggled to find the puzzle piece I seemed to be missing.

"I love you, Lailah Buchanan," he chanted.

He thrust deep into me, causing spirals of bliss to ricochet through my body.

Never breaking his agonizingly slow pace, he stayed steady, burying himself deep, as his mouth captured mine. His hands caressed my milky shoulders and squeezed my round breasts before finally sliding down to grip my hips as he continued to move against me. I felt my body clamp down, and I moaned, our kiss muffling my cries of passion, as Jude jerked against me, finding his own relief seconds later.

We redressed, and I curled up next to him once again, loving the warmth his body gave off. I never felt cold when I was in his arms. I drifted off to sleep, his arms closed around me, and I felt safe.

I HAD A DREAM.

Jude and I were walking hand in hand through an airport. With smiles plastered across our faces, we proudly handed over our passports to be stamped.

We got the keys to our rental, and with no directions or instructions at all, we hopped in our tiny toy car, laughing as Jude's head hit the roof. We were exhausted from our flight but so exhilarated and happy. We were here—finally.

He reached into a backpack and pulled out my old notebook before flipping through pages and pages of crossed-out dreams.

"The last one," he said, holding a pen out to me.

I looked down and saw, among the dark blue and black lines, number seventy-two sat untouched.

"Have my heart broken?" I said, looking up at him in confusion.

He smiled and nodded. "It is the last one. We wouldn't want to leave anything undone."

"But I thought..." I stumbled on my words as I watched his expression twist into something sinister. "You promised..." I whispered.

"I lied."

I woke up, startled, my arms reaching out...searching for him.

He was gone.

My hands brushed my arms briskly, trying to warm away the chill I had in his absence. I looked around the dark room, hoping to find his sleeping figure somewhere, but he was nowhere.

Out of the corner of my eye, I spotted something on the

tray table next to my bed. As my gaze shifted, I saw the small pudding cup with a plastic spoon beside it.

I smiled and picked it up before holding it against my chest like a prized possession. It was then that I saw the letter underneath.

In Jude's angular handwriting was my name written on a plain envelope.

My hand shook as I opened it.

> Lailah,
>
> Please know this is the hardest thing I've ever done. Loving you has been the brightest, most peaceful time of my entire life.
>
> Losing someone you love— I can't even begin to describe what that feels like. When Megan died, I died with her. I didn't think I'd ever come back from that.
>
> Until you.
>
> You showed me how to love again, how to live again.
>
> You gave me a reason for existing.
>
> That is why I can't stay here and watch you die.
>
> Because if I do, I don't think I'd survive.
>
> I'm sorry,
>
> Jude

The note crumbled in my hands as tears soaked my cheeks.

Closing my eyes, I remembered his tortured gaze and lingering touches as we'd made love last night. He'd known. As I had been trying to figure out why he was so melancholy, he had been saying good-bye with every kiss, every last caress.

And now, he was gone.

An echoed sob tore through the silence as the reality of my situation solidified.

He'd left me all alone.

No, he'll change his mind. He just needs time.

I searched around the room for my cell.

I'll text him and tell him to come back, so we can talk it over.

Once I explained my reasoning to him again, he would understand.

I jumped out of bed and found my backpack that Jude had packed for me. I rifled through it, finding clothes, toiletries, a journal, and my notebook.

But no cell phone.

It was gone.

He'd taken it.

Stopping dead in my tracks in the middle of the room, the enormity of what had happened finally came crashing down on me.

Jude was gone…and he wasn't coming back.

I turned back around, feeling wobbly on my shaky legs, and I pulled the notebook from the backpack on the floor. I walked aimlessly back to the bed. Pulling a pen from the drawer next to me, I opened it up and found the number I'd just dreamed about. As tears dripped onto the page, I dragged the pen along the paper and crossed out the one thing Jude had promised he'd never allow.

I pulled the notebook to my chest, curling into a ball, and I fell asleep with my newly broken heart.

THE COMFORTING WALLS OF MY CHILDHOOD ROOM NOW FELT claustrophobic and confining.

I used to lie in the hospital and dream of the soft feel of

my own sheets and the crisp smell of my mother's fabric soft-
ener on my pillow.

Now, as I stared up at the white popcorn ceiling and I felt
my legs drag against the freshly laundered soft sheets, it only
served as a reminder of what I was missing.

Jude's sheets never smelled like anything but Jude, and
they were anything but soft. Scratchy and cheap, the blue
fabric had several holes from years of use. But none of that
had ever bothered me because I was in his arms, safe and
warm in his arms.

Since he'd left, I hadn't felt warm in days. California was
on the verge of record heat, and I was burying myself under
piles of blankets, trying to replicate the feeling of his warm
embrace.

Nothing had worked.

Nothing would ever replace him.

No one knew where he was. He'd quit his job at the hospital, and Marcus had said Jude's apartment was empty.

He'd vanished without a trace.

A knock on my bedroom door signaled my mother's
hourly checkup. Between her and Grace, I was never alone. I
was perfectly healthy—for someone who was slowly dying.
But my emotional health was worrisome, according to
Marcus.

No shit.

I was not to be left unattended.

So, I had babysitters—again.

"Hey, sweetheart. I brought dinner," my mother said,
balancing a tray between her hands.

"Not hungry."

"Lailah, you have to eat," she pushed, placing the tray
down beside me.

I sat up, crossing my legs, as I looked down at the plate.
"Macaroni and cheese?" I inquired. "I can't have that."

She smiled. "I got a recipe online. I was able to make a
low-sodium version."

My face grimaced. "Awesome."

She huffed. "Come on, Lailah. I'm trying. You barely eat. You won't talk to anyone, and you cry yourself to sleep. I don't know what to do. Ever since he—"

"No! We're not talking about him," I said, raising my hands in protest.

"Fine. But you need to at least eat. I'm worried."

Tears trickled down her cheeks, making my chest tighten.

"I'm sorry, Mom. I'm going to be okay, I promise. I just need time. And see?" I picked up the fork. "I'm eating."

"Good." She gave a weak smile. "Can I stay here with you?"

I nodded, scooting over to make a spot for her on the bed. I grabbed the remote and flipped on the TV. I figured watching something mindless would be far better than conversation.

Nope. Definitely wrong.

My gut twisted as the food in my stomach suddenly turned sour. There, on the nightly news, in bright HD quality was Jude in a polished three-piece suit, walking into the towering skyscraper of Cavenaugh Investments. Cameras and microphones were being shoved in his face, and he pushed them away.

The caption at the bottom read, *Elusive Cavenaugh Son Returns to Spotlight.*

"Jude!" a reporter shouted. "Where have you been?"

"Is the recent downfall of your family's company the reason for your sudden reappearance?" another yelled.

He turned swiftly to address the crowd with glaring confidence. His eyes stared into the camera that was dead ahead, and my heart flip-flopped at the sight of him.

He looked regal. His tattoos were covered underneath the expensive fabric of his tailored gray suit. His hair had been cut shorter, accentuating his chiseled jawline and pale green eyes.

"While it is true that Cavenaugh Investments has had its

share of hurdles in recent years, like most Americans, I can assure you, we are on the mend. My number one priority at this time is my family and the thousands of people we employ. Thank you," he said, turning back, severing my view of his face.

I watched the last few seconds as the cameras followed him. Reporters shouted more questions that he ignored, and then he disappeared behind the double doors.

The TV shut off, but I continued to stare at the black screen.

"Are you okay?" my mom asked.

"No," I answered honestly.

At least I had my answer. I knew where he was. He'd returned home, back to his normal life and far away from me.

I was too hard to love, too difficult to be around.

He'd chosen the easy path, the safe route.

I guessed I had, too.

CHAPTER TWENTY-EIGHT
BOXES

The minutes ticked by as I sat in my office, staring at the computer screen.

Things were far worse than Roman had let on.

Financially, the family was still well off, thanks to the mastermind who had been my grandfather, but the company was failing.

If I hadn't come back when I had, layoffs would have been imminent. Even still, I would need to be pretty damn creative to keep people in their current jobs.

My eyes drifted up to the clock again and then back down to my phone.

Five minutes.

I tapped my pen against the glass desk, silently waiting, as the last few minutes wasted away, knowing I wouldn't get shit done until my phone lit up.

Seven o'clock on the dot, Marcus's name flashed across my screen.

I immediately picked it up and answered, "Hey."

"Hey, J-Man."

"How is she today?" I asked.

I could almost hear the smile through the phone line.

"You're like a broken record."

"Marcus."

"Okay, damn. She's okay. She's finally eating. Grace and Molly have been staying with her around the clock, and she's slowly returning to the land of the living."

"It's been three weeks."

"Yeah, I understand, but you left her—in the middle of the night. How did you expect her to react?"

Leaning back in my ridiculously overpriced leather chair, I pinched the bridge of my nose. "When are you going to tell her?"

"Tomorrow. I'm going over there for dinner, and Molly is going to announce that she sent in the appeal, and it went through."

"Think Lailah will believe her?"

"I don't know, but that's why I'll be there. I'll help back it up."

"Good."

"She's not happy," he confessed, his voice sounded tired and full of regret.

"That makes two of us. But I'd rather have her hate me and live a long, healthy life than have her love me and die tomorrow, knowing I could have done something to stop it."

"I hope you know what you're doing, Jude," he stressed.

I ignored his comment entirely. I didn't know what the hell I was doing anymore.

"You have the money. Make it happen. I'll talk to you tomorrow," I said before ending the call and tossing the phone onto the desk.

"You know, when you asked for immediate access to your bank accounts, I didn't think twice about it," my brother said as he entered the office. Hands in his pockets, he leisurely walked to my desk and took a seat in front of me. "Rich kid on the streets for several years? I just figured you'd had enough. But now, I wonder, what did you need all that money for, Jude?"

"None of your fucking business," I answered, rising from my chair.

His eyes wandered up my exposed forearms where the dark ink of my tattoos showed. "All right, but it will be my business if it turns into something illegal."

Bending down, I placed my hands on the desk in front of me, so I could meet his smug stare. "Like you're one to talk, jackass."

He flew out of his chair, and his face came inches from me. "Don't you dare judge me, Jude. You weren't here. You left me with a fucking loon of a father and a board who thought I was a moron. Well, it turns out, they're right. I'm good for one thing—public relations. Put me on a magazine, shove me in front of a camera, and I'm golden. But ask me to run a company, and this is what you get—absolute shit. So, congratulations, brother. I hope you enjoyed your extended vacation, pretending to be a commoner in California. This is your goddamn fault. Have fun cleaning it up."

I jumped over the desk, and my fist went flying, punching him hard across the cheekbone. He went flying. "You have no fucking clue what I've been through, what I gave up to be here!" I roared, pinning him down to the floor.

His lip was bleeding, and his eyes were fuming with hostility. "Seems we have a lot to learn about each other then," he hissed.

I pushed away from him, and I paced around the room. "Just get the hell out of my office—and leave me alone."

Wiping the blood from his lip with his collar, he got up and walked to the door and stopped. "You know, if this is going to work, we're going to have to work together. You might be smart, Jude, but you don't know shit about the public side of this company. As far as anyone knows, you've been in a cave for the past three years, and they're all dying to know why. We've got to give them something."

"I'm sure you'll figure something out," I sneered.

And I'd be damned if he didn't.

I woke up the next morning to see my face plastered all over national news.

"Next up, Jude Cavenaugh's tortured past. We have an inside look at how losing his fiancée turned this young man into a recluse."

"You've got to be fucking kidding me," I muttered, throwing the remote across the room.

I got out of bed and maneuvered around the untouched boxes toward the kitchen. Since arriving in New York weeks ago, I'd been staying in this furnished upscale apartment that Roman had found for me, and I still hadn't unpacked a single box.

Moving in would make it too real, too permanent, and I was having difficulties coming to grips with my new reality. It was the reason I counted down the minutes each day until Marcus called to check in, and it was the reason I still hadn't visited my parents after being home for three weeks.

Dressed in loose-fitting pajama bottoms, I made my way into the sleek, modern kitchen, shaking my head at the size of it. Why Roman had thought I needed all this was beyond me. He always had been over the top. His own apartment was twice this size and three floors up. We were practically roommates.

I started a cup of coffee and walked briskly over to the door where the weekend paper had been delivered. For three years, I'd lived virtually off the grid, and now, I couldn't go five minutes without turning on the news or picking up the newspaper.

I made a quick breakfast, grabbed my coffee and paper, and sat down at the table, prepared to read all about me and whatever clever story my brother had managed to whip up overnight. Flipping through, my fingers tabbed the crisp pages, and I had the briefest flash of Lailah lying in her hospital bed, reading one of her worn paperbacks, her fingers thumbing the frayed edges. She loved books, real books, just like I loved real newspapers. Something about the smell and feel of the words right in front of you was irreplaceable.

Like her.

My chest ached from that one tiny memory, and I no longer cared about what the paper said. Roman could do what he wanted—paint me as the poor, grieving broken man —but it wouldn't change anything.

I was here, and she wasn't.

I might have been that broken man after Megan had died, but Lailah had saved me, and now, I was saving her—by being here.

Food forgotten, I cleaned off my plate and walked up to a lone box standing in the corner of the vast living room. Taking a deep breath, I cut it open with a knife and slowly began the process of coming to terms with my new reality.

Breaking down the last of the boxes, I folded and hung the few clothes I had side by side, next to the closetful of suits my brother had had waiting for me upon my arrival. How he'd gotten my measurements I'd never know.

Seeing my old clothes stacked up next to my new ones was odd. My ratty old T-shirts, worn and faded with years of use, were next to priceless suits from top-of-the-line design-ers. As I stood there in my towel, readying myself for my first visit to my parents' house in over three years, it was like looking at two halves of myself—the old and the new.

But which was old? And which was new?

My entire life, I had been raised for one thing—the family business.

You are this company's future, my father would tell me as I traipsed behind him as a young boy.

It had been what I wanted, what I was good at, until the pressure got to be more than I could handle.

My three years in the hospital had taught me that I could be more than what I had simply been raised to be.

Now the question was, could I be both? Do I even want to be?

Looking at the closet again, I reached out and grabbed the nicest T-shirt I could find, deciding to bench the internal debate for another day. I had a family reunion to attend.

For as long as I could remember, our time growing up had been split between Manhattan and what my parents would describe as the country. For most of the year, my father had lived and breathed work, and during those times, which always seemed to coincide with school, we would live in the city. Although my father had been absent much of this time, my mother had been very atypical of our high-society life-style, and she'd immersed herself in the lives of my brother and me. When I hadn't been with a tutor or the occasional nanny, I had been with her. Growing up in a place like New York could be stressful on a shy kid, but she'd made it like a game, a giant mystery the three of us were employed to solve.

During the summer, however, when my father had taken much-needed vacation time, we'd be whisked away to the summer home upstate. It was there, in the country as my parents had called it, that I'd found my real childhood home. Far away from the noise and chaos of city life, everything had moved at a slower pace out there. Even my father's relentless drive had lessened in that house. I'd see him go on evening walks with my mother, pick roses for her in the garden, and laugh with her while they sipped lemonade.

As I drove out of the city that Saturday afternoon, heading down the winding roads toward the house my grandfather had built and passed down to our family, I realized I'd never get to bring Lailah here. I'd never walk her through the gardens my parents loved or pick roses for her like my father once had for my mother. It was the first time I doubted my decision.

Two long lives without each other—is it worth it?

Turning off the road, I drove down the tree-lined driveway until I came to the main gate. Hoping my security code hadn't been voided, I entered the six-digit combination and waited. The click of the gate had me lurching forward again. Apparently, they had retained some hope after all.

After entering the gate, the view was still as breathtaking as I remembered. Intricately laid bricks made a circular path down the palatial estate of my childhood memories. It still reminded me more of a castle than a house, but as a kid playing hide-and-seek in the cupboards and hallways, it hadn't mattered what it was called as long as I wasn't the one getting caught. If it weren't for my mother, I didn't think I would have gotten those rare moments away from tutors and textbooks.

The front door opened as I pulled up front, and I saw tears leaking from my mother's eyes as her hands went to her mouth. She'd aged since the last time I saw her. The dark blonde hair she'd always kept perfectly styled was now gray around the edges and cut short. Tiny lines had formed around her green eyes, and she'd traded her designer pantsuits for something a bit more casual.

Rising from the car, I slowly walked the short distance to where she stood.

"My baby boy," she choked out, lunging into my tight hold.

"I'm so sorry, Mom," I said, apologizing for everything from being a selfish person to a horrible son.

"You're here now," she replied, taking a step back. Her eyes roamed over me. "That's all that matters. Let's go inside, shall we?"

Her arm still linked in mine, I followed her through the double doors, taking a deep breath as I entered. There was always a faint smell of lemons and fresh flowers in the entry-way. As the smell hit my senses, I couldn't help but travel back a ways to long-forgotten summer days when Roman and I would torment the cleaning staff as they had spent hours polishing the ornate wooden banister.

"It hasn't changed a bit," I commented, taking a look around at the circular foyer.

A large bright bouquet of flowers sat in the center on an antique table that had been my grandmother's.

"No, not here," she said sadly. "But in other places, yes. Your father and I live here permanently now. We sold the penthouse in the city two years ago when…"

I nodded, not needing further explanation. Roman had already filled me in on the physical demise of my once formidable father. Early signs of dementia had set in a few months after the accident, and my mother had made the decision to relocate to the country, tucking him away from the board. It must have been obvious to the investors that my father wasn't well, but Roman had believed that the board held out hope I'd return and take over instead of my brother.

"I missed you," she said.

We took a seat in the grand living room together.

"I know. I missed you, too. I just had to…I couldn't come back."

"You don't owe me an explanation, Jude. I can't begin to understand what you went through when Megan died. It hurts me that you didn't come to me. It does, but I will never hold that against you. A heart does what it needs to in order to heal. Please tell me you've allowed yourself to do so?"

"Yes," I answered. "I was finally able to say good-bye."

She took my hand in hers. They felt softer, thinner than I remembered.

"Then, why do you look so destroyed?"

"It's a long story."

"No story is ever too long for a mother to hear." She smiled.

I didn't know where to start, so I started at the very beginning. I told her about the accident and losing Megan—how I'd never gotten to say good-bye and the pain I'd caused by forcing her parents out of the organ donations.

"They didn't reconsider after she passed?" she asked.

"No," I replied. "Megan's mother was so broken by her

death. I don't think either of them had anything left to give at that point."

I told her about my work in the hospital, about moving up and obtaining my license. She actually smiled and seemed proud.

And then, I told her about Lailah.

I told her about the way Lailah lit up a room, how she babbled when she was nervous, and that she had the most amazing heart—the most amazing broken heart of anyone I'd ever known.

"She's dying," I managed to say.

I went on to explain, detailing our late-night pudding conversations and how I'd discovered I was the reason she'd missed out on her first transplant.

"How did she even know?" she asked.

"Her doctor. He's her uncle. In his blind love for her, he told her before it was official."

"She should have never known."

"I know, but she does, and I can't blame Marcus for loving her. It's an easy thing to do," I said.

I moved ahead and told her about what Lailah had decided after the denial from the insurance company and why I'd left.

"Jude, I admire what you did, and I'm so grateful to have you back in our lives again. But are you sure you made the right choice?" Her expression was warm and comforting.

I looked down to the floor, gathering my thoughts. "If you had the choice, right now, between spending a lifetime alone or a single year with Dad, which would you take?"

"The year," she answered without hesitation.

I nodded without looking up. "But what if it were in reverse?" I questioned, meeting her gaze. "What if you had to choose for him? Only one year with you or a lifetime, Mom? Would you choose differently?"

Her lips pursed together, and I knew she understood.

"Why does it have to be one or the other, son? Why can't you have both?"

"Because I can't be in two places at once," I answered.

CHAPTER TWENTY-NINE

IT'S TIME

LAILAH

"You filed an appeal?" I bellowed, slamming my salad fork down on the hard wooden surface of my mom's solid oak dining table.

She startled slightly from the noise, and I watched her eyes widen in surprise.

"Yes, um…" she stumbled before blotting her lips with her cloth napkin and sitting up in her seat. She glanced over at Marcus, who had suspiciously joined us for the evening. With a nod, she turned back to me. "I know you asked us not to, honey, but this is your life we're talking about, and I—we couldn't just sit around and do nothing."

I looked at the two of them. "So, both of you were in on this?"

They nodded their heads.

"When?"

"When what?" Marcus's brows furrowed together.

"When did you submit the appeal?"

"A day or two after Jude left," he said.

My heart fell at his answer. For a split second, when they'd mentioned an appeal, I'd thought Jude might have been behind it as well. He'd been so angry, so firm against my decision, that I just thought maybe he would have done something.

I hadn't wanted him to, so I didn't know why it saddened me that he hadn't.

"So, you submitted an appeal. What now?" I asked, picking up my fork to push a grape tomato around the bed of greens on my plate.

"Nothing."

I looked up at my mother, who was smiling.

"What do you mean, nothing? Did they already deny it?"

"No, Lailah. They approved it."

My fork tumbled from my fingers, falling to the floor with a clattering clank. My eyes stung with repressed tears as I jerked them from Marcus's jubilant expression to my mother's.

"Approved?"

They both nodded, rising from their chairs with open arms that wrapped around me.

"Are you sure?" I asked as the emotional dam broke, and moisture dampened my cheeks.

"Yes." They laughed. "We're sure."

"But why?"

"I don't know. Change of heart. Divine intervention?" my mother said.

I looked up at her with a dubious expression, and she laughed.

"Who cares? It's approved!"

"Oh my gosh! I can't believe it!"

My mom took my hand, pulling me up from the chair. "Come on, I made something special for you. It's in the kitchen."

We all followed her into the small galley kitchen and watched as she moved things around in the refrigerator. Finally, she turned to face us, proudly displaying a bowl full of homemade chocolate pudding.

I stared at it, frozen in place.

"I always saw the empty containers in your trash can at the hospital, so I figured you had a thing for it even though those store-bought ones are so high in sodium. Really, Lailah, you should know better."

Flashbacks of Jude pulling out tiny packs of pudding, his dimple etched into his megawatt grin, before we spent the night talking over our spoonfuls of chocolate. The night he'd fed me in the hospital, and my stomach had turned into butterflies came blazing back and then fizzled into a moment not too long ago when we'd spent an evening in his apartment, licking the sticky dessert off each other's bodies.

"I'm actually not that hungry," I blurted out, turning my head away to flick away the tears that had begun to trickle down my cheek. "Maybe some popcorn later though?" I added quickly, looking up with a fake smile plastered on my face.

My mom nodded, looking over at Marcus, who just shrugged.

We settled down onto the couch and watched a movie together. Eventually, Marcus did make a bowl of popcorn. No one touched the pudding. I thought it had been blacklisted even though neither of them understood why.

It had been nearly a month since I'd seen him, felt his touch on my skin, and heard his deep voice whispered against my ear. Every minute had felt like a year. I'd always thought watching time go by in a hospital bed was agonizing. Seeing the seconds tick by without Jude was hell.

I couldn't turn on the television without eventually running into his face. He was everywhere. He was like the lost city of Atlantis for the financial world. Even the Hollywood gossip magazines and TV shows were picking up on it, taking photos of him on the street, as they told the story of his tragic past.

Will Jude Cavenaugh find love again?

The world all wanted to know.

"Will you tell him?" my mother asked.

I looked up to find her staring at me. The TV was off, and Marcus was gone. Two hours had gone by, and I had stayed locked up inside my head.

"Who?"

She raised her brow as if to say, *Really?*

I gave an exasperated huff. "No," I answered. "He left me, Mom. He wasn't strong enough to stay when things got hard. Just because I have the approval doesn't mean the road ahead is paved in gold. What if he came back, and the transplant didn't take? Would he leave again?"

"I don't know," she answered as sorrow etched her features.

"He chose his own life, and now, I guess I'm choosing mine—alone."

WAITING FOR A HEART TO BECOME AVAILABLE WAS A LOT LIKE waiting on a natural disaster. I knew it would eventually happen, but I didn't know when, and I didn't know how.

For weeks, I was glued to the phone and pager the hospital had provided.

After the third week, I started to lose hope.

It's never going to happen.

"It will happen, Lailah. Give it time," Marcus encouraged as we sat on the couch one evening, watching *The Vampire Diaries.*

"I know. But will I be sane by then?"

"Probably not, especially if you keep watching this ridiculous show. Seriously, it's horrible."

I hit pause on the remote and turned to him. "Say you didn't mean it."

"What?" He grinned.

"Turn to the screen, look deep into Damon's gorgeous blue eyes, and say you didn't mean it."

"Um…"

"I'll call you Uncle Marcus," I sang, causing him to laugh.

"Fine," he grumbled. He repeated the words, which were nearly inaudible due to the amount of mumbling.

"That was terrible, but I'll take it. Damon and I forgive you. Now, quiet, Uncle Marcus, and finish the show with me," I said.

I must have dozed off after the show had ended because I was suddenly being shaken awake.

"Lailah, wake up."

"What?" Why? Just let me sleep here," I protested.

"The hospital just called," Marcus said. "It's time."

I jolted upright, looking around the room, until I found him standing in front of me. My mom was racing around the apartment, packing things into a duffel bag. Absolute fear took over as I watched her.

This is real. No more waiting for the phone to ring.

It is happening—now.

I could die. I could die on that operating table, and this could be my final moments with my family.

I'd die never seeing his face again.

"Lailah, breathe," Marcus said gently, pushing my head to the floor, between my knees. "Deep, slow breaths through your nose," he instructed.

"I don't know if I can do this," I cried out.

Every single procedure, surgery, and test came racing back at that moment. I remembered every minute of recovery time, every second of pain.

"Oh God," I moaned.

Suddenly, I wasn't staring at Marcus's feet anymore but his face. Kneeling down, he grasped my chin and centered me.

"You are the strongest person I know, Lailah. UCLA has some of the best surgeons in the country. You're going to do just fine."

"Okay," I said weakly, nodding my head.

He cradled me in his arms like a child.

My mother followed us as we walked to the car, and he tucked me in the backseat. I stretched out and rested my head against the cushion as I watched the two of them work in tandem, throwing bags in the car. Marcus drove and pulled out of the complex. My mother was bent over her phone, her fingers furiously dancing across the keys. I didn't think I'd ever seen her use it for anything other than brief conversations.

"Who are you texting?" I asked.

"Grace," she answered, stopping briefly, before continuing again.

I realized, sitting in the back of that car, that this was probably the closest thing I'd ever have to knowing what it was like to go into labor. I'd watched my loved ones run around on my behalf, making frenzied calls and text messages, before the rushed late-night car ride to the hospital. The only difference was, at the end of the day, the only new life would be mine.

What would I do with it?

Within fifteen minutes, we were pulling into the UCLA medical plaza parking lot and walking through the glass doors of the transplant center. After signing about a zillion forms that I honestly didn't pay attention to, we headed to a room and waited for the surgeon.

Already dressed in scrubs and booties, a middle-aged man greeted us a few minutes later, shaking my hand firmly and introducing himself as Dr. Westhall.

"Nice to meet you," I answered softly.

He turned and did the same greeting to my mother. Then, he perked up when he saw Marcus.

"Good to see you again, Marcus."

"You, too, Todd," he replied.

"So, this is your niece?" Dr. Westhall said, taking a casual seat in the free chair near the door.

"Yes," Marcus answered. "She's the closest thing I have to a daughter, so please take care of her."

He smiled and winked. "We're going to fix you up good as new, sweetheart."

Well, at least one of us is sure.

Dr. Westhall proceeded to go over the procedure in detail, outlining the length of time and what would happen during the operation. After questions were asked by all of us, he excused himself, and we were left to wait while they finished prepping for surgery.

The waiting was always the hardest part, staring at the closed door while wondering how much time was left until it opened back up.

An hour passed until a nurse finally came to retrieve me. After a teary good-bye with a long group hug, I was wheeled into the operating room and prepped. They scrubbed and shaved the fine hairs from my chest and set up my IV. A friendly motherly-looking nurse stroked my forehead as I looked up at the ceiling. Breathing through my mouth, I counted the tiles above my head.

"We'll take care of you. Go to sleep now," she whispered.

And the world faded to black.

White clouds hovered above me as my eyes fluttered open for a brief second. I heard loud whooping and sharp beeps. Everything felt distant and out of place, like I was listening to myself from another room with cotton balls shoved in my ears.

"She's awake," I heard my mother say. "Or at least she was."

"She can't see me," a deep voice whispered.

"She won't remember any of this. Just hold her hand, and talk to her. I'll be outside."

A soft click added to the mechanical noises, and I felt a deep warmth spread through my fingers.

"I miss you so much, angel."

I know that voice.

"So much sometimes that it hurts to breathe."

He shouldn't be sad. I'm right here.

"I shouldn't be here, but I couldn't stay away, not today," he whispered. "You did it, Lailah. You made it through, just like I knew you would. Now, you'll have the life you deserve. It's all I ever wanted for you."

I tried to speak, but nothing came out—no words, no sound. I had nothing but good intentions. I wanted to tell him that it would be us, together, not just me. *We* would have the life we deserved.

"Please remember me when you look at the ocean waves or dip your toes in the water. Know that my love for you will never cease. It will only grow with each passing year. When you cross that last dream off your list, remember how we made pizza in the cafeteria kitchen and when we danced under the rain in your hospital shower. Remember late-night pudding debates, and when we made love for the first time, we felt our souls collide. Never forget the never-ending ways in which I love you and know that I will never stop fighting for you, no matter where I am or what I'm doing. I'll always keep your wings in flight."

A chair creaked, and as I tried to force my tired eyes open again, I felt gentle lips brush across my forehead.

"I love you, Lailah," he said softly.

I drifted deeper out of consciousness, wondering if my dream Jude would be there when I woke up.

CHAPTER THIRTY

LIFE'S A BALL

JUDE

The band faded into the background as I stared into the dark recess of my glass. Hunched over a bar stool in the corner of the bar area, I tried to disappear from the rest of the crowd.

"I'll have what he's drinking," a feminine voice said behind me.

I turned slowly and found Melody Scott. She was the reason I was sitting here and sulking over a glass of Coke, rather than hiding in my apartment like I did most weekends these days.

"You'd probably be better off ordering something else," I replied politely. "This is just soda."

She gave me a scrutinizing look and smiled. "There's a story, but I'm quite certain you're not going to share it."

That's for damn sure.

I turned back to the bar and watched as she slid onto the stool next to me. She continued to speak with the bartender, and her legs crossed in a slow, purposeful way as if she knew I was watching her. I turned back to my glass and checked my watch.

Fuck, have I really only been here for an hour?

"You know, you could try to be a bit happier, Jude. Look around, tonight is a huge success," Melody commented, sweeping her hand in the direction of the grand ballroom.

I'd hired Melody less than three months ago, and she'd managed to do everything I'd asked of her. When I'd returned from UCLA, I'd been broken beyond relief.

Honestly, I still was.

Seeing Lailah in that recovery room, knowing the heart beating inside her chest was no longer destroying her, had made every minute we were apart worth it. As I'd held her hand and kissed her skin, I'd known she would have such a bright future ahead of her, and it killed me to know I wouldn't see it. Leaving her for a second time had been like leaving my soul behind.

I'd returned even more confused.

I'd done what I needed to do. Lailah's surgery had been paid for and completed, and she was going to recover.

Couldn't I go back now? Take what was mine and still keep the family business afloat?

As I'd stepped into Cavenaugh Investments the morning after I'd returned from L.A., I'd found my brother waiting for me.

"Dad passed away last night," he'd said. "The board meets in thirty minutes."

That day, I'd lost my father, and my brother and I had inherited our legacy. Everything since then had been a blur of endless meetings along with helping my family mourn a man I barely remembered and negotiating all the paperwork that had come with it.

I couldn't go back to her.

Seeing my mother grieving over my father's casket as it had lowered into the ground made that clear. Walking into a boardroom of middle-aged men who expected me to save this company had solidified it. I had made my decision when I called Roman, and I'd chosen my fate.

Now, I was living with it—barely.

When I'd agreed to come home, I'd told Roman things would be run differently. I'd held him to that, and since the day I'd arrived back home, I'd completely restructured how everything in the business worked financially. It wasn't a perfectly oiled machine yet, but it was running better. We were making money again.

That was where Melody had come in.

I still remembered the look of complete shock and surprise when I'd told Roman that once we were back on our feet financially, I wanted to donate a significant percentage of our profits to charity. Not only that, but I wanted to hire someone to run the donations and also raise additional funds.

We would no longer be in it solely for the profit. We would give back.

If working in the trenches of a hospital for three years had taught me anything, it was that people were always in need.

Tonight marked the first charity ball organized by my newly hired Director of Charitable Donations, and if the one million dollars raised tonight said anything, I'd say she was good at her job.

She'd also been subtly hitting on me for weeks.

Melody saw me like the rest of the world did. With such a tragic past, I was the wounded puppy who needed to be cuddled and loved by just the right person.

Every woman on the Upper East Side thought she was just that person.

None of them were.

Warm breath tickled my ear. "Do you want to dance with me, Jude?" Melody whispered. She smelled like expensive perfume mixed with scotch.

I glanced up and met her hooded gaze. The dress she'd chosen was tight and cut low, exposing the perfect curves her body had to offer.

I felt nothing.

"I'd better go," I answered, rising from the stool as I slapped a twenty on the table.

"But the evening just started."

"I've got a pile of work waiting for me, and I still need to go visit my mom tomorrow," I answered before adding, "Sorry. Everything is great, Melody, really. I just have to get out of here."

I fled, loosening my bow tie as soon as I hit the cool chill of the outside, and I hailed a cab for downtown. My gut twisted as we passed a billboard sign covered in green hills, advertising Irish tourism.

Life really was cruel.

I guess no one ever said being a martyr would be easy.

My father had done one or two things right during his thirty-year rein of Cavenaugh Investments. One of those was relocating the main headquarters to its current location.

As I looked out of the floor-to-ceiling windows that put the New York skyline on full display, I felt a kind of kinship with the man I'd barely known. I remembered walking into his office, which was now mine, and seeing him standing in the corner with a drink in hand as he looked out at the buildings, thinking, planning, and plotting.

Family life was always split in our household. I was my mother's child, and Roman was my father's. It was the reason I was compassionate when my brother was greedy and the reason why I'd put myself above others when Roman would gladly just take everything for himself.

But our father had had one thing that Roman had yet to figure out. Dad had had Mom. That woman had kept his greed and need for power tethered. When it got too out of hand, she'd reel him back to earth. Granted, she could only do so much, but she was his anchor nonetheless.

My brother had nothing.

Nothing kept him tethered, and I worried that he might someday step so far over the line for something he wanted that he would get burned. Then, he'd finally understand what true loss was like.

"Somehow, I knew I'd find you here," Roman's deep voice said as he entered the dark office.

"Do you remember how Dad used to drink whiskey and count under his breath?" I asked without bothering to look up.

Footsteps sounded behind me until I saw the black of his tuxedo jacket out of the corner of my eye.

"Yeah, he'd stand here, just like this, and slowly sip his single malt and count. I asked him once why he did it, and he simply said it kept him sane."

"I guess we all need something," I commented as we continued to watch life go on beyond the glass.

"What do you need, Jude?"

I turned to him, surprised by his question. "What do you mean?"

"What do I mean?" he scoffed, taking a step backward. He began to pace. "I mean, you're spiraling, little brother. I see the work you're doing for the company, and damn, Jude, it's amazing, but then I find you here, late at night, like some creepy hermit. Why do I get the feeling that coming home was the last thing you wanted to do?"

"I'm here. Isn't that all that matters?"

"No, damn it. It's not!" he yelled, throwing his hands up. "I know you might think I'm some heartless asshole, and to most people, I am. What I did to you, after Megan died—I've been living with that regret for years. I should have flown out there and helped you, gotten you back on your feet, done something besides think of myself."

"What kept you? If you were so distraught over me, so filled with guilt, why didn't you just pick up the phone or fly out and see me?"

"Because I was angry. Dad got sick. You weren't here, and Mom—well, she couldn't handle it all. I was suddenly every-thing to everyone." He let out a choked laugh. "Cruel joke, right? The goof-off, the one everyone turns to for entertainment, was suddenly in charge of everything. They all wanted you, and all I wanted to do was prove to them just how wrong they were about me.

"When you called and said you were coming home, I thought my prayers had been answered. Finally, I could step back and be what I was supposed to be. But you know what? Those three years changed me. I can't leave now, and I can't stop caring about this company and the family that's woven around it."

I looked up at my brother as he came to a stop in the middle of the room. We looked alike in so many ways, yet we were so different.

"You can't limit yourself to only caring for us, Roman. Eventually, you're going to have to broaden your horizons and take in a few extras along the way."

He ignored my words, his eyes blazing. "What did you need the money for, Jude?"

I gave an exasperated sigh. "You know that day I went to go see Mom and Dad when I first came home? Do you know what Dad said to me when I saw him?"

He shook his head. "Probably, who the hell are you? He hasn't recognized me in over a year."

"No," I answered. "His eyes widened in instant recognition as I entered, and his lips puckered as he tried to find the words. Seeing him like that, so frail-looking after the many years I'd looked up to him as such a formidable man, was terrifying. It was like watching a god fall to the earth and become a mere human. It didn't seem real."

"I know," he answered.

"When he finally found the words, tears wet his cheeks, and he said to me, 'I'm so sorry, son. It's all my fault. It's all my fault.' He kept repeating that phrase until the nurse had to settle him down with drugs."

"What was his fault?" Roman asked, his brow furrowing in confusion.

"The accident. He sent us to California. I never came home. Mom said after he got over being angry at me for refusing to return, he fell into a deep depression, and that's when the dementia set in. He'd talk to me when I wasn't there, apologizing for everything."

"It wasn't his fault," he said softly, his head moving back and forth.

"I know that," I answered. "But he didn't. And because of the selfish decisions I made after that accident, because I stayed, I changed so many lives. This is me trying to make it right."

He walked to the door before turning back around. "You know, it wasn't your fault either. It's time you stop punishing yourself."

"Love is never a punishment," I answered.

CHAPTER THIRTY-ONE
PRETTY IN PINK

LAILAH

"Do you have it on yet?" Grace hollered from the other side of the door.

"Almost! Hold on. The zipper is caught." I bent down, trying to squeeze and pull the fabric tight to allow the zipper to move up the track. "I swear, I've gotten fatter since my last fitting," I lamented. I took a deep breath in, and the tiny teeth came together to close off my oxygen supply.

"Oh, stop it. You have not. And even if you did, who cares? The extra bit of weight you've gained because of the anti-rejection drugs have done amazing things to your figure. I wish I could gain a few pounds and turn into a sex goddess."

I snorted, smoothing the fabric down around my waist. "Sex goddess? I think you're delusional."

Without bothering to look at my reflection, I opened the door of the dressing room and stopped. Two sets of eyes widened as they took me in.

"Lailah, you look beautiful," my mother said, blotting tears from her eyes.

"I was going to go with hot. You look hot." Grace laughed.

Walking the short distance to the center of the room, I took a step, stood on the wide carpeted platform, and finally looked at my reflection in the mirror.

"You really had to choose pink, didn't you?" I smiled.

Grace ran up to me, squealing. "It's perfect! And yes, I had to choose pink. It's the best color ever. You look amazing in it. You can't argue with that."

The dress was actually beautiful, but I had to give her a hard time. Any girl who themes her wedding Sophisticated Princess deserves a bit of hassling. The sweetheart neckline and high waistline gave way to a flowing blush-colored skirt that reminded me of the silk scarves my mother always loved to wear. It ebbed and flowed as I walked and—well, yeah, it made me feel kind of like a princess.

"I'm just glad you chose subtle over something in the cotton-candy spectrum of the color wheel."

"I did say, Sophisticated Princess, not Barbie Gets Married."

I laughed as she started playing with my long blonde hair, throwing out ideas on what we could do with it.

"Do you want it up or down?"

Looking at my reflection, I took a deep breath. The neckline of this dress left nothing to the imagination when it came to the scars of my past. The pink line that bisected my chest was now darker from the recent surgery, and it stood out prominently against the pink fabric. Having my hair down around my shoulders would take the attention away from it.

"Up," I said, knowing I had to face my fears one at a time.

Life was no longer about hiding in the shadows. If I wanted to experience all the normalcies of it, I had to embrace the darker sides as well, and that started with a few stares and whispers.

"It will be beautiful," Grace said, holding it away from my face.

The three of us looked at my teary-eyed smile staring back.

The girl who had never cried now couldn't seem to ever turn off the damn water works.

I'd always been so good at keeping things together and in check. I wouldn't break down, and I'd never shown my weaknesses.

But now, I let it all out. When I had been in pain during recovery, I'd cried out for help and cursed fate for making me go through so many obstacles. As I'd recovered, I'd cried for the ability to have a second chance. And late at night, I would cry because I missed him.

Six months had gone by, and I still awoke each morning, reaching out for his warmth. The dream I'd had in the recovery room wasn't the last. I would see him nightly when I closed my eyes, but they were always memories—pizzas and pudding, laughing under an indoor rain shower, and feeling his tender touch as he made love to me while saying he'd never leave.

But he had.

"Beautiful dress," a deep male voice echoed from behind.

I looked up, and my breath caught.

Jude.

But on second glance, I realized his hair was a bit too dark, his eyes were a little too hard, and he carried himself differently.

"Holy moly, that's Roman Cavenaugh," Grace whispered, turning quickly to see if the reflection she'd seen in the mirror was indeed real.

"Pleasure to meet you," he said, taking a step forward to take Grace's hand.

A slow, sensual kiss was placed on her palm, leaving her awestruck and tongue-tied.

"Grace," she murmured. "I'm Grace."

His lips turned upward, and he smiled as he took her in. His eyes roamed over her hair and curvy figure until they finally settled on the engagement ring on her left hand.

"Lucky man," he commented.

A faint blush colored Grace's complexion as she pulled her hand away, shaking herself from the trance she'd stumbled into. "Thank you."

He gave a polite smile and then looked up, setting his eyes on me.

His eyes reminded me so much of Jude.

Closing the distance between us, he held out his hand, and I took it.

"Roman Cavenaugh," he said. "You must be Lailah Buchanan."

His gaze shifted briefly down to my scar, making me feel naked in my dress.

"Yes," I answered.

"Good. Well then, is this your mother?" he asked, looking over to where my mother was standing, silently observing everything.

"She is."

"Great. Do me a favor, will you?" he asked, stepping forward toward her. "Run home, and pack Lailah a bag. Maybe enough for a week or two. Whatever you can find. Anything else she needs, we can provide for her."

My mom's eyes widened at his bold request.

"Excuse me? I don't know who you think I am, but I'm not going anywhere with you!" I exclaimed.

He turned back around, his face transforming into a wide grin. "Oh, sweetheart, after what I have to tell you, you'll be begging me to get on that plane. And if you don't, I guess you're not worth everything my brother's done for you after all."

After I changed out of my dress, Roman and I headed to a coffee shop across the street while my mom and Grace headed home. He'd promised to deliver me safely back to my mom's in an hour after he explained himself.

He might look like Jude, but the domineering attitude he carried made me want to dropkick him. He had exactly twenty minutes to reveal exactly why he had flown all the way across the country to pack my bags and order me around like one of his employees.

We stood in line, and I shifted from one foot to another as I read the menu posted above.

Number thirty-three—order a ridiculously priced cup of coffee.

I'd never been in a coffee shop—let alone, ordered a cup of coffee. The names baffled me.

Why couldn't they just call them small, medium, and large?

"Are you okay?" Roman asked, obviously sensing my distress.

"What?" I startled. "Oh, yes. Um…what are you getting?" I asked.

We got to the counter, and I almost chickened out by saying I'd have what he was ordering, but I managed to get through it, ordering a grande mocha something or other. I didn't know. It sounded decadent.

We both ordered scones as well, and we made our way to a small table in the corner by the window. I smiled, thinking about yet another thing I'd be able to cross off my list.

"So spill," I finally said. I started to pull the corners off my chocolate scone before popping them into my mouth.

Yum. Real food is awesome.

Roman repeated my actions and took a bite of his blueberry scone. "When Jude called me last summer and said he was coming home, he was very specific about a few things."

Taking a sip of my mocha, I watched him run his fingers over the edge of his cup. "Two things actually—one, he wanted more control, more power over what we did…and didn't do."

"Why does this involve me?" I hated every word, every sentence that involved Jude. It was like a lance to the heart, pulling me back, making me remember those beautiful few months where I'd felt soul-defining pure love—until he'd left.

"And the other," Roman continued without bothering to answer me, "was immediate access to his account that I'd frozen years earlier. Now, I didn't think much of it at the time, and I agreed to both on the spot. You've seen the news, I'm sure. Cavenaugh Investments wasn't in a good place, and I would have agreed to just about anything, so I could hand over the reins to my younger brother."

"Again, I don't understand why we are having this conversation."

He smiled. "You're very impatient."

"You would be, too, if you'd spent your entire life stuck on the outside, looking in."

"We all have prisons and chains that keep us from the one thing we really want in life, Lailah. Yours were just bigger and stronger than most."

"And what do you want most in this life, Roman?" I challenged, raising my eyebrow. I took a slow sip of coffee.

"Freedom," he answered. "Just like you."

"Handing everything over to your brother hasn't turned out the way you expected?" I smirked, watching the pleasant smile on his face disappear.

"He might have solved our problems, but he's not happy. He's goddamn miserable."

I shook my head. "He doesn't appear to be miserable in the gossip magazines. Apparently, he's dating a coworker. They're very happy," I sneered.

His eyes heated in anger. "Don't believe everything you hear on TV or see in the papers, Lailah. Leaving you destroyed my brother. He's nothing but an empty shell."

"Well then, why isn't he here, telling me that himself?" I asked a bit too loudly, causing a few people to turn their heads.

Roman looked around and cursed. "Do you think you could be a little more discreet?"

"Sorry," I muttered.

"Why do you think Jude needed all that cash? All of a sudden? When he got home and I saw he'd traded his Sperrys and Polos for grungy jeans and tats, I figured he'd gotten himself into trouble. But the more I was around him, the more

I realized it had less to do with him, and more to do…with you."

"Me?" My eyes widened as everything started to settle into place.

I will never stop fighting for you

"Oh God, it wasn't a dream. He was here—after my surgery. He was here," I blurted out as my eyes began to blur.

"Did you really believe the insurance company would reverse a denial that quickly?"

"He paid for my transplant?"

"Yes," Roman answered. "I finally did a bit of digging and discovered where he was wiring all those funds to. With the aid of a few friends, I was able to track the bank trail back to you. My mother filled in the rest, bursting like a dam when I showed her all the evidence. Apparently, she's been carrying the secret of you around for a long time."

"Your mother knows about me?" I asked, blinking away tears.

"Yeah," he answered. "She'd really like to meet you."

"He didn't abandon me," I said as an overwhelming feeling of hope spread through me. For once in my life, the feeling didn't scare me. Hope was a terrifying risk for someone like me, but as many times as I'd been disappointed or overwhelmed with joy in life, everything had brought me to that hospital for a reason.

"So, what do we do now?" I asked.

"Now, we catch a flight, and you save my brother the way he saved you."

"Good. Let's go."

Number eight-seven—Fly on a plane.
Check.

CHAPTER THIRTY-TWO
AN UNWRITTEN FUTURE

JUDE

Warm California sun drifted lazily through the windows, illuminating her long tawny-blonde hair like a halo. She smiled up at me, as the bare skin of her shoulders peeking out from under the dark cobalt sheets.

That was how I always remembered her.

I pushed back from my desk and turned away from the photo. I'd placed it there weeks ago because I needed to see her face again, and I needed a reminder of why I was here and not in that bed, holding the woman I loved.

Maybe it was a bit sadistic, having a token that constantly showed me everything I'd lost and didn't have. But every day since I'd made that call to Roman and walked away from her had done the exact same thing. Just sitting here in this office was enough of a reminder.

At least seeing her beautiful smile, her love radiating in her tender blue eyes, confirmed everything I was doing, the reason I was here.

She was alive.

Somewhere in Santa Monica right now, she was starting

over, having the life she'd always wanted, and none of that would have happened if I wasn't sitting here.

I looked at my watch and realized I was nearly late for a meeting. I pressed the intercom button and waited for Stephanie, my secretary, to respond.

"Yes, Mr. Cavenaugh?" she replied.

"Jude, Stephanie—it's just Jude." I laughed.

"I'm sorry, Mr. Cavenaugh—Jude...sir?"

Stephanie had been my father's secretary before she inherited me, and I thought the loss of formality I'd instituted with the few employees who worked directly for me confused and scared her.

When I'd told her she was free to wear whatever she'd like to work from now on, her response had been, *Do I have to?*

She'd stuck to her pencil skirts and tailored jackets while the rest of us would throw in casual days every once in a while.

I had been Californianized—at least, that was what the staff had said.

"Is lunch all set for my meeting with Roman and the board?"

"Oh, um...actually," she stammered. "Your brother—I mean, Mr. Cavenaugh canceled the meeting late yesterday."

I raised an eyebrow at that. He'd never canceled anything I'd scheduled.

"He canceled it?"

"Yes, sir."

"Did he say why?"

"He did, yes. He said he had some business to attend to, and he wouldn't return in time."

"What the hell? What kind of business?" I clamored, instantly regretting my tone. "I'm sorry, Stephanie. Forgive me. Thank you for the message. I'll be sure to immediately follow up with my brother."

"Um...well, actually—"

"Thank you." I hit End before the anger in my voice rose again.

I quickly tried Roman's cell phone, but it went directly to voice mail.

I should have known better than to trust him. For the last six months, he'd been nothing but doting and dedicated to our plans to revive and refurbish this company. We'd been on the same page.

Now, he'd bailed without notice to me, canceling a very important meeting with the board.

Rising from my chair, I stalked to the windows and stared out at the bustling city down below.

"One…two…three…" I started, trying to see the method behind my father's madness. "He probably picked up the first woman he could find," I muttered. I pictured my brother on some far off island, boozing it up, while I sat around, scratching my head.

"Actually…" a sweet voice echoed from behind me.

I turned around and lost the ability to breathe.

"I probably wasn't the first woman. It did take him six hours to reach me, and he did see Grace first, so I don't know what that would make me, but definitely not the first," she babbled.

Finding the words to respond escaped me as I took her in while she stood in the doorway of my New York office. She'd gained some weight, filling in curves I never knew existed. Dressed in a simple green sweater, tight jeans, and boots, she looked like perfection.

"You're here," I managed to say.

"Yeah." She smiled.

"You're really here," I said again, the reality setting in. I moved quickly, taking several long strides toward her.

Lifting a shaky hand, my fingers grazed her cheekbone. My eyes squeezed tight, emotions overwhelming my parched soul. "Dear God, if I'm dreaming…I don't ever want to wake up," I whispered.

"You're definitely not dreaming. But if you need proof…"

My eyes opened just in time to see the palm of her hand make contact with my face.

"Ouch!" I yelled. "What the hell was that for?"

It wasn't exactly the reunion I had expected.

"That," she said, her eyes blazing, "was for making important life decisions without me, Jude."

"Nice," my brother's baritone voice said as his towering figure appeared behind her. "I like her." He grinned. "Not even five minutes here, and she's already putting you in your place."

"Get out," I growled.

"Oh, I will. You two have fun. By the way, Jude, you're welcome."

He pivoted around, and I listened to his chipper whistle evaporate down the hall.

I turned and walked over to the plush sitting area my father had put in for small business meetings. I'd used it for a bed on several occasions when I hadn't felt like catching a taxi home. Right now, I thought we could both use a comfortable place to sit and talk.

Still rubbing the sting out of my cheek, I watched her slowly lower herself to the sofa, her beautiful blue eyes meeting mine as she settled. Right then, everything in me that had been lying dormant for months roared back to life.

Take her.

Take her now.

My fists balled at my sides as I showed the greatest physical restraint of my life. I'd dreamed, fantasized, and pictured her in my mind nearly every second since the day I left her bedside. Seeing her here, healthy and recovered, made me want to do every sort of cliché caveman thing to her.

"So, you want to explain yourself?" she asked, her foot bobbing up and down as she sat with her legs crossed.

"Explain what, Lailah?"

"Why you decided to leave me?"

"Obviously, you know why," I answered.

"I do. Your brother is apparently a good investigator…or he has friends who are. I didn't ask specifics. So, yes, I know exactly why you left, but I still don't understand why you couldn't have just told me."

I let out a deep breath. "Would you have let me go?"

Her mouth opened quickly and then closed again.

"Exactly," I said. "You would have never let me leave, Lailah. You had thrown in the towel, given up, raised your little white flag in surrender to your fate. And I understood that, I did. You've been through more shit than most people experience in an entire lifetime. But understand it from my perspective. Put yourself in my shoes. You were dying with no hope for a recovery unless you got that surgery. I did what I had to do to keep you alive. It was the only option for me."

She nodded, her eyes glistening with unshed tears. "But why didn't you come back?" she asked. "I remember now—when you were in my hospital room after the surgery. You wanted to stay. Why didn't you stay with me?"

"I should have known you'd remember that," I said with a slight grin. "I wanted to, more than you could possibly imagine. Walking away a second time, especially after you'd just undergone very risky surgery, was like taking a bullet to my heart for every mile I put between us. But I can't run this company from Santa Monica. This was my deal to Roman for returning, my penance for giving you a life you deserve. I can't abandon my family, not again."

"So, where does that leave us?" she asked, her eyes meeting mine.

I took a deep breath, letting the air slowly vacate my lungs. "I don't know, Lailah."

Silence settled between us before I heard her lilting voice again.

"Did you know that NYU has an excellent cardiology department?"

My heart skipped a beat.

"I didn't know that," I answered, trying to gauge her blank expression.

"They do. Marcus says that transferring my care to the East Coast would be relatively easy if—"

"If you moved here?" I finished, my eyes widening.

She nodded, her expression brimming with excitement. "It's already done. My things are being shipped next week. See? You're not the only one who can make life decisions all on your own."

"You're moving to New York?" I asked in bewilderment. *This can't be possible.*

"Yeah, but I can't decide where to live. Do you think you could help me find a place?" She grinned.

Reaching out, I grabbed her around the waist and pulled her to me. She let out a high-pitched yip and laughed as her legs fell around my thighs.

"You will be living with me," I said. "Forever."

Our lips met, and I was in heaven again with the sweet taste of her kiss and the way she molded her body against mine. She was my salvation.

Life—it really did go on, even after insurmountable grief, debilitating sorrow and a life waiting to begin. As long as we were able to love and be loved in this world, no heart would ever be beyond repair.

Love had brought me to her and there, within her arms, I had found a reason to live again. She was my angel, my Lailah, my love.

EPILOGUE

LAILAH

Beep, Beep, Beep…

My eyes still shut, I listened, focusing on my surroundings, as I felt the sheets, smelled the air, and did my mental checklist.

"Oh my God, Lailah! Turn off that damn alarm!" Jude mumbled.

I laughed, remembering exactly why I'd stopped doing the mental checklist a long time ago.

There was no need.

Every morning, I awoke in the same place.

Home.

It didn't matter if we were in our high-rise Manhattan apartment or in a hotel room on the California coast. The man next to me would always be the only home I ever needed.

I opened my eyes to find Jude buried under our covers with his pillow firmly covering his head.

"You know, you could turn it off," I suggested with a smirk.

The pillow lifted, and I saw his doubtful expression change as he looked over at the alarm clock on my side of the bed. A wicked grin crossed his face as he suddenly sprang, pinning me underneath him, while he reached across to cease the loud beeping. His hard naked chest brushed against mine, and I felt my nipples pebble instantly.

"That was an excellent idea," he said, surveying his new view like a king.

"It's never good to be lazy," I whispered.

His mouth took mine. My hands dived into his short hair as my legs wrapped around his waist.

An hour later, he'd thoroughly proven just how necessary alarm clocks were.

I raced around our hotel room, looking for my lost shoe.

"This is all your fault!" I yelled, pushing my head under the bed in search of the long-lost nude pump.

"You weren't complaining last night," he scoffed. "In fact, I seem to remember something along the lines of, 'Oh God, Jude, never stop…please never stop.' Can't blame a guy for trying to follow directions."

My head reappeared from the lower recess of the bed, and as I stood, I turned away to try to hide the blush he'd caused. I felt his tender touch wrap around my waist as he turned me around.

"I love seeing that. Don't ever hide it." He smiled, brushing his thumb down my reddened cheek.

"I can't find my shoe," I said with a pout.

His smile widened as his eyes narrowed in on my bottom lip.

"Focus, tiger." I laughed. "Shoe. Me. Need it."

"Right," he answered. "Okay, one shoe coming up!"

After ten minutes, he was on the bed with his shoulders slumped in apparent defeat. "Are you sure you can't just go barefoot?"

I gave him a hard stare.

He shook his head, lifting his hands in surrender. "Okay, give me the shoe."

I handed him the left shoe, and I watched him walk to the hotel phone. He punched a single digit and waited.

"Hi, yes. I need someone to go retrieve some shoes for me —and fast. Size seven and a half. Nude. Maybe a two- or three-inch heel?" He looked up at me for confirmation.

My dumbstruck face just nodded.

"Good. Thanks."

"Oh my God, what did you just do?" I asked, laughing.

"I used the benefits of this ridiculously expensive hotel."

"That was like watching a deleted scene of *Pretty Woman*."

"Except?" He moved from the bed and stalked forward.

"Except you're way hotter," I answered.

"Good answer." He stopped himself several steps from me and turned back around. "If I touch you again, we're never going to make it there on time."

"Well then, stay over there. If we're late again, Grace will kill us."

"It was the rehearsal dinner. It wasn't even the rehearsal, and it was, like, five minutes." He waved a flippant hand as he slumped down in the desk chair and began to tie the silk tie around his neck.

I went into the bathroom and finished curling my hair, loving the way the soft coils tumbled down my back. Taking a new interest in clothing and makeup, I'd turned into quite the girl since my recovery. Grace had been thrilled, constantly emailing me sales and brands she loved.

Being in the hospital, I'd never had an opportunity to dress myself the way I'd wanted. Everything was made for comfort, and although I still loved my sweats and yoga pants, I enjoyed dressing up for an evening out. This body of mine had been through the ringer, and it had always been something I was proud of, just not particularly interested in adorning it.

Now, I was proud and showing it.

I finished attaching the back of the diamond earrings Jude had bought me several months earlier, and I looked at myself in the mirror one last time just as a knock came to the front door of our hotel room.

That couldn't possibly be the shoes.

"Hey, angel, your shoes are here!" Jude called from the other room.

I walked out and found a stack of shoes at least six boxes high.

"Holy crap," I said, gazing up at the display.

"Well, with sizing difference, I wanted to make sure you had options. So, pick what you want to wear now, and keep the rest."

I tried not to let the designer labels deter me.

The second day I had been in New York, he had taken me shopping. I'd nearly had a stroke, short-circuiting that brand-new heart of mine, when I came in contact with some of the price tags I'd been handed.

Money was part of Jude's life now. It had taken him a while to adjust again after living with so little for so long, but now, he had a different outlook on all of it.

It was a gift, and he enjoyed sharing it, especially with me.

Finding him in a pair of jeans and a ratty old T-shirt on the weekends still made my heart flip-flop, but I would trade a pair of scrubs for a suit any day.

That man was made for suits.

When he'd insisted on paying for my tuition, I'd fought him on it. It had been one epic battle. Eventually, he'd won out, arguing that I would never be able to work as a counselor without a degree. I'd finally decided my life calling was to help those out there like me—the people who felt cheated and hopeless because they were born different from the rest of the world. I'd had an amazing counselor when I was younger, and I hoped I could make that kind of impact on someone else's life one day. It was a long ways off, but someday, I'd get there. I had originally planned on working to pay off my tuition. I could also have taken loans and found scholarships. Jude had given me a firm no to all of that.

"Go work at McDonald's, for all I care, but do it only if that's what you really want to do," he'd said. "You've spent your entire life buried. Now, it's your time to finally do whatever it is that makes you happy. Go to school, Lailah. Be whatever it is that you're destined to be."

I had nothing but time now, and what an amazing gift it was.

Time was not our friend this morning though, and I quickly made a decision, picking a pair of peep-toe pumps similar to the ones I had packed—or I thought I had packed.

We raced out the door and prayed traffic would be in our favor as we drove toward the sandy beach.

What a beautiful day for a wedding.

JUDE

"See? Right on time," I said as we pulled the rental car into a parking spot along the boardwalk.

Looking out at the water's edge, Lailah's eyes searched around until she spotted the small gathering of white chairs, and she smiled. "There it is," she said.

"I really wish they had let us help set up last night," I replied.

I jumped out of the car to grab her door. If I wasn't quick about it, she always beat me to it. She'd roll her eyes when I did this, but I thought she secretly loved it. A faint blush would blot her cheeks as she exited, and that was exactly why I kept doing it.

"Might want to take those shoes off when we get to the sand," I suggested as we walked arm in arm toward the stairs leading down to the sand below.

"Oh, good call." She bent down and slipped them off, exposing her cotton-candy pink toes. "I wonder if I should go check on her." She looked back at the hotel behind us.

"You're here!" a bubbly voice cried, running up to steal a hug.

"Your belly!" Lailah exclaimed, looking down at the tiny round belly of her best friend.

"I'm finally showing!" she squealed, running her hands over her enlarged stomach.

Lailah laughed, placing her hands over Grace's.

"I think you might be the only woman on the planet who was upset about not getting a belly right away."

Grace's eyes twinkled as Brian, her husband, came and joined us.

He wrapped his arm around her waist. "She wanted to go shopping for maternity clothes the second the stick turned pink."

I watched as Lailah shook her head, laughing.

"That sounds like you," Lailah said.

Grace was only four months along, and her little belly was on perfect display in her gauzy floral dress. I had no doubts she'd bought it three months ago just for the occasion. That woman was a planner.

After some long overdue catching up, we were told to take our seats.

Lailah and I excused ourselves and walked to the front as the minister joined us.

"I can't believe this day is actually here," Lailah said softly in my ear.

We all turned, Marcus came to join us.

I gave him a brief nod and grinned. "It's about time."

His gaze warmed, and I felt his hand cup mine. Looking down, I watched him drop a sleek white gold band into my palm.

"Can't be the best man without that," he said. "I wouldn't be here without you, J-Man."

"Maybe not today, but it would have happened eventually."

My hand closed tightly around the cool metal band just as the music began to play softly in the background. I took once quick glance toward Lailah and caught her gaze. She smiled, clutching the small bouquet of sunflowers in her hand that Grace handed to her at the very last moment.

We both turned just in time to see Molly making her way down the sand. I heard Marcus's breath catch as he first caught sight of his bride.

Her hair was braided beautifully down her back, and her simple ivory gown made her look sophisticated and regal. As she slowly moved forward to the front, she passed the intimate gathering of friends and family. Then, the entire world seemed to melt away as Marcus and Molly took each other's hands.

All I could see was Lailah.

As the minister spoke words of love and eternal commitment, I saw Lailah's eyes glisten as she watched her mother and Marcus exchange rings. My heart beat faster as the ceremony came to a close, and Marcus and Molly kissed each other for the first time as man and wife.

Everyone clapped and cheered, but all I could think about was Lailah and what I was about to say.

So much planning had come to this one moment.

Hugs and congratulations were shared as the few guests joined the couple under the arch.

I shook Marcus's hand, and he grinned, knowing what was coming.

"Are you all packed?" Molly asked, holding Lailah in her arms.

"Packed?" she asked. "We aren't leaving for a few more days."

Molly smiled, turning to me.

"Actually," I said, pulling the envelope from my pocket, "we're leaving tonight."

I handed it to Lailah, and she opened it. After pulling out the first-class tickets, her eyes skimmed the words written on them. Her lip began to tremble as her hands shook.

"We're going to Ireland?" she asked.

"Yeah. No more placeholders, Lailah," I said. "We're really going."

"But..." She hesitated, looking up to her newly married mother.

"We've known for weeks. Now, get your butts out of here!"

Molly laughed, and Lailah engulfed her in a huge hug.

"Don't forget me," Marcus said.

Lailah pulled him into their family hug. "I'd never forget you...*Dad*."

Marcus's hand tightened around her before letting go. "Get going, you two," he choked out, his eyes blinking several times, as he tried to compose himself.

I took her hand, and we made our way to the car.

She stopped us just as I opened her door.

"I can't believe this. You're just full of crazy surprises," she said, her expression joyous.

"Oh, you just wait," I said, grinning, as I helped her into the car.

We made our way to the airport to make yet another one of Lailah's dreams come true.

Two days later, among wildflowers and castle ruins as the sun peeked through the clouds on our perfect Irish day, I got down on one knee and made all my dreams come true with a single question.

And she said, "Yes."

Will Lailah and Jude find their happily ever after? Find out in Beyond These Walls...

BEYOND THESE WALLS

PROLOGUE

LAILAH

The cool ocean air rushed through the hills, tousling my hair and sending a chill up my spine, as we climbed a bit higher toward our destination.

"How are you doing?" Jude asked.

With his hand firmly wrapped around mine, we traveled through the vibrant green grass.

"Good, really good." I smiled as my hand danced across the tops of purple wildflowers scattered everywhere. I took a deep breath through my lungs, letting the air swirl around my rib cage, and said a small prayer of thanks, knowing there had been a time in my life when a simple deep breath wasn't possible.

"We're almost there. Do you see it?" he asked, pointing with his free hand toward the water's edge.

"Oh my gosh, yes!" I exclaimed.

In the distance, overlooking the ocean was a small church—or the remains of one. Three walls still stood, and as we walked closer, I could see the remnants of the fourth spread across the ground in piles. The roof and floor were long gone, but in its place, nature had taken over. Tiny daisies and beautiful blue sky had woven perfectly *through the weathered foundation and walls, creating something that seemed almost part of the land.*

Neither of us spoke for a long while. We just stood in the center, absorbing its quiet beauty. This was how I'd always imagined it. When I'd sat in my hospital bed, fantasizing about faraway places and exotic trips to destinations unknown, this was what I'd always pictured in my head.

And here I was, standing in my own dream.

Because of Jude.

I turned, and our eyes met. There, in the middle of the church, surrounded by wildflowers as waves crashed below us, the love of my life dropped to one knee.

"What are you doing?" I asked, my voice shaky and thin, as I looked down at him.

"Exactly what I've wanted to do since the moment I met you."

"I don't know what to say."

"Don't say anything." He smiled warmly. "Just listen."

I nodded as he took my hands in his own.

"I know you think that I saved you, but in all honesty, it was you who saved me. Anyone with the same amount of wealth could have paid for that surgery. It wasn't hard. But you pulled me out of the darkness. If it weren't for you, I would have spent the rest of my life in that hospital, hating myself for the mistakes of my past. You are my light, my angel, and now, I want to make you my wife. Please say yes, Lailah. Please make me the happiest man alive and marry me."

Tears welled up in my eyes as he reached into his pocket and pulled out a tiny black ring box. As he lifted the lid, I felt my new heart skip a beat at the sight of the dazzling ring tucked inside.

Traditional and timeless, it was exactly what I would have picked out. I couldn't help but reach out and run my fingers over the top of the single solitaire set on a thin gold band.

"Yes," I answered softly as happy tears trickled down my face.

I watched as he slipped the ring on my left hand. It was a perfect fit. Happiness and joy shone in his eyes as he stood, scooping me up into his arms. I knew forever with him was exactly where I should be.

"I love you," I said, running my hands through his messy blond hair.

"I love you—hey, did you hear that?"

What? That's not how this is supposed to go.

"Hear what?" I asked.

"I swear, I heard a child cry out. Didn't you hear it?"

"No, I don't think so."

This never happened.

Dread flared to life in my chest as he looked around.

"Come on. Let's go look."

Suddenly, I heard the faint cry of a child. I looked around, but all I saw were hills and miles and miles of green countryside.

Another cry.

"Wait, I think it came from over here!" I pointed and turned right, which took us farther inland toward a group of trees.

I don't remember a forest.

We entered the large cluster of trees, and suddenly, it grew dark. The tall tree limbs seemed to come to life, reaching out for us, as we walked deeper and deeper.

"I think I heard it again," Jude said, moving faster.

His speed approached a run, and I tried to keep up. Huge tree roots leaped out of the group, blocking my path, and soon, we were separated.

"Jude!" I cried, looking right and left.

"Lailah! I'm right here!"

"I can't see you!"

I turned around in circles, the rising panic taking over.

"Jude!" I screamed. Feeling my breath beginning to weaken, I stood frozen in place as the dark walls of the forest began to close in around me.

The child cried out again, and this time, it was a cry of anguish. I suddenly felt torn.

Where do I go? Who do I run toward?

"Jude! Help me!" I managed to say before collapsing.

Seconds later, the darkness swallowed me whole.

LAILAH'S SOMEDAY LIST

1. Fall in love
2. Earn a college degree
3. Learn more about my mom
4. Get a job
5. Stand in line for something
6. Go to a carnival
7. Take a vacation
8. Go a day without medication
9. Watch a high school football game
10. Go on a roller coaster
11. Apply to college
12. Watch fireworks
13. Sing at a karaoke bar
14. Put my toes in the ocean
15. Mow grass
16. Be a best friend
17. Live on my own
18. Dye my hair pink
19. Get hit on
20. Go to a baseball game
21. Help a friend move
22. Go skinny-dipping
23. Go grocery shopping
24. Buy a car
25. Be kissed until I'm breathless
26. Spend a day at the farmer's market

27. Visit a foreign country

28. Get my ears pierced

29. Ride a bike

30. Go to the library

31. Adopt a dog

32. Paddle boat around a lake

33. Order a ridiculously expensive cup of coffee

34. TP a house

35. Play miniature golf

36. Eat cotton candy

37. Go to the drive-in and make out the entire time

38. Go to prom

39. Experience a hangover

40. Pay bills

41. Buy my mom a birthday present

42. Go to a roller-skating rink

43. Dance in the rain

44. Get a bad haircut

45. Jump in a bouncy house

46. Have a sleepover

47. Get a bikini wax

48. Make love

49. Dance in my living room

50. Go caroling during Christmastime

51. Have an entire conversation in only text messages

52. Go furniture shopping

53. Babysit a child

54. Buy lingerie

55. Visit an art museum

56. Make snow angels

57. Eat dinner by candlelight

58. Do a Lemon Drop

59. Try sushi

60. Go to an ice cream parlor

61. Learn to ice-skate

62. Make a meal from start to finish

63. Go to a bachelorette party

64. Get a pedicure

65. Spend an afternoon fishing

66. Spend an entire day outside

67. Go on a hayride

68. Take salsa lessons

69. Try on wedding gowns with my mother

70. Make an apple pie

71. Go to a movie theater

72. Have my heart broken

73. Learn to use a hammer

74. Have a makeover

75. Eat fast food

76. Ride a Ferris wheel all the way up to the top

77. Get married

78. Catch lightening bugs

79. Go camping and sleep under the stars

80. Get a massage

81. Learn to stand up for myself

82. Have a picnic

83. Change a diaper

84. Take a hike

85. Fail a test

86. Run errands on my own

87. Fly on a plane

88. Adopt a child

89. Have someone to miss

90. Plant a garden

91. Make a sand castle

92. Celebrate an anniversary

93. Take a yoga class

94. Go boogie boarding

95. Go someplace humid

96. Go on a hike

97. Get a speeding ticket

98. Hail a taxi

99. Go to an adult store

100. Go trick or treating

101. Volunteer at a children's hospital

102. Ride a horse

103. Go to a gym

104. Learn to eat with chopsticks

105. Take the subway

106. Burn an entire batch of cookies

107. Get a Facebook profile

108. Walk a mile start to finish

109. Read a "dirty" book

110. Go to a birthday party

111. Have a girl's night out

112. Go on a date

113. Go to a strip club

114. Get a tattoo

115. Go apple picking

116. Drive a car

117. Get a tan

118. Go swimming

119. Rake leaves

120. Fly a kite

121. Ride in the back of a cop car

122. Vote in an election

123. Take a writing class

124. Sleep through the night

125. Eat ice cream for breakfast, lunch and dinner

126. Go bungee jumping

127. Be a organ donor

128. Watch the sunrise from a mountain top

129. See a waterfall

130. Go kayaking

131. Save someone's life

132. Paint the walls of my own house

133. Go to Disneyland

134. Scuba dive

135. Go hot tubbing

136. Go skiing

137. Spend an entire day on the beach

138. Visit someone in the hospital

139. Learn to shoot a gun

140. Go on a road trip

141. Serve jury duty

142. Make a new friend

143. Live until I've seen it all

ACKNOWLEDGMENTS

Writing a book is like giving away a tiny piece of your soul. Every word is precious, every sentence is sacred and at the end…all you can do is hope and pray the world understands the level of responsibility you've given by entrusting them with such a gift.

To my husband—my forever #1 fan, I love you. You are my soulmate, best friend and the inspiration of every hero I create.

To my two kiddos—Thank you for being the most awesome cheerleaders a mother could ask for. Hannah—Thank you for writing me the panda poem. You are now a published author! Go brag to your friends! Em—Never stop being you.

My parents and family—Thank you so much for the endless support and love.

To my awesome beta readers—Christy, Michelle, Danielle S, Danielle B, Carey, Melissa, Sarah, Jennifer, Staci , Shera, Whitney and Becca. Thank you so much for helping me make WTW the best it could be!

Bloggers—Thank you. Seriously. Thank you for everything you do for indie authors everywhere.

Jovana and Ami—Thank you for being awesome. I couldn't have picked a better editing team. Each and every book I write is perfected and flawless because of the two of you.

Sarah Hansen — Thanks again for an amazing cover and thanks to my photographer and cover models for making this photo possible!

To my amazing readers—Like dessert, I always save the best for last. Thank you supporting me and my family. Thank you for loving my characters and the stories I create. And mostly, thank you for being you.

Never stop dreaming.

—J.L.

ABOUT THE AUTHOR

J.L. Berg is the *USA Today* bestselling author of the Ready Series. She is a California native but currently lives in Virginia. When she's not writing, you will likely find her spending time with her family or watching Doctor Who. J.L. Berg is represented by Jill Marsal of Marsal Lyon Literary Agency, LLC